MEET DELPHIE DOUD:

"I could cry. I could cry till I was shaking all over and my head ached. Because Bruce couldn't ever be President, or me make a trip to South America, like Doug Cunningham, or have a parlor with a rug. Because we came from Arkansas where everyone was poor as a church mouse and because people made fun of you if they found out you were born there, and Mama and Papa were always letting the cat out of the bag. Because we had such a peculiar last name, a little old stub of a name, that simply asked the kids to laugh at it and call me Delphie Doudy. I could see the way Papa and Mama lived, and I could feel their way hardening around me like a crust I couldn't break. I was caught. I wouldn't ever get away. So I didn't try to stop my heart if it wanted to break. I let it cry into my pillow until at last it lay down inside of me with a sigh and went to sleep, being too tired to fight and hate and resolve and despair any more that night . . ."

But tomorrow is always a new day for Delphie Doud. She's out to be her own person, and anyone who gets in her way had better watch out!

ABOUT THE AUTHOR

Edna Frederikson was born in Arkansas and spent her childhood in Oklahoma. She was educated in these states and at the University of Iowa, the University of Nebraska, and the Graduate School of the University of Kansas which awarded her the Ph.D. degree. Her professional life has included the teaching of English at Madison College in Harrisonburg, Virginia. A world traveller, she makes her home in Harrisonburg. This is her first novel.

THREE PARTS EARTH

Edna Frederikson

POPULAR LIBRARY - TORONTO

To the memory of
my husband
Otto Frovin Frederikson

BOOK ONE

Quite a Bit of Growth,
Almost Unthoughted

CHAPTER I

Out of the Dimness

Summertime on the farm at Urbanette was more interesting than the fall. In summer I could prit nigh always play outdoors, and Jennie and Sallie were at home all day, too. Even when they ran off and left me, there'd be something for me to do. Like play with my chicken. I'd hold him close to my mouth and he'd bob his head and take a peck or two at my teeth. Probably he thought they were grains of corn. If I tapped a finger on his head, he'd say, "Chuck-chuck," sort of deep in his stomach, which showed he'd be a rooster when he grew up. Only he didn't live to grow up. One day I was playing with him, and Mama hollered at me from the house, so I turned a tin can down over him to save catching him again. But I forgot, and coming back after a long while, I found him all limp, with his eyes shut. He felt ugly on my hand, and I slung him as far as I could into the weeds and rubbed my hand on my skirt to get rid of the feel of him there. Then I ran around and around the house, laughing and hollering so much that I couldn't think of him any more.

In hot weather also I could chase butterflies. I wasn't very good at catching them. Sallie was, and with one of the prettiest, bright blue or maybe velvety brown with orange spots, between her fingers, she'd bite off its head. This was supposed to mean she'd get a dress the color of the butterfly. Try as I would, I couldn't remember about the colors long enough to be sure that either of us ever got the dresses afterwards, but it didn't seem to me that we did. So it was probably just as well that I caught very few butterflies, since biting off their heads wasn't a thing I pleasured in exactly.

Better than butterfly-chasing was to have Jennie and Sallie persuade Mama to let them walk into Urbanette and get her a spool of thread, say, or it might be some baking powder if

7

she'd run out. They didn't want me along, but Mama's hands were so full with our new little baby girl that often she made them take me. They'd choose the shortcut through the fields going in, and we'd pull some wax off the waxweeds for chewing gum, but coming back they'd keep to the road and we'd stop for a rest at the Stinkamafoddas place. The name of the people was really Philbeck, of course. Mama just called them Stinkamafoddas for her mischief. They were dirty and no-'count, according to her, the younguns had sticky fingers and their mother was fitified. If we didn't go to their place, they wouldn't feel encouraged to come to ours. So Mama said. But we had to pass right by their house, and there was such a flock of Stinkamafoddas children that one of them was sure to spy us and call out for us to come see some new little kittens or a calf or something. We didn't overlook the dirt and the danger that Miz Philbeck might have a fitty spell, but we couldn't resist the invitation. Then, too, Sallie was always hoping for a chance to steal back our checkerboard.

The summertime was full of such interesting things to remember out of the dimness of other things around them. But, oh, best of all in the summer was for us Douds to gether up and go to visit at Granpa and Granma McNabb's place at Tomahawk. Papa'd hitch the team to our little red and green spring wagon, Mama'd take Alma in her arms, all of us would clamber in, and away we'd go. Granma McNabb never paid me much mind, but I was supposed to be Granpa's favorite grandchild. He'd diddle me on his knee, saying, "Did you ever see a p-p-possum in a p-p-paw-paw p-p-patch, p-p-pickin' up p-p-paw-paws, p-p-puttin' 'em in his p-p-pocket, p-p-poor little p-p-pitiful p-p-puke?" as fast as he could, and have me try to repeat the words after him, until Mama said, "Hush your mouth, child, nobody wants to hear it a-goin' like a clapboard in a goose's hine end." I'd feel like crawling off in an auger-hole, but Granpa'd only laugh and stand me on the floor.

I would light out for the cookroom, in hopes of overtaking Jennie, Sallie, Aunt Myrtle and the uncles. There were four of them still at home—Will, the oldest, then the twins, Ras and Bras, who were a little bit ahead of Myrtle in age, and last of all Troy, who was some older than me and, being a boy, always got to go with the others whether I was allowed to or not. Their special play-spot was a deserted house beyond the creek. The others hopped across, but I stopped on

8

the bank and began to cry. Bras was the only one who noticed. Once he came back and fixed me a little mill-wheel, which he wedged between two rocks in the beautiful clear dancing water. How it did spin, around and around and around, that little wooden wheel! I was almost entirely comforted, and loved Uncle Bras very much.

Now at last fall had come, and there were no more trips to Granpa's, and no little yellow chickens, and only a few butterflies to shake and shine at noontime above Mama's pink and purple asters. Jennie and Sallie started in to school again, and while they went on with their play-town under the sweet-apple tree, it had a bad location for me, at yon end of the orchard next to the barn lot and not far from the straw-covered shack for the cattle. A few weeks ago Papa'd found some of the straw on the ground, raked together for a bed, with the prints in it where some strange man must have slept all night in the dark near the cows. I wasn't scared in company with Jennie and Sallie, but not for love nor money would I have gone to that end of the orchard by myself.

The girls picked the place because its very distance from the house discouraged Mama from staving out every so often to see about matters she wouldn't understand. The sweet-apple tree was a fine big one, however, with limbs bending over till they almost touched the ground. I was never allowed to play, but I'd sit in my wooden box at the edge of the town, watching and listening hard. When I knew how to join in, I fancied that Jennie and Sallie wouldn't mind my being with them.

The drawback now that school had begun was that the girls weren't able to play in the orchard except on Saturdays and sometimes a little on Sundays, which caused them more than ever to wish to be by themselves, and I had to watch them like a hawk or they'd sneak off without me. So when one of the Saturdays finally got there after a lot of school days, and Mama said, "Yuns needn't be in such a killin' big rush about breakfast, yuns ain't a-goin' down to that ol' orchard till the dew dries off," I didn't let out a cheep. Finishing my bowl of nice warm oatmeal and Little Reddie's milk, I went onto the back porch to wait, perched on my box, while Mama tried a dress on Jennie, and Sallie washed the dishes.

" 'Frog went a-courtin' an' he did ride,' " I sang, to keep myself company, and thumping my heels against the box.

What a lovely box it was! with big red and black letters on the sides, and a lid that fitted, just right to hold my treasures. At present these consisted of part of a catalogue of wallpaper samples and a small piece of almost-new screen wire, but who could tell? I might obtain more any day.

" 'Sword an' a pistol by his side,' " I sang on, leaving off to make room for Sallie beside me on the box. She'd brought the turpentine to dob some on her sore foot.

"Dob on some more," I said earnestly. "You don't want to get the blood poisonin' from that rusty ol' nail you stepped on the other day." And I mentioned that I myself might have died a few days ago, though not from blood poisoning.

"I swallered a pin. I was a-rockin', an' I had the pin between my teeth, an' after a while the chair came down extry hard, an' when I happened to think of it, I didn't have no pin in my mouth no more. So Mama an' me looked on the floor an' in all the cracks, an' they wasn't no pin there, so we knew it was in me."

"You're still alive, though."

I felt quite guilty about it, and explained that the only reason I hadn't died was that Mama'd made me eat a lot of cabbage and take some castor oil to work me. "She thought the pin'd catch on the cabbage an' go out that way. An' I guess proberly it did," I said. Sallie seemed interested and in a pretty good humor, so I asked could I come with her and Jennie.

"No."

"I'll give you somethin' if you'll let me."

"What?"

I answered the almost-new piece of screen wire, and that wasn't satisfactory, so I had to admit that I also owned some wallpaper samples.

"I'll have the wallpaper," said Sallie. "I'll cut my paper dolls out some dresses from it."

So far, so good. Jennie appeared, and I set off down the orchard path close behind her and Sallie, dragging my box and trying not to call attention to myself. Since the girls had make-believe families living under every tree and must pause to pass the time of day with every family, it took some while for us to reach the play-town under the sweet-apple tree. I was feeling more and more hopeful about my prospects, but now Jennie wheeled on Sallie and said, "What's *she* doin' here?"

Sallie had a lumpy rag doll named Billy Cobweb who lived in a shoe box. "Come on," she said, busily arranging him in it. "Let's p'like I'm Billy Cobweb. Mornin', Mr. Turnipseed, how you come on?"

"I ain't Mr. Turnipseed yet," said Jennie, who saw through everything. "I want to know what call you got to let Delphie come without askin' me."

"You was in the house." Sallie screwed up her eyes and pretended to spit tobacco juice into the weeds. "This is Billy Cobweb. He wants to know what Jeff Turnipseed aims to do about them chickens o' his'n that got into Miz Cobweb's garden an' et up all the tomaters."

If only Mr. Turnipseed would stroke the place where he was supposed to have chin-whiskers, and politely reply something like, "I swear to God," and had them ol' dominickers been a-doing that! But no. Jennie wasn't playing while I was there. I didn't know what had got into her. Generally always it was Sallie who caused me the most trouble.

"I give her my wallpaper to let me come," I said, my chin trembling.

Sallie promptly pointed to my box. "She's got a piece of almost-new screen wire, too."

"I'll look at it," said Jennie, and did, deciding that she could bend it and tie a string to it and have her a little surrey for Jeff Turnipseed to ride around in. "It ain't much," she added, not quite satisfied, and eyeing my hair. "I tell you what. You let me comb an' pleat your hair after dinner, an' you can stay down here till then."

If there was one thing I hated, it was to have that girl monkey around with my hair. But she dearly loved to do it, and I could always undo the pleats afterwards, so I got me an apple out of the grass and crawled into my box, the single treasure I had left, and Jennie pulled some imaginary spectacles to the end of her nose and told Mr. Cobweb he could have some turnips out of Miz Turnipseed's garden to make up for the tomaters.

The girls were warming up on the old fellows and would soon be ready for Ruben and Struben. These two lived on a prong of Bear Creek, and Ruben was sparking Struben, but it seemed like her friendship for him had growed cold, leastways that was what they were telling around. The girls'd had to break off at this stage last week, and unless they'd done some playing since that I didn't know about, which I doubted, they'd go on from there today. At that moment I noticed half a worm wiggling in the bitten place in my apple, and my stomach heaved and I began to hack and spit, trying to get out of me every bit of what it looked like might be in me. Meantime, the girls must have got onto the subject of sparking all right, for the next thing I knew Sallie was dancing up and down, being nobody in the world except herself and quite careless of her sore foot while she sang out, "Jennie's got a feller! Jennie's got a feller!"

"I ain't no such!" said Jennie hotly.

"He give her a little red ribbon at school the other day, an' she tied it around her wrist! Pud Philbeck!" sang Sallie.

You wouldn't have thought she'd stoop to teasing her own sister about such a boy.

"I just wore it 'cause he give 'em to all the girls." Jennie was almost crying. But Sallie never paid much heed to warning signs, so she got slapped, and the noise coming from her mouth changed without a break from singsong to straight howl.

"Did I really hurt you?"

At the thought Sallie bawled louder than ever.

"Don't take on so," Jennie begged. "I didn't aim to hit so hard. You'll have Mama down on us in a minute."

"Don't care if I do," said Sallie, but having quit hollering long enough to speak, she stayed quit and glanced around and saw me where I'd got out of my box in the excitement. "It's *her* fault," she declared, and headed towards me. "Allus pokin' in where she ain't wanted an' gettin' folks upset." I shied away from her, and fell backwards into my box. "Go on up to the house," she ordered, standing over me. "You can keep your ol' wallpaper."

"Go on," Jennie chimed in, also standing over me. "You can keep your screen wire, too. I'd ruther have my freedom."

I went, but bellowing at every step, for if Sallie hadn't already roused Mama up, I aimed to do it myself and maybe she would 'tend to those girls.

"What ails you, youngun?"

She was on the porch to meet me, a piece of Jennie's blue

12

sateen dress in her hands, and rather cross, afraid I'd wake the baby.

"They made me go away. I wasn't doin' nothin'. They just made me go away."

"Well, I wouldn't try to stay around 'em if they didn't want me. I'd have too much pride."

"I don't want to have no pride," I sobbed, lugging my box up the steps. "I want to have some fun."

She studied me for a minute, then suggested it'd be nice if I stayed with her this morning. "I enjoy your company, Puss," she told me.

"Well, I enjoy yours, too, Mama," I said. "But you don't do nothin' to entertain me."

"Do you have to be entertained ever' minute of your little life?"

All the same, she went indoors and returned with a scrap of blue sateen and a needle with heavy black thread. "Here. Do you think you can enjoy yourself with these?"

"Oh, yes, Mama, I know I can. I'll set right here on my box."

Humming to myself bits from an old song of hers, about one Monday morning John did go down to the meadow for to mow, whilst swinging my legs to shoo off the flies that still sailed around so heavy and bitey in the chilly mornings, I sat and sewed, and after a while Jennie and Sallie came up to dinner. I let them arrive at the porch without one glance from me.

"What you doin'?" said Sallie interestedly.

"Emborderin'," I replied coldly.

"Let's see what you done." Jennie took my scrap of goods and held it out. "Gee, honey, you're gettin' so you do real good. Look, Sallie, ain't that good for her?"

I explained that I'd intended to make me a little pocket-book, but Mama wouldn't let me borry her scissors, so I'd decided just to emborder. I couldn't keep from grinning. The black thread did look pretty against the blue cloth, or would if the cloth hadn't got a mite dirty or had a few dots of blood from the places where I'd picked my fingers with the needle.

"Would you like to come down an' play with us after dinner?" said Sallie.

I almost cried goodie before I remembered. "What do I have to give you this time?" I said suspiciously.

13

"Not a single solitary thing. All you have to do is loan us your box."

"You want my box?"

"Just to play with," said Jennie. "It'll still be yourn."

"I don't think I want you to play with my box."

"Oh, yes, you do." Sallie was very mysterious. "We have an idy for the most fun with it!"

In spite of experience, I let myself be persuaded.

After dinner, accordingly, I got my doll Pearl and the girls took my box and we all went down to the sweet-apple tree again, Jennie climbed up to lodge the box between some limbs and the trunk, Sallie handed her the biggest of the rag dolls, a rather special one made from an old red flannel underskirt of Mama's with eyes, nose and mouth stitched on the face with the same strong black thread I'd been using, and Jennie set him inside the box.

"There!" she cried. "That's God an' His house!"

What imaginations she and Sallie did have! Their idea filled the day with excitement. It lasted through Sunday and carried over into another Saturday. Every possible kind of thing was going on, especially dying. At first people were scared, but then they held a protracted camp meeting, with everybody repenting and singing,

"*Are your garments spotted, are they white as snow,*
Are they washed in the blood of the Lamb?"

so they'd be sure of going to heaven, and after that they prayed to die. If their prayers weren't answered right away, they went out and ate dirt or exposed themselves to bad weather so as to hurry matters along. One of Sallie's men even pretended he was fitified, and fell down and rolled on the ground like Miz Philbeck up the road. But God wasn't to be fooled a bit more than hurried. He simply sent one of Jennie's angels down to give the man a look and say, "Just for that, you ain't a-goin' to die at all, mister, not in the near future. You're a-goin' to stay right here in Urbanette, Arkansas, for the rest o' your born days. How do you like that?"

The trouble was, such a lot of people had died, there were hardly any to live in Urbanette any more, and Jennie and Sallie were spending most of their time hopping around in the tree, being angels. This left me alone on the ground, my head thrown back to follow their movements while I hugged Pearl in my arms. She was my store doll, and had a china head with yellow hair painted on, china hands and feet with tiny little black boots also painted on, and her name dented in on the china at the front of the neck where it was glued to the part of her that was cloth and stuffed with sawdust. I wished very much that she could go to heaven, too, but the girls were firm that I'd fall out of the tree and break my neck if I tried being an angel for her, so I could only hover beneath the boughs, craning upwards and saying, "Why don't you p'like," and "'Fise you."

So I was glad to have yet another Saturday rock around and the girls agree to give God and His angels a rest for the day in favor of fun on earth again. "This is ol' lady Cobweb, I'm a-comin' to see you, Miz Turnipseed," said Sallie. They'd chosen to limber up on old granmas rather than granpas, it appeared, and I thought I saw my chance.

"This is Pearl," I announced. "I'm a-comin' down the road to see Miz Turnipseed, too. Let's p'like you-all got up an' come to meet me, you was so pleased to see me."

"It's a fur piece to Miz Turnipseed's," said Sallie. "It's too fur for Pearl."

"No, it ain't," I said. "She's already here. Howdy, Miz Turnipseed, I brought you some onion sets for your garden."

"Now ain't that onfortunate," said Jennie. "You tell Pearl, Miz Turnipseed ain't got no garden."

"She had one the other day!" I cried, and reminded her that Mr. Turnipseed had given Mr. Cobweb some turnips out of it.

"Well, after that the Turnipseeds dees-continued their garden," said Sallie. She and Jennie were grinning at each other, because it was so easy for them to get the better of me, or so they thought. I planted myself in front of them.

"I'm here. I'm Pearl, an' it's goin' to be onfortunate if you don't let me play, too."

"You ain't here," said Sallie. "You're over there. Can't you contain yourself for a minute?"

"No, sir, I got as much right to make up talk an' stuff as you."

"You ain't either. Whose play-town is this, anyhow?"

"It's your play-town, but God's house is mine, so there!"

15

"It is not! God's house is God's house. It's been His'n so long He ain't got no memory o' when it wasn't. An' just for that, you can't stay down here no longer."

Too late, I saw I'd gone too far. "I can, too, stay, can't I, Jennie?" I pleaded.

"No, you been tormentin' us long enough. I reckon we've earned God's house. You go on now."

"I'll take my box if you make me go," I sobbed.

"Just you try touchin' God's house," said Sallie, "an' He'll show you whose house it is! Somethin'll happen to *you*, all right. You might as well go on. It ain't a-goin' to do you one particle o' good to stand around here this mornin' bawlin' for buttermilk."

It didn't do me any good that morning, and I had to bide my time all through that day and Sunday. But on Monday morning, after Papa'd gone off across the fields to see if any of the long slim minks playing up and down Bear Creek had got into his traps, and Jennie and Sallie'd trudged away to school, swinging their shiny little tin dinner pails beside them, Mama told me to skedaddle down to their play-town and get my box. "An' don't let me hear you foamin' an' faunchin' around about it no more, Delphie, or I'm a-goin' to blister you good."

I'd been half-expecting her to come with me. Could she have forgotten about the cattle shack beyond the orchard where that unknown man had slept? Or was there really no danger any more? Eyes now to one side, now to the other, I moved away from her along the orchard path. How cold it was, and silent, here this morning! and how strange and gray the trees were! They looked as if during the night some of the mist had got caught among their curly dry leaves and the little withered apples still clinging to their boughs, and it occurred to me that each tree had kind of huddled itself together to stay warm against being scared, like me in bed at night when I was afraid of Raw-Head-and-Bloody-Bones. What sound was that from the cattle shed? A cow mooing? And that snapping in the weeds—was it only a chicken? I wanted to run, but then I couldn't watch out so well, nor hear if something was sneaking up on me. Slowly I went on setting one bare foot ahead of the other on the frost-wet grass and ground. I'd hardly realized in advance what a big brave act I was undertaking. If I hadn't loved boxes so much, and if

I hadn't had to show those girls in any case, as a matter of pride, and beyond all, if I hadn't gone on reminding myself that Mama wasn't far off, that she was thinking of me this minute and would come quick as lightning if anything started to get me—if I hadn't had all that to screw up my courage by, I'd never have made it to the sweet-apple tree.

Only when I was there did I remember Sallie's threat about God, and I took a quick look up to where He sat in my box, staring straight out through His stitched-in black eyes. But whether or not He frightened me, and whether I mightn't break my neck in a fall from the tree, I had no time to consider. At that moment something stirred in the barn lot, or I thought it did, and in a flash I had skinned up the tree, swept the box to the ground, and with a few thumps and scrapes to myself—nothing important—was down again and speeding along the path towards Mama and safety, hauling my box and not failing to keep one sharp eye to the back. There was no cause for alarm behind me, however. The barn lot went on being silent and deserted, while the girls' red rag doll that was supposed to be God stayed where He'd been tossed face-down, His stitched-in black nose in the dust.

CHAPTER II

Close Together

Getting back God's house, with Mama's help certainly, was just about the most important act I could ever afterwards recall doing in my life, up to that point. And it just about broke up the girls' play-town in the orchard. It was high time for us younguns to come in out of the cold anyway, Mama said, and she hardly ever let us play outdoors. The house wasn't much fun with Jennie and Sallie there, and practically none without them. For one thing, the baby was always crying, which upset Mama and she'd take it out on me as Alma was a puny child and had to be coddled all the time. And if she wasn't crying, she was sleeping and not a sound must disturb her. So it was still a relief to have a Saturday roll around, with Sallie tending the baby and Jennie helping Mama, and maybe winning a reward.

"Can we go play in the barn now, Mama?" they'd coax.

From the orchard their imaginary families had moved into the barn, the Cobwebs making their home in the corncrib and the Turnipseeds in the stalls. The girls also had programmies in the loft. They never had programs, they held that programmies were more stylish. Jennie played a make-believe piano, thumping her fingers all along the keyboard, and bouncing on her tee-hiney from the energy it took, while Sallie pretended to scrape a fiddle, twisting and bending every which-way, and humming the tune in order to let the audience know what it was.

The audience was me. I had to sit in the hay with the kittens and keep quiet until the music was over and then clap to beat the band. For a change the girls spoke pieces, and once in a long while they let me speak one, too. Oh, it was fun! I folded my hands in front of my stomach and grinned with the pleasure of it.

> "We have a cow all red and white
> We love with all our hearts,
> She gives us milk with all her might
> To eat with apple tarts."

I got tired of the piece, but it was the only one I knew, and the girls were all for it because it was short. What I liked was to make up a story about my doll Pearl. But Sallie always got the fidges, and I had to quit all of a sudden, saying, "An' that was all of hit." As a general rule, however, I stuck to the cow or the girls didn't allow me to speak at all. And first of all they had to get us to the barn.

"Why do you want to play in that ol' barn?" Mama'd say.

She was always suspicious of anything we appeared to enjoy too much. As for Papa, he was just suspicious. And on a Sunday, when he and Mama were sitting around the house all day, we children could might nigh count on having to sit around there with them. They tried to keep us satisfied, we gave them credit for that, but all they could think of was to ask riddles which we knew the answers to already, or for Jennie and Sallie to do some chording on the organ. Both of them could play, they took right after it even though it was by ear. "I surely would pleasure in some good organ music," Papa'd say. "I don't reckon you girlies know who could supply me with some." One of the girls would sit down and start pedaling, and the organ would puff out the first sweet wheezy notes of Papa's favorite piece, *When the Roll Is Called Up Yonder*. From that they might go on to the prisoner's song or to another about the picture that hung on the wall, one girl playing and one singing.

I'd crawl under the bed in the corner of the room, listening to the music and whispering to myself, little stories sort of, or maybe just words and nice thoughts, and after a while Mama and Papa would begin to talk of times when they were young and about people dead so long that I had never seen them, like Granpa and Granma Doud, and two little boys named Dow and Orien, who were my brothers and would have been older than Jennie if they'd lived. Then sometimes Papa would be telling, slow and grave, about the night his father passed away, how he said, "Son, I think I'm goin' to have a bad night," and Papa went to wipe the blood from his mouth, for it was the consumption that he had, and Granma Doud began to cry, but Granpa said, "Here now, Frances, I don't want none o' that," and all at once I'd remember that Raw-Head-and-Bloody-Bones was under this very bed at night, and out I'd roll so fast that Mama couldn't help laughing and asking who'd been pulling Delphie's tail-feathers now.

The move into Urbanette changed all that. We lived in a place that Papa put up midway between the depot and the schoolhouse, and during the week people came and went, selling us eggs, chickens and the skins of possums, skunks and minks they'd trapped, and buying back our flour and feed. The produce store was in one side of the building and our quarters in the other, but there was an extra room at the back for storing skins until they were shipped to St. Louis. Sometimes they weren't quite dry. Then if the wind blew from that direction, they almost stunk us out.

What did I care? Compared to the farm, everything in Urbanette was fun or at least more pleasant, the same as summer was better than fall out there. Among other things, Alma wasn't so fretful, and would stop whimpering entirely if Sallie took her on her lap in the big rocking chair, and rocked and sang to her. Most wonderful of all the changes for me, though, was that I got to go to school for the first time, not

19

every day, but whenever the road wasn't muddy, or if I'd got my shoes on the wrong feet and Mama had to hold out some inducement for me to unlace them and put them on right. I tried to get them on wrong on purpose, but I couldn't tell them apart. So it was just up to God what days I went to school.

My eagerness didn't mean I was so bent on learning. I simply liked being at school. The primer class stood at the back of the room and read to one of the older girls. When the grubby tattered old book came down the row to me, I stared hard at the picture and said, "Bz-bz-bz, cat an' dog," which was what the others had said as well as I could make out, and the girl seemed to think I had read a line, so I thought maybe I had, too, and gazed around the room some more.

Pretty soon Papa sold the produce store and we all gethered up and went on the train over to Berryville and lived for a month in a big old house there. This town had sidewalks, and I went to school all the time. Staying such a short while I didn't learn much here either, but there were interesting things at that school, like a girl who instead of ears had a hole in each side of her head. And at home there was a whore who lived next door to us. She walked past like an ordinary woman, but she was a whore all right, because Mama spied on her and found out, and a whore was one of the worst things a person could be, whatever it was.

Then Papa quit his job at the stave mill and we all got on the train again and went away over into Oklahoma, to a town called Bridgewater. Here we stayed in a hotel, but only for a few days as it cost so much money, and then we moved into a little gray house at the top of a hill right where the town ended and the country began. It was a mighty poor excuse for a house, the wind came in through cracks and holes, and there was a good house down the street which we could have had for five dollars a month. But the house on the hill went with the land that Papa was going to farm, and he said it wouldn't be long till the weather would moderate. There were two rooms and a lean-to kitchen, and Mama papered them all with fresh newspapers so they wouldn't be so dirty-like. In addition, she got some white sandrock, which you could find in the fields around there, and with it she scrubbed the floors until they were clean enough to eat from.

"The place still looks like it's ready to fall down," said Jennie, and was warned by Papa that she was complaining too much for her own good.

Again, for my part, I didn't so much mind about the house. Every school day I was carrying my very own books clear across town to the grade school, and once every month I had my very own report card to show that I was learning something at last. Sometimes at school a boy might holler at me, "Redhead, gingerbread, five cents a cabbagehead!" but not very often any more. And though it was a damp cold spring in general, at length it rolled around to Easter, a fine sunshiny day, followed by another which was going to be of the same order to judge by its morning start, and I could sit on the back steps with my report card in my hand, admiring it. It wasn't Easter vacation, however, for Mama, elbow-deep in the family wash on the porch behind me. As for Jennie and Sallie, they were having a holiday the same as myself, but it wasn't affording them the same pleasure either since Jennie had to help Mama while Sallie tended the baby, rocking to and fro with her in the swing which hung from the big oak tree before us.

> "Darling little Nell, darling little Nell,
> Many hearts are yearning for thee . . ."

Alma was singing, and Mama straightened up from the washboard to enjoy the sight and sound of her. "None o' the rest o' you younguns knew songs an' could sing like that when you wasn't much more'n two years old," she remarked. Her face pinkened, and she stole a quick look at Jennie and me, as she'd almost plagued herself out with her bragging. But Jennie said, "Almie's pretty, too. She puts me in mind of an apple bloom."

She was ranching the suds out of the clothes in a tub alongside Mama's. I followed her glance back to the baby, on Sallie's lap in the sunshine falling down through the little green leaves of that old gray oak. She was very pretty, I could see, with that pink-and-white complexion like Jennie's apple bloom, hair shining soft and goldy red, and eyes not too different from the sky, so bright and gleaming blue this morning. It was a fact that her teeth were a little black from the medicine she'd had to take all her life, but that didn't show from this distance, and how clear and sweet she was

21

singing on about darling little Nell! lisping a bit but never missing a word of her song. At the same time, wasn't I right here, atilt on the steps with a good start on my education, and a grade card to prove it? I ran to hold it under Mama's nose.

"See, I got *very good* in phonies!"

"You remarked it before," said Jennie. "Little Braggy."

"I'd a little ruther it'd been *very good* in writin' or 'rithmetic," said Mama. "I reckon phonies are all right, but you can't even tell me what they are. I don't see how you can be so good in 'em."

Neither did I, and tried again to see if we hadn't read the teacher's handwriting wrong. But I couldn't make anything out of it except p-h-o-n-i-e-s, which was phonies.

> *"Though you walk the streets of gold*
> *By the prophets told of old . . ."*

I ran out to the swing. "Want me to push?"

"No," said Sallie, above Alma's voice.

> *"Still we miss you from this world of ours,*
> *Little Nell."*

Oh, it was sad! Mama called out to Sallie to button that baby's sweater, and I went back to the porch. "'Pears like Almie's had more colds'n common this spring," she said, wringing out one of her big white underskirts and handing it to Jennie. "It's the drafty ol' floors in this house." She pulled a section of white countapin onto the washboard and rubbed her big fat bar of yellow homemade soap up and down against it, then crumbled a little white sandstone on to make extra sure it'd come absolutely clean like she had to have it, going on to say that Alma ought to have a little flannel cloth on her chest right now. "Once the washin's on the line, I reckon I'd better fix her one."

"I use to wear a little flannel cloth like that, didn't I?" I said, coming to stand beside her. "With turpentine on it, an' some lard to keep it from blisterin'."

"Yes, you was real good about it." It was me Mama was enjoying the sight and sound of now, and she gave me one of her special sweet smiles. "We was livin' on that poor ol' forty-acre farm up above Allerton, Arkansas. You'd be out

22

playin' an' it'd come off. Then you'd come a-sizzin' in with, 'Mama, I lost my little flannel cloth,' an' I'd have it to put on again."

"What was some other things I did?" I said, pleased.

"Oh, you sneezed before breakfast," said Jennie, "so you didn't catch cold, an' nobody had to werry about you."

I got my breath, to argue about it. "They did, too. Mama werried when I had the three-months' colic, didn't you, Mama?"

"I don't know as I was so much werried as bothered. It was in the hotel at Allerton where you was borned. For three solid months I walked the floor with you o' nights to keep you from cryin' an' disturbin' the folks who was stayin' with us."

It made me a little sad to think that I'd only bothered people instead of worrying them, and I returned to the steps and watched Sallie and Alma sliding slowly back and forth through the brightness and blueness. Having run out of regular songs, Sallie was making them up. "Away up in heaven," she sang, "Almie will be."

Alma sang the words after her, and their shadow rocked across my feet. It was too much for me, sad as I already was, and surprising myself as much as anybody, I broke suddenly into song, the happiest one I knew, about if her father's cottage turned into a palace, she'd be none the happier, happy little Alice; though what, I couldn't help thinking, if I should discourage God from changing our house into a palace! supposing He had any such notion in the first place.

"Make Delphie hush!" cried Sallie, mad as a hornet, and Alma gave a whimper.

"Hush up, Delphie, you know you can't sing to do no good," said Mama. And reminding me that Sallie had to keep the baby quiet till the wash was done, she added, "If you can't be good, settin' there in that nice sun, I'll find somethin' for you to do."

It wasn't fair. She might have done a little better than to let one child be pretty and smart and a singer all at one time. She ought to have divided things up more. I felt like a singer inside, too, like bursting if the feeling couldn't get out. I would listen hard to myself singing, and it sounded nice. I didn't know why it didn't have that effect on other people. There'd been a time when I was cute, Mama herself said so. I'd heard her say I'se the cutest little short thing when I was

23

born. But this was a long time ago, in the hotel at Allerton where I'd had the three-months' colic.

That hotel was another place which Papa put up for us. It was a good two-story frame building with a long porch running clear across the front, downstairs and up, painted white, and directly facing the little red depot across the street. I couldn't remember the hotel, yet it was nearly the same as if I could, I'd heard so much about it and about the cold January night when I was born. Mama'd been doing the washing the day before, exactly as she did it once a week of the live-long year, and at three o'clock in the morning Papa rousted himself out to go for Ol' Doc Grimes, who hadn't studied medicine for more than a year down at Little Rock but who knew how to bring babies into the world well enough.

Then there was Mama's Sister Hat. She thought her family was better than ours, but came to help Mama out for a week or two, one result being that I wound up with her name. Thank goodness, it was my middle name, and I didn't have to go around being called Hattie. "I had to speak my thank-you some way, Delphie," Mama'd excuse herself to me. She hadn't any excuse for taking my other name off a Delpha shoe box that happened to be standing on a shelf across the room from her bed. She thought it was a pretty name, to go with Doud.

The Doud Hotel, in Allerton, Arkansas. I got quite a bit of growth on me there, almost unthoughted, I imagined, while Papa sat around gassing with the drummers in the office but with his ear primed to catch any important sound from other parts of the house, such as the kitchen, where Mama was doing the cooking with the help of a woman named Lutie Elder. Ol' Lutie, as Mama referred to her. She was some sort of kin to Aunt Hat's husband. They all thought I was cute then. Once the governor of the state and the members of his staff laid over at our hotel between trains, and Mama and this old Lutie fixed dinner for them, a chicken dinner set out with napkins and toothpicks and all the style Mama'd ever heard of, including a coconut cake placed in the middle of the long table just to be fancy till it was time to cut it. The governor had some papers sticking out of the side pocket of his coat, and I toddled up to his chair at the table, pulled them out and was playing with them on the floor when Papa noticed, and returned them to the governor. Soon everybody went back to eating, and I crawled over and got the papers again, and would have played with them some more but that I fell against the stove and burned the back of my head, so that I had a tiny little bald spot there to this day, but fortunately where it didn't show.

The governor's papers was a story I'd often heard Mama and Papa tell and laugh about from the time when I was little and cute. Mama had another from the farm above Allerton which she'd been speaking of a few minutes ago. For some reason, nobody had ever told me what it was, Papa sold our nice hotel and bought this poor old forty-acre farm on a hill just outside Allerton. It was hard to fathom, because, according to Jennie, we'd been so happy in that hotel compared to afterwards—at Christmas the people who lived in Allerton set up an evergreen tree in our yard, it was for everybody and was decorated, oh, so pretty, with presents on it for all the children, among them Jennie, who received a big doll with eyes that opened and shut and a little go-buggy for it and candy and nuts to last a week; and this, as I myself knew, was a lot more than any of us children ever got nowadays. Whatever the cause of our leaving the hotel, there we were on that scrubby farm above Allerton, and at times Mama'd have an errand in town and come home to find all three of us younguns waiting for her stacked up on a stump in the yard, Jennie on the bottom, Sallie on her lap, and me on top. To hear Mama tell it, we were an awfully cute sight, me in particular.

Then Papa had a long spell of sickness, which was another odd thing about that time as he was never sick nowadays, and we sold the farm, at best it was scarcely possible to make a living on it, and Papa having got well enough to travel, we sashayed over into Oklahoma for the first time, to Muskogee, or maybe it was Checotah or Sapulpa, or maybe all three in turn, I could never keep it straight how it was supposed to have been. Was it about there that Alma had come in? Or was it after we returned to Arkansas to live? I stared again at the baby and Sallie in the swing, then down towards the long field stretching off to the back of the house where Papa was planting cotton, and at last around at Mama and Jennie on the porch. Still the answer escaped me, and after a minute I asked Mama.

"Where did I get Almie? Why, out of a holler oak tree.

That's where I got all you little tadpoles." She laughed till her face was pink, it was such a good joke our being tadpoles and her finding us in a holler oak tree. She mixed me up.

"I don't mean that. I mean—I mean—"

"You mean where was she borned," said Jennie. "It was at Urbanette. On the farm there. Surely you recall that."

I was prit nigh certain I did. I knew I remembered her in the rocking chair with Sallie after we moved into the produce store in town, which meant that she was also with us in the big house at Berryville. And it was in there somewhere, among all the places we'd lived since Allerton, that I must have come to the end of being little and cute, leastways I couldn't bring to mind any more entertaining stories about it.

Casting my eyes around once more, they came to rest on Papa, guiding the mare up one row and down the next, holding onto the handles of the cotton planter and hollering haw or gee at the turnings. Such a pretty field it was, or would have been, with its border of pale green scrub oaks in among a lot of little wild plum trees, all fluffed out now in white bloom, if it hadn't been for the cloud of yellow dust which the planter and the mare were stirring up around Papa. "Easy there, Net! Easy, girl!" he called out as he leaned back on the reins, tied together and looped around his waist.

"Papa's got awful long legs," said Mama sociably, "but he sure has to take big steps to keep up with that mare."

For her to be so tickled over Papa, sort of staggering along in all that dust, was a bit of a surprise to me, and I twisted around in order to see her better. But her pleasure was fading almost before it had arrived.

"Now what ails him to be a-runnin' up here at this time o' mornin'?" she exclaimed.

"He wants a swig o' fresh water, I expect," said Jennie.

We watched him get it at the pump, then come to join us on the porch. "That dust sure makes a feller dry," he said, smiling around at us all, and pulling off his old felt hat, he wiped his face against the sleeve of his shirt. I scooted over so that he could sit beside me, and from the top of the steps we both gazed down at Net, tied in the shade of a tree at one end of the field, and switching her tail as she nibbled little green leaves along the fence row.

"What time do you want me to come up to dinner, Mama?" he addressed her after a minute.

I felt that he was only making pleasant conversation, but

Mama said, "Now don't begin werryin' about dinner at this hour o' mornin', an' me with all this wash to get out." Rubbing away stronger than ever as if to show him, she also said that he thought he had it hard, but he just orter wash this family's dirty duds for once.

"You wouldn't like cotton-plantin' down there in the dust neither unless I'm mighty fur wrong," said Papa. "But I guess we both work hard enough, Brittie," he added gravely.

It was sad to think they both worked so hard, and I did not wish to begin it myself.

"Seems like the clothes won't never come clean," said Mama. She wouldn't argue with him now, but she'd tell us children later that her work was, too, harder than his, or at least it lasted longer. "Maybe it's 'cause it's the first o' the month," she went on, with the corners of her mouth turned down. "Dirt's harder to get out the first o' the month."

"But that ain't accordin' to reason," said Papa. "'Pears like dirt'd be as hard to get out one time as another."

"I don't know why it is. But I've heerd ol' women say it was harder to get out the first o' the month, an' I been a-watchin' it ever since I started doin' the family wash down at Calico Rock in Arkansas when I was nine years old, an' it sure is so, all right. An' I don't see no real call for you to go on conterdictin' me, Papa."

Alma was whimpering again. "Oh, all right," said Sallie, who'd paused in her songs to hear the talk between Papa and Mama, "here's your ol' Christmas song for the *second* time!" and resuming with jolly old St. Nicholas, turn your ear this way, she dashed through what the other children wanted down to

"*As for me, my little brain is not very bright,*
Choose for me, old Santa Claus, what you think is right."

The last came out in a perfect bawl as Sallie swung vexedly to and fro. Alma clung close. "What's Ch'istmas?" she lisped.

"Why, that's supposed to be the day Christ was borned on," said Mama, being especially nice so that Sallie should think she was enjoying herself. Besides, she was more content now that Papa was on his way back to the field, to get to work once more, like herself.

As for Sallie, her little brain might not be very bright, but it was made up. "That's all for today. I'm tired." Unwinding

27

Alma's arms from around her neck, she stood the baby on the ground, where she commenced to cry dismally.

"Now, Sallie, they's all them colored clothes for us to get out yet," said Mama. "What you got to stop now for?"

"I got to stop some time, hain't I?"

"Listen to that! Such language! 'Hain't I!'"

"I heard you say it."

"You didn't no such, an' you don't need to say you did."

"Yes, I did."

Mama looked harder at Sallie than she had at Papa. "What I say is a little different from what you say," she brought out at length.

"I don't see why, but all right." Sallie was well aware that the only reason she hadn't got boxed was her inconvenient distance from Mama. "*Ain't* I. Is that better?"

"That's a whole lot better. Now take that baby up an' pacify her."

There were two nice neighbor women, Miz Woods and Miz Carr, living at the bottom of our hill, and Miz Carr had a girl, Thelma, who was my age, and we used to play together. Among Thelma's play-pretties was a bunch of paper dolls, of stiff cardboard that was slick and shiny on the front side, and all very beautiful, the pink-cheeked girls having blue eyes and yellow curls as a rule, and wearing deep blue dresses with pink sashes or else the other way 'round, pink dresses with blue sashes, while the boy dolls were apt to have brown eyes and brown curly hair, and usually dark blue velvet suits. Miz Carr said that if I'd promise not to ruin them right away, Thelma could give me one girl in pink and one in blue as well as one boy in blue. I promised, and did take very good care of them, storing them in a shoe box on the front porch and not letting anybody touch them except me. Mama knew all this, yet only a few days later as I was toiling up the hill from school, the first view meeting my eyes was Alma on the front porch, put down there by Mama with my box. From a good ways off I was already becoming mad, and when I came onto the porch and saw that Alma had bitten a corner off my boy doll and got dirt on the girl with the pink silk dress, I became even madder. Then, too, I'd had a very trying day at school, and before I could stop myself I just reached out and gave that baby a slap. It wasn't so very much of a slap, after all, it was no more than a quick little

28

tap for her to learn by, as Mama'd have said, but Alma broke into sobs as if I'd really hurt her.

"I'd be ashamed to treat my little sister thataway," said Mama, coming out of the house to gather Alma into her arms and soothe and pet her. "I'd be glad to have her feel well enough to want my play-pretties."

"She allus feels well enough to want 'em." I was trying to clean and straighten them.

"Take your things then, Selfish," said Mama.

She carried Alma into the front room, where I could hear her sobbing still. I felt like crying myself, from the pitiful sound of her, and from being called Selfish. If it hadn't been so unfair, almost I'd rather have been slapped in my turn and made to give up the dolls entirely. But I knew that I was in the right and that Mama ought to take care of my things when I was away from home instead of turning a baby loose on them, and when I'd got them wiped and flattened as well as I could, I went around the house and Sallie and I pumped to and fro in the swing. As we flew through the air, standing up face-to-face, we noticed how it was in streaks, cool one moment and warm the next, until we churned it up, and how all of it was weighted down with the smell of the wild plum blooms, so sweet and heavy that together with the swinging it turned us rather dizzy. Soon I forgot everything else except that it was getting on towards supper, and I was right down hungry.

Coming from school the next afternoon, I remembered my dolls and began staring hard from the foot of the hill. The baby was nowhere in sight, which didn't prove anything, and I wasn't easy in my mind till I'd opened the shoe box and found everything in good order. Alma was in the front room, covered up in the bed she slept in with Mama and Papa. She stayed there the rest of the evening and the days and nights following. If I woke up during the night I'd see Papa or Mama, one or the other, sitting beside her very quietly, the lamp turned low, and sometimes without fully waking I'd hear one of them get up to poke a stick of wood into the stove. To me, however, the house seemed chilly and dark even in the daytime when the sun shone against Mama's stiff white lace curtains, and I didn't like the smell of medicine. I would run outdoors, into the air that was gold from the sun and blue from the sky and that smelled so sweet from all those wild plums and from the lilac which had also burst into

29

bloom. Thelma Carr came up with her mother and Miz Woods, and we two children went to sit on the warm rounding red clay top of the storm cellar.

"My sister's sick," I told Thelma. "She's got the double pneumonie fever."

"I know," said Thelma, adding, "Do you think she'll die?"

"Oh, no." I tried to think why. "Doc Blaine come with another doctor today."

It sounded important. Yet somehow I felt all out of sorts, and I got up and said, "Would you like to have some lilacs to take home with you?" Mama'd said I could give her some, but be sure to take them from the purple bush.

"I'd rather have white," said Thelma.

"Well, they ain't many of those. I'll have to ask."

The only ones in the front room were the two neighbor women, Miz Woods with the baby in her arms. Neither of the women paid any heed to me, and I went on into the next room, where Mama was lying down on the girls' bed. This was strange enough, but then I noticed Jennie and Sallie sitting very still across the room, their eyes on the floor, and in the corner Papa, standing beside Mama's quilts, which were folded and stacked high on top of the bureau. How queer it was to see him leant over there, elbows on the quilts and forehead on his hands! I didn't know what to do, but Mama opened her eyes and stretched out her hand to me and said, "What is it you want, hon?" Before I could speak, Miz Carr came in and stopped by the bed, laying her hand on top of mine and Mama's, and saying something very softly. What I thought she said was, "Your little girl is gone." Then Mama, who'd lifted her face from the pillow, let it fall back and cried harder than I'd ever seen anybody cry. And across the room Jennie and Sallie were crying. And in the corner Papa dropped his face onto his arms and cried as well. I'd never heard such sobs. I thought they'd break my heart. I began to cry like the others, but Miz Carr led me into the kitchen and cleaned my face with a towel, put two of the big brown cookies she'd brought us into my hands and sent me to the yard again to be with Thelma.

"What's the matter?" said Thelma.

I gave her one of the cookies and bit into my own, chewing hard against the tears which were still hurting behind my eyelids. "I can't tell you," I said, but I went and picked the lilacs from the white bush because they were what she wanted.

30

After a while a man they called the undertaker came, and Papa pushed Mama's sewing machine out of the corner in the front room, putting a small board at each end to raise up the low places and make the top level, and Mama brought one of her heavy white countapins folded to fit and laid it there. And Miz Woods washed the baby and dressed her in her little white lawn dress with the lace insertion, all freshly washed and ironed, and pulled on her long white stockings. Jennie, Sallie and I were in the kitchen. Papa came out and said, "You girls may want to kiss your little sister, but the undertaker says you mustn't do it." They let us go in and look at her, lying on the sewing machine with her eyes shut and her soft goldy red hair combed out on a tiny white pillow. But she wasn't pink-and-white complected like an apple bloom any more, she was white like the pillow, or a wild plum bloom, and I was glad to have the undertaker bring a white casket, which looked very small, but then so was the baby, and put her into it and close the lid. Miz Woods and Miz Carr had pleated some pretty wreaths out of bridal wreath, as they called it, and in among the flowery white plumes they twined a few of the blue flags which were coming into bloom. These were laid on the casket, and we put it into the spring wagon with us and took it to the graveyard.

The sun had quit shining and rain was starting to fall. It was lonesome and gray and cold, and the rocky river bluffs on the far side of the graveyard, and the woods that were fulling from pink into green, and all the fields around seemed to grow quiet and to wait. We waited, too, while Alma's wet gleaming box went down into the deep hole that had been dug for it and the dirt was shoveled in after. You could hear the clods as they struck the little white casket. " 'Pears like they're hittin' me, inside," Jennie whispered, with a sob. We were all gathered close together under Mama's big black umbrella, all except Papa, who just stood and let the rain come down on him. When the whole grave had been filled in and a hump of red clay earth built up on top, we drove home again.

In the front room the fire had gone out and it was colder than ever. "Ain't you glad you was good to your little sister while you had her?" said Mama, looking with her red eyes at Sallie. I was at the window. Just outside was the big old oak where Alma and Sallie had swung and sung together such a short time back, and the rain was sliding down through its

31

young green leaves and falling over the long dark cotton patch which Papa'd been planting that day. I remembered other things, how Alma had lain so still in Mama's arms to be bathed the last time I'd noticed her very much, how I'd given away the prettiest of the lilacs and there weren't any left for her coffin, and that I'd slapped her. I remembered, standing for a while at the window with Sallie and gazing down towards the cotton patch. "The white plum blooms are all gone," said Sallie. "I guess the rain has beat 'em to the ground."

CHAPTER III

What Boys Were for

Alma's high chair was still in the kitchen. Lots of times as we were sitting down to a meal Mama's eyes would fall on it and she'd start to cry. "When people love each other so much, it don't look like they orter be separated," said Papa, and his eyes, like hers, would mist over. He blamed himself. He should have rented that other house for us to live in, it wasn't but the five dollars a month. "We thought we could save it," said Mama. "It ain't no more your fault than mine."

Presently the high chair was gone from its place, and school let out, and I had been promoted to the second grade, and it was summer. Then Mama got sick, it was from her stomach, Doc Blaine said, and he had her eat something called *Shredded Wheat*. Once in a while she'd give me one of the biscuits with milk and sugar, and it was simply wonderful. Finally, in the fall, men came with machines and dug a great pit in the red clay ground where the new high school was to be built on our hill, and before long our house would have to be torn down. So as soon as Papa had his cotton picked, we made another move, but this time not far off, only seven miles away from Bridgewater to a farm Papa rented on the banks of the Arkansas River. During the winter Jennie, Sallie and I walked two miles to a country school at Bonnot's

Grove, which wasn't much more than a broad place in the road, and the next spring Papa put in a really big cotton crop.

I knew a little about cotton-planting already, from watching Papa as I sat on the back porch there on the hill at Bridgewater, or as I waited in the shade at the end of a row for him to come up if I'd brought him some fresh water. Later on I'd thought that cotton was a pretty sight in bloom, with all three colors all over each green stalk at the same time, the big flowers that were white at first, then pink, and then red, before they withered and fell off. I'd admired it in the fall as well, seeing the soft fluffy white cotton full out in the sharp brown bolls, and it was fun to get to go with Papa to the cotton gin with a wagon load of the snowy stuff. But this spring at Bonnot's Grove I was beginning to grasp the difference between a cotton crop made at a distance, as you might say, by others, and a cotton crop made close to, with me taking part.

"In my opinion God didn't rightly know what He was about in creatin' weeds," said Sallie, on one of the hot sunshiny afternoons that found us children in the field hoeing along in our customary order, Jennie in the lead on one row, Sallie a little behind on the next, and me at the tail-end on another. "It's chop-chop-chop the gol-durned ol' weeds all the time."

"You ortn't to refer to God thataway," said Jennie, straightening up and slinging her heavy red pigtail back over her shoulder.

Like Sallie and me, she was wearing a funny-looking straw hat with a tall peak-ed crown sprinkled all over with big shiny red, green and blue butterflies. Papa'd bought one for each of us, he thought them pretty. Leastways, that was what he said. Mama declared that the stores kept all the gaudy truck for the Mexican trade, and that the clerks'd never tried to sell them to Papa except they saw he was green. She didn't mean any harm by saying it, but that must have been what they thought. Nevertheless, once bought, we had the awful things to wear in the field. Time and weather were toning the butterflies down, but not enough to soften the disgusted look which Jennie let fall on hers as she pulled it off and wiped her sweaty face on the sleeve of her dress.

"It'd be on the part o' wisdom," she went on, to Sallie, "not to let Papa hear you say 'gol-durned' neither."

"I don't care," said Sallie. "I'm hot. I been hot all day. I been hot for a week. I don't cool off at nights even. I wish we had some boys in this family. Then they could chop the cotton. That's what boys are for."

"'Fise doin' it, I'd just not create no cotton," I offered, from behind, but Sallie was faunching on about why Papa had to go off and leave us by ourselves down here.

"You know he went to see how Mama's feelin'," said Jennie impatiently.

"Well, I thought he allus claimed he didn't want us younguns toilin' in the field unless he was, too."

"He'll be right back."

Sallie grinned to me. "Jennie's a nanny goat. Takin' all that sulphur-an'-molasses for her blood o' late is turnin' her into a nanny goat. Ba-a-a! Ba-a-a!"

"Stop your bleatin'," said Jennie, adding very reasonably that she didn't care for chopping either but Papa needed our help. "You know he ain't been able to find anybody to hire, so I wish you'd hush up."

"I won't hush up," said Sallie. "I'm sufferin'." However, as Papa appeared on the bank of the creek at that moment, she did hush up, and in fact we all did, applying ourselves to work again without another word. Papa had that effect.

"Finish your rows, girlies," he called to us cheerfully. "Then we're knockin' off for the balance o' the day."

Sallie's mouth fell open, and stayed so. But Jennie, who never could leave well enough alone, it 'peared like, glanced up at how high the sun still was and wondered out loud what we were quitting so early for.

"It ain't my idy to have you childern in the field unless I'm there with you," said Papa, as if to prove Jennie as right as she so often was.

Even Sallie didn't have it in her to ask why he wasn't going to be in the field, and after a moment, as he took up a hoe and began to chop towards us on my row, he told us. He had to go over to our neighbors, the Edmistons, and use their telephone.

"Why?" said Sallie, unable to hold herself back one second longer.

"It ain't nothin' that'd interest you."

He knew very well that down here on this lonesome old cotton farm on the Arkansas river where nothing ever happened except work, as it seemed to us, we children would be mightily interested in anything important like a telephone call. He wasn't a person you could tease for an answer, though, as you could Mama, and meekly finishing our rows, the three of us started down the path to the creek. He was taking the path its other direction towards the Edmiston place.

"Just a minute, childern."

Still holding ourselves in until he should be out of hearing, we turned our faces towards him again.

"Your maw ain't feelin' as well as common," he said kindly, "an' so yuns won't be disturbin' her, I'm goin' to let yuns go swimmin' in the horse tank."

"Hooray!" Sallie whooped, and bounded across the creek. "It sure is nice of you to let us, Papa," said Jennie. My mind was working like Sallie's, and before Papa could change his, I was down the path and over the creek. Where the girls had leaped, however, I chose the log. A thick smelly coat of crude oil from wells that had been drilled farther up was moving slowly along on top of the water, and I didn't want to land in it in case my legs were too short for the jump which was so easy for the girls. They were already at the pasture gate and climbing over, careful to keep off the catapillars which were crawling thickly on its rails. They might become butterflies some day, but at this time they were worms, quite pretty in colors of yellow, brown and orange, but worms all the same that could sting you. And if you stepped on one of the soft fuzzy things, your whole inside closed its eyes and shrank together and shuddered.

"What do you think's come over Papa?" Sallie was saying as I overtook her and Jennie. "He never let us play in the tank before. Claimed we'd ruin the horses' drinkin' water."

"It's usin' the telephone stumps me," I joined in.

"Well, the sensible thing," said Jennie, rather cross and grown-up as she was apt to be nowadays, "is to put it out o' our heads an' get into the tank an' enjoy ourselves. But we can't go in as nekked as we was born."

She was gazing severely at me and Sallie. Halfway across the pasture we'd already got our dresses unbuttoned down the back and here beside the big steel tank we were on the point of completing the job and hopping right in.

"Nobody'll see us," said Sallie, and it was true that the tank was hidden from the house and the road by orchard

35

trees and that nobody was then living in the tenant house beyond the barn.

"I'll get us some dresses out o' the dirty clothes pile," said Jennie, frowning. "You wait."

We watched her go on past the barn and up the hill through the orchard towards the house. "She acts like the dresses we got on wasn't dirty," I remarked. "Ba-a-a!" said Sallie. "Nanny goat Jennie!" The horses were in the barn lot, their heads over the gate in our direction. "It'd embarrass that girl," said Sallie, "if the horses saw her nekked."

Giggling, we shucked off our top layer, and still very tickled, somehow found ourselves shucking off the underneath layer as well. The side of the round gray tank was hot against our stomachs, and after a few minutes in which Jennie still remained absent, it came to us that there wasn't much sense in being naked out of the water rather than in it. "Fact is," said Sallie, once we'd acted on the thought, "we're more out o' sight in."

I didn't answer. I had just received the biggest shock of the afternoon. Hanging on backwards to the rim of the tank, my full length drifting outward and upward in the clear cool water where sunbeams danced in zigzags and broken golden gleamings against the dark green moss below, I saw that I was beautiful. I wouldn't have believed it possible. It was wonderful to know what pretty people felt like. They must enjoy themselves all the time. With regret I drew on the soiled dress which Jennie now tossed to me. As much as my sisters, however, I realized how awful it would be to have Papa get back and catch us naked in the horse tank. He might even whip us on our wet skins. Anyhow, Jennie had further news. Mama said that after supper we could go up to the Cummins place to play.

"Me, too?" I quavered. I knew I couldn't. Mama'd only say, "You're too short, Puss," which was supposed to content me.

"You, too," said Jennie. "I don't even have to help Papa with the milkin'."

"I simply don't fathom ît," said Sallie. Neither did I. First Papa, and now Mama, giving thought to us children's enjoying ourselves. "It ain't natural," Sallie declared, and added, "It upsets me."

I knew what was bothering her. Was it all somehow because Mama was sick?

36

"She ain't, actually," said Jennie. "She's just layin' down with the kind of stomachache. Miz Cummins is up there with her."

The stomachache was no cause for real worry, and we studied the whole business some more. Sallie suggested that Papa probably wouldn't countenance Mama's idy, after all. He hardly ever let us go anywhere in the evening, he was so scared of some boy's sparking Jennie, and would he give a hoot what Mama'd promised us? I agreed. Papa'd already been what you'd call overly nice once today. It didn't stand to reason it'd keep up. But Jennie said no, we should calm ourselves, and as a matter of fact Papa seemed in an awfully big rush for us to finish our supper and go on.

There was no getting around how peculiar it all was. But sure as I lived and breathed, I knew where I'd be tomorrow —back in that hot old cotton patch, chopping weeds—and applying Jennie's sensible view about the horse tank to the present situation, I let no grass grow under my feet but hastened after her and Sallie out of the yard and along the lane.

The Cummins children were expecting us, and going into the clover field between their house and the river, the lot of us fell to hard playing, at black-man, last-couple-out and crack-the-whip, until I at least had had all the pleasure I was capable of having of that one kind at a time. It was nice to be tired from something besides work, though, I was thinking, as I sat down on a rock to wait for Papa to come for us girls. Shep, the Cummins collie, came to sit beside me, I put my arm around her neck, and together we watched the sun go down like the big red eye of God at one end of the field while the moon rose at the other, to look the sun straight in the eye for one long minute. And the big red eye didn't blink, but sank down fast beyond the river, and then the moon was easy and swam up into the sky, growing ever whiter and brighter, and laying her silvery shine over the playing children and all the world around. What a remarkable day it had been, I thought, staring along the fence-row cedars which were standing in pools of shadow so black that you couldn't tell where the tree ended and the shadow began; and as fireflies set up their twinkling, bright in the deep shade but pale in the moonlight across the clover, my mind hovered with the same sort of flickering, on and off, over the possible reason for so much remarkableness collected into one day for us three

Doud younguns. Then Shep growled. My hand on her throat felt the growl before my ears heard it, and in one motion the collie and I shot up and ran to join the others. They, too, were becoming tired from so much fun, and presently we all went trooping back to the house.

Papa had come. In the front room he and Miz Cummins were laughing and talking, very delightedly for the end of a long day, it seemed to me, and Mr. Cummins, who'd been in bed asleep, was entering from the next room, tugging his galluses up over his shoulders. "Well, now, Mr. Doud," he was saying with a jolly smile, "don't keep us waitin'. Tell us which it is."

Which is what? I wondered, gazing up at Papa, who was brushing at his moustache, sort of embarrassed and pleased and proud all at one time. "Yes, sir, I will," he replied to Mr. Cummins, then turning towards Jennie, Sallie and me, "We've got a fine big new brother for you girls down home," he told us.

For the second time that day Sallie's mouth dropped open and she forgot to close it. Miz Cummins chuckled more heartily than ever. "You'll like havin' a boy in the family, won't you, Sallie?" she teased.

"I guess some things happened today, all right," said Sallie at last, and for once she did sound pretty well-satisfied.

It was Jennie who heaved a sigh. "It'll make more work," she said, "but it'll be right sweet to have him."

For another time on that unusual day I, too, was speechless with shock. Stumbling sleepily down the lane, however, as I clung to Papa's hand, suddenly I remembered tomorrow and the cotton patch. A fine big new brother, was there? What did Jennie mean—more work? I knew what boys were for. My sleepiness passed off and uncontrollably I gave a hop and a skip.

"Goodie!" I cried. "Now I won't have to chop cotton any more!"

CHAPTER IV

Things Good and Bad

Soon after Bruce was born some darkies came to live in the tenant house across the creek. They agreed to stay through the cotton-picking in the fall, but about the middle of the summer they took a notion to leave. Papa got his shotgun and sat with it across his knees on our front porch on the hill. Down beyond the barn the darkies were busy carrying their stuff out of the tenant house. After a bit Papa stood up, raised the gun to his shoulder, aimed it in their general direction, and let it go off with a frightful bang. Then he sat down again. Back of the window curtains I was shivering and shaking, for if he hadn't killed one of them, surely they'd try to kill him now. Mama laughed.

"He ain't shootin' at nothin' but a hawk in that ol' dead cottonwood, youngun. But I reckon them darkies have took his meanin'."

They were rapidly moving their stuff out of the wagon and putting it back into the house.

Some time later my half brother Frank showed up. He was Papa's son by his first wife, who had died. Frank had been gone from home since before I could remember, and if I hadn't been told I'd not have known he was kin to me. His coming must have been the reason Papa let the colored people move, after all. With them out of the tenant house, Frank and the woman he'd married and their two little younguns began living in it. I never got really acquainted with any of them, Mama keeping me and Sallie as strictly on our side of the creek as she had when the darkies were there. She said Frank's woman was lazy and dirty to match the way Frank'd always been, and that we wouldn't learn anything from either of them that she was in favor of. We saw the woman on her trips to our pump for a bucket of drinking water. Her name was Vannie, but Mama referred to her as Brollium. Why, I didn't know, unless it had to do with her sassy style of walking, and to me the woman seemed rather pretty, or would have under better circumstances.

Poor as those circumstances were, Frank and Brollium stayed on in the tenant house through the summer months, until it was time to pick the cotton. Then they moved, the tenant house was vacant again, and Jennie, Sallie and I were set to work at a job that couldn't wait. We picked from the day the work started, with the cotton a little wet and hard in the green bolls, to the time when the last soft white cotton flowers were spilling out of bolls become stiff, sharp and brown. We helped on Saturdays and often on school days, and in all I picked four hundred and twenty pounds. "That's good for a youngun not yet eight years old," Mama encouraged me. Papa said he'd save my pay to buy shoes for me. "We can't 'shoe the horse, an' shoe the mare, an' let the little colt go bare,'" he said. "Can we? Not after cold weather sets in nohow." That was a nice friendly way of putting it, but secretly I planned to spend some part of the four dollars and twenty cents I'd earned for something I especially wanted for my own self, I hadn't quite decided what.

I was in the third grade now, Jennie and Sallie had thought that was where I belonged, and had persuaded the teacher to promote me. "What are you learnin' in the third?" said Mama. "Besides how to call the other childern 'kids'?" For the life of me I could think of nothing I'd learned recently except about the sinking of a big ship called the *Titanic*—the teacher had told us the story and shown us some terrible pictures of people about to drown and begging to be saved. But as Jennie was quick to point out, was it strange that children kept out of school as much as we were should be ignorant? We thought the day would never come when all the cotton would be picked, all the peanuts dug, all the dried navy beans hulled, and all the apples cored, quartered and dried. Suddenly, however, it did come, and with it our living at Bonnot's Grove was over. Papa readied the wagon for a trip, arching a line of wooden bows across it and stretching a canvas top over them. He also arranged for an auction.

How exciting it was! The auctioneer drove the seven miles from Bridgewater, his surrey loaded with a batch of tin cups and plates and some iron cooking vessels for the free lunch. Mama and Jennie fixed one of the big black pots with beans and another with coffee over a camp fire in the yard, while Papa laid planks across his carpenter's sawhorses and set the plates and cups on that, along with bread and a flock of brown whiskery coconuts which he cracked in particular for the kids, who'd sidle up and say, "Gimme a hunk, mister." The lane was thronged with buggies and wagons, and people wandered about the yard and barn lot, inspecting the furniture, produce and livestock. At last the auctioneer got up on a box and began his singsong. He turned his head and pressed an ear forward with one hand to help him hear the bids, and the articles he was selling he described as so valuable and good I could hardly believe they were ours. On finding such was the case, I looked at them with more respect, and was sorrier to lose them. Among other interesting events of the occasion, I became acquainted with a little boy whose baby sister had died. He told me about it as we sat together on the stairway to the loft, and I told him about Alma. We grew to be fast friends in the telling, and when we parted we promised never to forget one another.

It had been a brimful day, yet it had flown past and evening was nigh. Buggies and wagons were rattling away, carrying off the last stick of furniture, and the last pig, and the last bag of peanuts. The place looked too dead to skin, and I said to Mama I wished we could leave, too. "One more night with a roof over your head ain't goin' to hurt you," she replied, as she put down pallets for us on the kitchen floor. The dark bare room gave me a queer feeling as I lay beside her and Bruce, but soon I forgot everything in sleep except for something about the little boy whose baby sister had died. From this I opened my eyes on another day and, sitting up, discovered that I was alone in the empty house. Even the pallets of the others were missing. Had they gone off and left me? My heart skipped a dreadful beat, and I rushed out into the yard.

Papa was backing Old Prince and Net up to the wagon, Jennie was rocking Bruce in her arms, and Sallie, over a small camp fire, was trying to help Mama boil coffee and fry salt pork. The food smelled wonderful in the chilly air, but Mama got smoke in her eyes and hollered, "Get right back in there an' stop draggin' the tail o' that nightgown through the dirt, Delphie!"

I hurried, and was ready to eat with the rest of the family.

41

Still chewing on a tasty piece of bacon rind, I climbed into the wagon and tumbled onto the quilts which had been spread out over a couple of mattresses behind the seat.

"Get right out o' there, Delphie!"

It was coming to be a regular tune with Mama.

There was the trunk yet to be shoved under the seat, in between a big flour sack full of dried navy beans that Mama'd saved back from the sale and a box for the cute little collie pup which the Cummins children had given us to remember them by. So Sallie got a chance to plant herself in the middle by the puckered opening in the canvas above the tailgate, and Jennie and I had to squat alongside, peering over her shoulders for a last look at the green frame house we were leaving, at the vacant tenant house where the darkies and then Frank and his family had lived, and at the windmill above the tank where we girls had played the day that Bruce was born. The wagon lurched down the hill and the horses splashed through the creek at the bottom, slowing more and more as they pulled the next slope.

"I don't reckon we'll ever lay eyes on this place again," said Jennie, and let out one of her big sighs.

"I don't want to ever lay eyes on it again," said Sallie, chomp-chomp-chomp on a piece of coconut left over from yesterday. "They ain't nothin' for me to remember about this place but work."

It wasn't so, there was lots else to remember. There was eating watermelon on the back porch, for example, each of us with a long slim slice, and spitting the seeds out into the yard where the chickens were on the wait to gobble them up. There was the beautiful big peach which Sallie'd chanced on, the only peach borne the whole past season by that fine-looking Elberta peach orchard on the hillside below the house. She was so proud of herself for finding it, and went racing to Papa, who took his knife out of his pocket, rubbed the blade clean on the palm of his hand, to and fro, and then peeled the peach and cut it, slow and smooth and careful, into six equal parts, one for each of us, including Bruce. There was watching Jennie and Sallie card fluffy cotton bats for a new quilt, plying the carders which Mama'd brought from Arkansas. Later they joined her in sewing the bats into the quilt. Stretched on a frame which hung from the ceiling in the front room, it was rolled up when not in use and lowered again for the quilting. Mama and the girls would draw up their chairs, and I'd hover around, admiring the straight rows of pretty little stitches they were putting in to make a pattern, and pointing out among the quilt blocks scraps from dresses one or another of us had at one time had. Sallie didn't fail to let it be known, of course, that what meant pleasure for me meant work for her.

But then I also had work which was different from hers. And look how much pleasure me and her'd had talking play-people together, after Jennie declared that she was too old for such nonsense and Sallie said that her and me'd start over with some entirely new families. The first set we made up was composed of the Blacks and the Whites, who were very elegant and so proper in everything they did they wouldn't dream of dropping a *g* even, carrying it to such a comical extreme that they regularly said things like *cotting* instead of *cotton, buttings* instead of *buttons,* or *mountings* rather than *mountains.* Both families were rich, but the Blacks were the richer. This was because they were Sallie's property, and she compelled me to say first how much money the Whites had. Then she simply went me one better. The Blacks also had a black automobile, and after considerable argument I obtained a white one for the Whites. My argument was that I had as much right to automobiles as Sallie. Hadn't we seen our first and only one at the identical moment in Bridgewater, a big black affair with red straps holding down the top in front and an enormous horn?

With our second set of families we balanced off all that elegance in the first, the Daveyshons and Andershons being so silly that they pronounced all their *s*'s like *esh*'s. It could be very funny, and we laughed a great deal. We also fought. Once in a while, however, a make-believe fight between Beshie Daveyshon and Jeshie Andershon could turn into a real one between Sallie and me. Sallie'd whack me too hard and I'd just politely do the same to her, then we'd grab each other and topple over onto the floor, for I was becoming almost exactly as strong as she was and neither of us could overpower the other. There on the floor we'd lie, unable to budge, until Mama somewhere not far off roused herself to the situation and came to pry us apart and stand us on our feet. "Mark my words," she'd warn, "you'll have your papa out here in a minute." Alone once more, Sallie and I would maintain that it was every bit and grain the fault of the other

43

one, repeating *'tis* and *'tain't* for so long that presently they became grunts to save breath and we both got tickled. I'd see her gleaming at me out of the corner of an eye, I'd gleam back, and we'd both give one big grunt right together, which finished the quarrel with neither of us forced to give in.

As a matter of fact, such disagreements seldom occurred, the farm was so lonesome and both us girls were so keen to talk play-people. I was keenest of all on Sunday, for that day, as everywhere with us, was the dullest and most lonesome of the entire week. I liked to go to Sunday school but wasn't permitted to walk into Bonnot's Grove by myself, and often neither Jennie nor Sallie could be prevailed on to take me. Weather could also keep me at home. Like rain. Like rain one Sunday morning only a short while back. . . .

Everything had gone wrong that morning, beginning with the rain, which held on by fits and starts right up to time for Sunday school. Then, as soon as it was too late for that, out shone the sun, hot and getting hotter, and Mama had me and Sallie skin up onto the roof of the back porch, handing us up the white cloths filled with half-dried apples which we'd had to bring down in a hurry an hour or two before at the onset of the rain, and after we had them all laid out again for the drying, why then she told Sallie she and Jennie could go to the field over by the river and find us a mushmelon, but me she set to tending Bruce on the back porch.

Tending him was one of my regular jobs, part of that work which was different from Sallie's. I also ironed his clothes for Mama, standing on a little box to make me tall enough for the ironing board, and not minding the job either. I did mind her calling on me to wash out his didies for her. She couldn't brag on me enough to make me not mind. And while I had no objections to shooing flies and seeing to it that he didn't roll off his quilt, I was tired of the amount of it I'd been doing this summer and fall, and said as much to Mama. Well surely, she replied, I could shoo flies just this one time more as I was so good at it, and she'd feather into that nice grape cobbler she was fixing us for dinner. But as I said no, I was still tired of it, she boxed my jaws to persuade me.

Bruce wasn't helping matters any, doing I couldn't recall what-all except that he was after my cigar box and somehow got hold of it. I took it right away from him, and of course he

44

had to holler fit to wake the dead. The upshot was that for once Papa lived up to Mama's predictions, and came staving through from the front room. I hadn't realized he was that close.

"My box!" I gasped. "Bruce had my box!" You had to be quick with explanations around Papa or the whipping was over before he knew there were any.

"Let him have it," said Papa. "It ain't worth a continental."

"No!" Shaking my head and holding the box behind me, I backed away.

"We'll just see about that." He broke a switch from the little ellum tree at the corner of the porch.

I was going to catch it, but I couldn't help it. It was my box. An Irishman who'd worked on the road had given it to me with the remark, "It's got a nice clane cigar smell if you want to kape it," which had been something for us to mock and laugh at ever since. I'd never have thought it of Papa that he'd make me give up that box. It might not be worth a continental, but it was a thing I thought considerable of. I didn't know how to give up something that was so much mine. I didn't know how to be meek about it, like Papa wanted. He wasn't meek. Nobody in our family was meek, not even Jennie, really. So where should I have learned how? I hung onto the box until he wrenched it away.

When the switching was over, I sat on the steps and looked at the flies crawling on a whitish patch of ground where some milk had been spilled. I'd get even with Papa. Not just for the little lines of blisters his switch had raised on my bare legs. I could stand them. I could even keep from touching them to find out how bad they were so long as he and Mama could see. But I'd get even with him for making me give up something that was my very own, for making me hop and say, "Yes, sir, I'll be good, please stop, Papa, I'll be good," putting a begging into my voice that I hated and promising two or three times before he let go of my shoulder. Because he was able to do that to me. In my own mind I'd taken back every promise to be good as soon as I'd made it. In fact, I aimed to be worse than ever, and this time I'd be really mean, not just a little old get-my-box-back mean. Not that I cared for meanness, but to show him. Only I had to be sly about it in order not to get caught, and to know what I was doing myself wasn't enough. He had to know that I had

45

got even, and more than even, and he would some day. I couldn't see how at this moment, but I'd manage it. The hotness inside me said I could.

And I'd show Mama. She'd brought it all on by being unreasonable. As for Bruce, I turned my back on him. It was his fault, too, and he'd watched me hopping and begging, and hadn't known what I was thinking, not to mention that right now he was chewing the lid off my box, cutting his teeth on it.

Wait till I go away, I thought, while I dried up from the crying. You'll be barking up another tree before I come back. You can bake all the cobblers you want to, Miss Mama. I'll be having a whole case of Van Camp's pork and beans all by myself. I don't know just where I'll be having them, but it'll be a good piece up the road and don't you doubt it. You wait.

But I had to wait just as long as she did, which took most of the pleasure out of the thought. Besides, my legs had stopped hurting, and after some further time I was being kindly invited to fill my stomach round and tight as a little snare drum with Mama's nice dinner. Then, too, Papa began saying something about if Delphie there'd quit sulling around with that underlip hanging out far enough for him to step on it, he'd see if she couldn't come along on a load of cotton to Bridgewater next Saturday. All of it took my mind off getting even, and I'd actually forgotten about having to do it until today, when I'd more or less stumbled onto the memory as I gazed back at the green frame house we were leaving and thought of the many things, some good and some bad, to be remembered from there.

CHAPTER V

On the Go Again

How could I have neglected a thing I'd felt so strongly at the time? I wondered this morning as the green house on its hill sank out of sight below the higher one on the other side of the creek. But then hadn't I forgotten an earlier occasion when I'd slapped my baby sister and taken some paper dolls away from her, until, talking with that nice little boy yesterday, I'd been reminded of it? Of course, neither event nor the feelings that went with it had really slipped out of my mind, and some day, no doubt, when, as Mama said, I'd developed the judgment to know more truly which things were good and which were bad—when that time came I'd recall them all much as she and Papa did what had happened to them in a long-ago of their own. Mama was uncommonly good at such remembering, and during the days of the wagon trip I had many chances to listen to her and Papa. Meanwhile, as we slowly but steadily put behind us the well-known seven miles into Bridgewater, all of us had to quieten down from the bustle of the auction and the hustle of our early morning start.

Papa and Mama also had a piece of business at the bank. It concerned a note, and they were discussing it back and forth over Bruce, propped on a pillow between them, all the way to Bridgewater.

"What's a note, Papa?" I'd crawled up behind the seat and was leaning forward over Bruce in order to hear.

"A note stands for money somebody borried at the bank," said Mama, after a minute in which Papa didn't say anything, "an' the time comes when somebody has to pay it back."

She sounded awfully grim, for her. And had she said somebody, or somebody *else*, had to pay it back? I was afraid to ask. We pulled into Bridgewater, stopped in front of the bank, and Papa climbed down and went inside. Was he paying off a note for us, with money from the auction? I imagined so, and forgot about it as, on the go again, we rattled north out of Bridgewater over a way new to me. Frontwards, if I gazed out above the horses' pretty pointed bobbing ears, I saw the two roadsides that were so narrow in the distance gradually spreading apart as we came, while if I cast my glance backwards, out beyond Sallie's head of black hair, I saw that the track closed itself to a point behind us again, and in either direction I had a feeling that it was kind of unfriendly and secret, like the whole big outside world that I knew so little about. Yet it was a pretty road, tilting now up and now down, and the fall day was pretty, too, which made the unusual stiffness and silence between Papa and Mama all the more disturbing. Noontime arrived, and how much longer

47

they were going to remain uncomfortable with each other would have been hard to guess. Then my hard-boiled egg blew up.

We'd paused alongside the road to eat our dinner, which was cold, but Papa built a small fire to warm ourselves by, and it occurred to me that I could heat my egg in the live coals at the edge. So it blew up. There was a pop, and pieces of egg and shell flew through the air. I was as scared as the rest of the family, thinking that somebody was shooting at us, though we didn't know why. Mama and Papa were still laughing when we got back into the wagon, and as the afternoon wore on they limbered up even more towards each other. Therefore my egg had been lost to some good purpose, I thought, drinking in their talk, which presently roamed back to times so far away they were unknown to me save through what I'd heard tell, like now.

As luck would have it, Mama'd got onto the subject of work, and was relating how she used to go once a week over to her Granny McNabb's to wash for her. She wasn't but twelve-fourteen years old at the time, but she'd tie up all her granny's dirty clothes in one big sheet and carry it to the old wash place on the creek. There were two large wooden tubs and one big black boiling kettle, and she dipped water from the creek, spreading the clean clothes out to dry on the grass and bushes. For this job her granny gave her a piece of salt pork about the size of her two hands, and Mama was glad enough to get it, since lots of times they wouldn't have eaten much at home if it hadn't been for what she brought with her. That was the kind of provider her paw had been, and able to quote Scripture about it, to boot.

Her paw was my Granpa McNabb, if you please, and I'd heard him quote Scripture and often seen his letters to her which always began *Dear Dau. and Fam.* and closed with God's blessing and the mention of some special chapter and verse from the Bible. It seemed strange that such a man could have denied Mama a pig which she'd raised and which was the only thing of her own she'd ever had at home. But Granpa said, she was marrying the rich miller down at St. Joe, wasn't she, and couldn't he buy her a pig hisself if he wanted her to have one? The rich miller was Papa. He couldn't understand about Mama's paw either, his people had been well-to-do, they'd had Negro slaves. And Mama replied yes, and after the slaves were freed, Granpa'd had to go to work in the field and he hadn't liked it.

"All his brothers an' sisters was still pretty well-fixed," said Papa. "Take his sister, Jen. She married Henry Shelby, an' to this day they own might nigh half the county down there around St. Joe."

Mama declared that she just didn't know. Granpa'd started out as a Methodist preacher but had a falling-out with his congregation and became a hard-shell Baptist, only then he didn't have a congregation, just this little old farm they lived on, and he was better at preaching hellfire and damnation than at farming, and put most of the work onto his younguns as soon as they were knee-high to a grasshopper. Her and her brother Albert were the oldest and got the worst of it, although their maw helped them as much as she could, with more babies coming all the time.

This accounted for Mama's eternal talk about work, I guessed. It tired me to hear, besides worrying me that I might bear a favorance to Granpa in this respect.

"Tell about your Cousin May Shelby when you was young girls," I broke in, thinking what a wonder it was that Mama had ever actually been a young girl, "back there before your hair turned brown, an' you hated it 'cause people poked so much fun at red hair in them days, even more than they do now. Tell about your bustle."

"That wasn't nothin', youngun. You've heerd all that before."

She was a little pink and smiling though, because she liked my remembering and asking her to remember things like her bustle when she was young. The bustle was a shirt sleeve which her Aunt Jen and Cousin May Shelby stuffed and fixed with a string at each end to tie around her waist beneath her skirt and hold it in place behind. But Granma McNabb was opposed to bustles, she didn't care if they were all the rage, and when Mama got home from her visit with the Shelbys wearing one of the things, Granma made her take it straight off and put her down on the back porch carding and spinning wool or cotton for socks and sheets and clothes, and whichever it was, the work was a great deal harder than any Sallie and I were called upon to do, regardless of the fuss we made about it.

49

"*Nothin'* could a been harder'n our pickin' cotton," said Sallie, who'd joined me behind the seat. "My back still aches from stoopin' over, an' my hands are a sight to behold."

Were we never to get away from that blessed concern with work? Thank goodness, Papa had other interests, and clucking to the horses, shook the reins over their round brown shiny-smooth rumps and remarked to Mama that her Uncle Henry Shelby had influence, he could trade it with somebody and get his childern almost any government post they wanted in the county, and sometimes in the state.

"That's how your Cousin Alf Shelby got hisself elected to the state legislature before he was twenty-one years old," Papa recalled.

Mama agreed that her Uncle Hy had aimed for those childern o fhis to amount to something, all right. He educated them for that.

"You was educated, too," said Sallie jealously.

"Yes, I was mightily educated. I went to a three-months' country school runnin' through July, August an' September, an' had to drop out in August to pull fodder off the corn."

"An' Papa was educated," said Sallie, paying no heed. "Papa taught school, didn't you, Papa?"

"It was just a little ol' country school like the one I went to," said Mama. "You only got twenty-five dollars a month for teachin' it, didn't you, Dave?"

"Them was right good wages at that time an' place," said Papa. "It was a good school, too, Mama, or was when I taught it."

"I know it was a good-enough little ol' school, I didn't aim to say it wasn't, Papa. I was just sayin' straight out what you got, that's all I was a-sayin'."

If she'd got matters patched up, it didn't show in Papa's next remark, to the effect that there was a lot of bad in them Shelbys, when you stopped to think. Take Bob Shelby, he was a brother of Mama's Uncle Hy, and he ran a whiskey still. One time he got drunk on his own whiskey, and killed a preacher while he was preaching. "He stood at the door an' fired in over the heads o' the congregation," said Papa, to clinch his point.

"It wasn't 'cause he was drunk, Dave," said Mama earnestly. "Bob had a grudge against that preacher."

"That didn't justify, Brittie."

Papa was firm, even if her uncle's brother Bob had got out of it all by running away to Texas, and I had a notion Mama'd think twice before belittling Papa's schoolteaching again. As she saw the justice of her side, however, she began to grow pretty firm herself, observing that Henry Shelby and his brother Bob weren't kin to her nohow but by marriage, then, following a general line already used by Papa, that she didn't know as the Shelbys were any worse than other folks in them pioneer times and places, and finally that Papa's own cousin, Little Dave Doud, was crooked as a dog's hine leg.

It was Papa's turn to stand up for his kin, maintaining that Little Dave Doud wasn't crooked, he was just a gambler by profession.

"I don't see where professin' it keeps it from bein' crooked," said Mama. "Gamblin' sure ain't no yardstick straight profession, in my opinion."

It wasn't in Papa's either, I knew that, he wouldn't allow a pack of playing cards in the house. After a minute he remarked that Little Dave was his second cousin.

"You was his namesake, Dave," said Mama, not letting him out of a thing.

"That don't make him nothin' but my second cousin, Mama."

Here I had a chance to ask a question that had been bothering me. Did they call him Little Dave because he was so little?

"They called him that 'cause he was six-foot-two, child," said Papa.

"Tall like Papa," laughed Mama.

The story was that he'd been a gambler by profession, and one evening down in Springfield, Missouri, he gambled with Wild Bill Hickok and won his watch. "Wild Bill tried to make him give it back, but Little Dave declared he'd won it fair an' square," said Papa, not looking at Mama but you knew he had her in mind, "an' he wouldn't do it. Words follered, an' Wild Bill dared Little Dave to put the watch on his chain an' wear it across the street the next mornin'. 'Make it nine o'clock,' says Little Dave."

"An' did he?" Sallie prompted, her mouth hanging open rememberingly. I could hardly draw breath, I was so scared and sorry for Little Dave.

"At nine o'clock the follerin' mornin'," said Papa, "Little

Dave appeared on the court house square, the watch on his chain. Him an' Bill both drew, but Bill fired first an' killed Little Dave."

Sallie gulped. "Little Dave was kin to me, too, wasn't he?"

"It ain't nothin' to be proud of," said Mama.

"It sure is pretty weather for a trip," said Papa.

It stayed pretty all that day and the next and the next— three days running, or perhaps it was four, they were a good deal alike and it was hard to keep count. Day after pretty day the wagon bumped and complained along the road, and if Papa and Mama had made up their minds where they were going, they hadn't let us young ones in on the secret yet. Sallie thought we should take a good look at every town we came to, in case it turned out to be the one for us, but none had so far, and the road remained about the same to either side, although we crossed from Oklahoma into Kansas, and then back into Oklahoma again. On both crossings I looked hard for the state line, and it must have been in there somewhere, as Papa mentioned it, but I couldn't find it any more than I could locate the big dipper which I'd understood him to say was in the sky at nights, and which I fancied might resemble our large granite-colored drinking cup with the handle. Papa, Mama and Bruce slept on one of the mattresses underneath the wagon, while Jennie, Sallie and I were bedded on the other mattress inside. As I lay on my back and waited for the sleep-feeling to come sighing down and fold me away for the night, I studied the sky through the tailgate opening in my canvas roof, hoping that the big dipper would float past among the stars, and listening to Papa and the girls. They'd be sitting as I'd left them, dreamy and fire-colored in a circle nearby, harmonizing such old songs as *In the Sweet Bye-and-Bye* or the one that began, "Some folks say that a nigger won't steal," and anything they sang would be very beautiful in their way of singing, gentle and sad. Cradling Bruce in her arms, Mama'd be looking on and listening as well, I guessed. She preferred her own old songs, usually something lively like the one that went, "There was an old man lived out in the West, he had an old woman was none of the best."

Mornings were cold, there'd be gray mist hanging in the hollows or drifting in ragged shreds across the road. We girls

52

would hover by the fire, eager for whatever breakfast Mama was able to bring up, presently the sun would rise, frosty-bright and not very warm at first but gradually clearing the fog from the earth, and we'd drive on. During the day very little happened, we children sang until we wore out our songs, played all the sitting-still games and asked all the riddles we could think of, or teased the collie pup in his box. At noon we ate cold boiled navy beans and ham hock or some other food Mama'd brought from the farm. In the afternoons she and Bruce might come back onto the mattresses, which gave two of us girls a chance at the seat beside Papa, or, occasionally, Papa might hand the reins to Mama and get out to stretch his legs, allowing us girls to walk with him alongside the wagon if we wished.

One day stood out because something very pleasant happened in it. On this morning Papa went for a bucket of water to a nearby farmhouse, and the woman there sent us a panful of hot biscuits for our breakfast. She'd heard our voices raised in song the evening before as we sat around our campfire, and she'd wondered about us. Papa said she was an awful nice woman, Mama declared the biscuits were might nigh the best she'd ever et outside her own, and Jennie said, "Somebody like that you never laid eyes on, but you'll allus remember."

Another day was remarkable for an opposite kind of occurrence. We were passing a schoolhouse in a small town, and it was recess time, with the children playing outside. We girls were crowding together, as was our wont, at our lookout at the back of the wagon, and one little bunch of children on the sidewalk was struck by the glimpse of us. All at once two or three of them were hopping up and down and pointing their fingers at us and hollering. In the beginning I couldn't make it out. Then I did.

"Wagon tramps! Wagon tramps!" they hollered.

"Yi-yi-yi-yi-yi!" Sallie yelled in return, and popped out her tongue and wiggled her fingers at her ears and even put her thumb to her nose, making sure first that Papa wasn't looking in her direction. Jennie sank back into the dimness. I'd have thought that she was brushing flies from around her eyes, except that there weren't any flies in the wagon. I turned back to my station at Sallie's shoulder. I was capable of making some pretty good faces myself and was aiming to do it, but already the children were out of view, and Sallie sat down by Jennie with the words, "I reckon I fixed *them*, all right." Had she? I didn't know, but I surely hoped so.

After that it seemed to me that most of what took place was mishaps. Usually we could see a funny side to them, as on the day when my egg blew up, but sometimes the one who had the mishap didn't find it laughable at all. This was the case with me on another noon when I singed the tail of my red flannel coat. I had my back to the fire, warming myself this time, and all of a sudden Mama slung a bucket of water over me from behind. I sprang into the air. "Don't you know you'd a been on fire in another minute, youngun?" she excused herself fast, but went on laughing with the others. I stalked over and got into the wagon, out of my wet coat and under a quilt. And there I stayed the livelong afternoon. If I raised up, the girls pushed me down again, saying did I want to catch my death of cold. The upshot was that at suppertime I had to eat the little there was to be eaten with a crick in my neck.

This was the day the fine weather came to an end. Next morning it was altogether gray, wet fog clung to the ground and you could little more than guess at the trees which you knew must still be burning red- and yellow-leafed to either side of the road. By noon such a drizzle had set in that we couldn't leave the wagon, and as the day advanced it began to put down in good earnest. All of us were stiff and cold, and entering a town of some size, Papa said we'd better stop over-night in this here little wayside hotel.

Wedged between him and Mama on the front seat, I had my stocking cap pulled to my brows and was clutching the quilt over my knees with both fists. The man from the hotel opened the barn doors for Papa and helped him unhitch and lead the horses into their stalls. He was so nice and friendly that as he peered up at me and Mama in the wagon and said weren't we coming in to supper, I was on the point of climbing straight down. Mama held me back.

"I guess your little boy is hungry, Missus," the hotel man told her with a chuckle.

"It ain't a little boy, Mister." Mama drew the cap from my head to show my long hair, and the man said well from the looks of my hands he'd thought I was a boy.

To be mistaken for a boy because my hands were so rusty and red and scratched didn't please me at all, and I was still hungry and cold. Overhearing Papa tell the man real cheerful and polite that we were much obliged but we'd eat in the wagon tonight as we had a right smart of victuals on hand to clear up, I hurriedly whispered to Mama didn't he know there wasn't anything left except lightbread and Karo.

"We got a-plenty right here for tonight, Mister," Papa repeated, a little louder and heartier than ever. "We'll be in to our room directly we've et."

I couldn't get over the notion that we were being invited, and tried to argue with Papa after the man was gone. Papa answered that the invitation would have cost us a pretty penny, and a great big girl like me ought to know when to hush her mouth. Mama broke off a piece of dry cold lightbread and poured a bit of white Karo syrup on it. "Let's see that disappearin' down the red lane now."

We'd already had it once today, as we crouched in the wagon at noon, and at first I couldn't bring myself to eat it again, fast as you must if you meant the syrup not to drip. Soon a string of sticky silky-looking drops was hanging on the front of my red flannel coat, which still had a burned place behind, and alongside this chain was another, composed of shiny tear drops which were sliding down my chin and falling off one by one.

"It'll help some, won't it," said Mama, "to be sleepin' under a real roof again tonight?"

It would have helped more if the bed she put me, Sallie and Jennie into hadn't fallen down during the night—a mishap which tickled none of us girls, least of all Jennie, who was on the bottom of the pile on the side that struck the floor. Breakfast in the hotel brightened us all, however, and a good thing, for the day was worse than yesterday. Rain fell without stopping, wind blew the rain, heavy wet leaves let go their hold on the trees and dropped to the ground while the trees themselves bent over till their limbs scraped against our canvas top. Sallie and I watched the horses splash forward with their heads lowered and water running in streams down their good backs, or else we followed with our eyes the tracks which our wheels were cutting in the black mud behind, but after a while we were content to quile down under the covers with Jennie. She consented to tell us a story she'd read on the farm in Mama's monthly magazine, *Comfort*.

From her looks, Mama could have used some of a commodity called comfort right then. She seemed to be shrinking down tighter and smaller all the time on the seat up front, and there was hardly a cheep out of her. Papa wasn't saying much either, beyond get-up to Old Prince and Net. But Bruce cried, and the collie pup chimed in. And the hotel breakfast got to be so far off that it was only a memory.

At noon Mama handed us each a chunk of dry bread to gnaw on. There wan't even any syrup on top. And it kept on raining. And at last, just as night was falling, we began to smell a very bad smell.

"It's from the radium wells in the vicinity," said Papa.

The vicinity was Claremore, Oklahoma.

We drove into a wagonyard, the first in the experience of any of us girls. Through the mist and twilight we made out a big open square yard, arranged on two sides for wagons, horses and feed, on a third side with rooms for folks who were travelling in the wagons, and on the fourth, facing the street, as the home of whoever was running the place.

"That's how it's organized," Papa explained.

Close on Mama's heels, we girls left the wagon, picked our way across the deep smelly ooze which was miring down the wheels, and stepped onto a dry spot. We were so stiff we almost creaked, and for a minute we only huddled together, peering, and waiting for Mama to lead us into the room we were to occupy that night. It had a small iron cookstove and two beds with mattresses. Mama gave Bruce into Jennie's arms and got a fire going. We crowded near. None of us had taken off our coats.

"Don't yuns propose to stay a while?" said Papa, coming in from the yard, and no more testy than he had a right to be probably.

Mama looked at him. "We'll get bugs in here, Papa."

"They ain't no need o' takin' on," he told her, as he stretched his hands out with ours to the warmth rising from the stove, "just 'cause you're all wore out."

"I ain't a-takin' on," said Mama. "I'm just remarkin'."

"What do you expect for twenty-five cents?" said Papa.

"I expect bugs," said Mama.

She did at last remove her coat, however, and lifted the mattresses and inspected the walls, but she didn't find any bugs, and Papa didn't call her attention to it. Presently he went out and bought us a gallon of milk, Mama warmed it in a bucket on the stove, and we had it for supper, standing

56

around and dipping our bread into it. In the morning Mama set to frying us some salt pork for breakfast while Papa went out for more milk. He was gone for quite a while, and on his return wore a changed, fairly excited expression.

"What do you think o' the looks o' this place by daylight, Brittie?" he said, and before she could answer, added that he'd been talking to the old widder-lady who owned the yard. "She'll rent it to us for twenty-five dollars a month. That includes the livin' quarters up front."

Mama held the smoking skillet away from the stove and gazed out through the dirty window and the thin sunlight to the yard, which from here seemed to be purely mud and manure.

"You ain't thinkin' o' rentin' this place, are you, Dave? You never run a wagonyard before."

"I've run a livery stable, Mama, an' this is a livery stable an' feed store as well as a wagonyard. Operatin' a hotel was good experience, too."

Mama's lips drew together a bit tighter, if that was possible, but we heard no more from either her or Papa, and after breakfast they went off together to talk further with the old widder-lady and decide how it would be with us. In their absence Sallie and I explored, climbing into the mangers of empty stalls, and peeking into the vacant rooms, in one of which Sallie found a poke of corn meal. Jennie'd gone out to the sidewalk in front. Following her, we stared up and down the street, at the railroad tracks across from us and at a hotel over by the depot, until at last Jennie said, with a sigh, "I don't know which is worse, the smell o' wet manure an' straw inside, or the stink o' the radium wells out here."

"Won't neither one make no difference," said Sallie, "if we don't locate in Claremore."

Her hopes were soon smashed. Mama came to report that Papa was settling the deal, and that same day the widder-lady moved out of the living quarters up front and we moved into them.

CHAPTER VI

All I Had to Work from Really

They consisted of two rooms, these living quarters. The kitchen was a regular room, though small, but the other, which was our front room and a sort of office for the yard, had a corner missing. It was sliced off by the driveway, which cut at an angle into the yard. The front room was still of fair size and except for its peculiar shape did very well.

Papa'd taken the canvas top down from our wagon, its use now being to deliver feed, and given away our collie pup. He ate too much. But the hateful thing that befell me directly and right off the bat in Claremore, Oklahoma, was at school, where I got put back into the second grade. Mama said I should speak to Miss Kitty about it. Miss Kitty taught the second grade. She had curly brown hair and was pretty, and she said, "I rather think you'll be promoted at the end of the semester, Delpha." I'd never heard of a semester before, nor had Mama, who said, "She orter let you go in the third now," and bade me keep after Miss Kitty. I did so, and learned that the end of the semester would be soon after Christmas.

Oh, it was fun to have Christmas coming! I didn't care if Papa did go on saying that Santie was as poor as Job's turkey this year. Whenever I walked along Main Street under the red and green decorations and looked into the store windows at bicycles and roller skates and rocking horses and big brown teddy bears and beautiful curly-haired dolls, one of the dolls being the largest I'd ever laid eyes on, in a rocking chair fit for a child—at those times I simply couldn't resist the Christmas feeling bubbling up in me, and I hopped and skipped along until suddenly I remembered Papa's cautioning, Don't skip, it's hard on your shoes, I swear to God I don't

58

know where the next pair is coming from. That sobered me for a minute, then the special Christmas feeling was sparkling and dancing around inside and making me happy again.

At school we drew pictures of Santie Claus with our crayons, and a tingling ran all along my backbone and down to the very tips of my fingers as I colored the funny old fellow. For a special treat the last afternoon of school before vacation, we children in the second grade were permitted to go in with those in the third, and their teacher read us a story. Her name was Miss Brady, and she was old and didn't enjoy herself very much, and I couldn't help thinking that but for having to be promoted into the third in order to get educated as fast as possible, I'd be happier in the second. Miss Kitty and Miss Brady let us children decide on the story to be read, and we chose the one about a bull that did wonderful acts for its master, who would whisper his wishes into its ear.

Afterwards the kids whooped and hollered like crazy things, the boys particularly, as they ran off the schoolground, they were so pleased over Christmas and our two weeks of holiday. Me, I went on studying about the wonderful bull and how it helped its master, and along Main Street I lingered in front of all the store windows one time more, gazing longest at the beautiful doll in the little rocking chair, yet never quite forgetting as I gazed that my red flannel coat had a patch behind where the burned spot had been. This condition always made me uneasy if I turned my back to people, and I tried not to turn it unless I had to.

Sallie and I were hoping and praying that it would snow in time for Christmas, and one evening it did start in just a-throwing the white stuff down. It was still at it the next morning. Observing me and Sallie going over our old wool toboggans against holes, Mama repeated that it wouldn't do us a lick of good to set our caps for Santie this year, she could tell in advance that when there wasn't enough grease in the house for her to make biscuits with hardly, there wouldn't be any gifts for us, not even a stick of candy. That took the bounce out of the Christmas feeling again, but again only for a while, soon it crept back and danced up in me, oh, so blessedly! Partly it was because the snow never quit falling soft and steady outside, covering the mud and manure in the wagonyard and shaking across the depot and hotel up the street like a lovely slow white curtain. Partly it was from my continuing hopes of Papa.

59

I was on the wait for him at the window which looked out from underneath the roof of the driveway and along the new white street. In the other room Mama was boiling some of the dried navy beans from the farm, and the warm smell floated in on the dampness which caused the panes of my window to sweat. There was also a drying smell from the clothes she was ironing, and I could hear the thump of her iron on the board together with her advice to Jennie and Sallie concerning some candy they were fixing to cook. It all felt and smelled and sounded nice, like home, and I listened with pleasure to the talk about the soda and molasses which Mama was selling to the girls for five cents each. Where Jennie's nickel came from was a mystery to me, but Sallie's was from the sale of the poke of corn meal she'd found. For although the worms in it made it unfit for cooking, the meal was all right for chicken feed, and Sallie'd peddled it from door to door until she finally sold it for fifteen cents. This left her a dime after bearing her share of the cost of the molasses and soda, and I'd understood her to say she aimed to spend it for Christmas.

And with Santie laying down on the job like he was this year, I had in mind to go uptown and spend a little my own self, which was why I was waiting for Papa. I hadn't forgotten that hot old cotton patch last fall, after my half brother Frank had left us, and Papa, Jennie, Sallie and I finished making the crop without any help at all. I remembered very well how we went up and down the rows, each of us dragging a long canvas bag for stuffing the cotton into, and how my bag, although somewhat shorter than the others, was plenty long to suit me. Even my shoulder had a recollection in it, of the canvas strap pulled so tight that it hurt. And though once in a while, if Papa wasn't noticing, I might be able to stretch out on top of my bag in the shade down between the rows, it wasn't for so many minutes that I still hadn't done four-dollars-and-twenty-cents' worth of picking.

Wiping the sweat from the window glass with one sleeve, I stared out into the snowiness, and all of a sudden the loose snow in the driveway rose up from the ground and whirled out and away down the street like the thin white veil of a ghost in a hurry, and through the veil came Papa in our wagon. The seat had been taken out, and he was balancing and bracing himself on wide-apart legs behind Old Prince and Net. I ran to open the door and stand on the top step,

60

and Papa whoa'd the team alongside to hear what I was after.

"A dime? What do you want a dime for?"

In his voice it sounded so unreasonable that if I hadn't already worked myself up to a considerable pitch, I'd have quit then and there.

"I thought I'd buy myself a play-pretty for Christmas," I got out.

He was blowing his long red nose, the finger of one stiff red hand now to this side and then to the other. Hadn't he heard me? Yes. "I ain't got no dimes today, Delphie."

He lifted the reins, and I said fast, before the lump in my throat could get any tighter, "Couldn't I have one out o' what I earned pickin' cotton last fall?"

He'd whoa'd the horses again, however, and his voice wasn't so high. Had my words carried him back to the cotton patch, too? Was he remembering us kids hauling our bags up to the scales which hung from the limb of a tree at one end of the field, and himself weighing the bags in, afterwards dumping the cotton out onto the big white accumulation beside the scales? Did he see in his mind's eye as plainly as I could the image of that little red notebook which he carried on purpose in his pocket, with a page for each of us girls, and did he recall how he took his stubby pencil and wrote down the exact amount each one had picked that particular time? He might have been remembering. The snow falling thick and soft as cotton itself would have helped him to remember. His long old leather wallet was in his hand, and he was peering into its thinness.

"Mind you don't waste it. They ain't much more where that come from, my girlie."

I knew it was wrong, I knew I oughtn't to have that dime, I knew I'd waste it and maybe help cause us to starve, but not all the warning in that *my-girlie* of his could stop me from taking it or put the damper on that old Christmas feeling much longer than for me to get my coat and cap and tell Mama where I was bound for. Nor was I well out of sight of the wagonyard before I was hopping and skipping along through the soft snow on the sidewalk as if I owned two pairs of shoes, both pairs good, and it mightn't have occurred to me that I oughtn't to skip at all if the motion hadn't shaken my garter strings loose.

Oh, those garters! slowing me down and making trouble in spite of their being bran-new ones, torn by Mama from a piece of stout muslin only yesterday upon my showing her how rotten my old strings were, and all knots. Mama didn't ordinarily pay much attention to the problem of garters, she wore long skirts and could roll her hose, twisting each top into a knot and tucking it neatly under the edge of the roll below a pretty white knee. It was different with short skirts and long underwear. You had to tie the strings as high above your knees as possible to prevent their showing, and over a union-suit it was hard to tie any knot tight enough to hold if you ran and played. I re-tied my new strings as best I could without overly pinching my legs, and was hurrying on when I spied a handful of orange peels. They weren't a bit dirty, somebody must have dropped them into the gutter only a few seconds ago. Pretending to hitch up a garter, I got a fistful with one quick grab. Nobody saw me. The swirling snow was too thick all around. By the time I reached Main Street I had the moist fresh white insides well gnawed out, and tossing the peels back into the gutter, I entered the notion store.

It had a world of notions. On the first counter were toys which wound up, and most of them were things I'd have liked to have, but none was exactly what I was willing to give up my dime for, and yet I might have chosen one after all if it hadn't turned out that every item in this group was twenty-five cents. I moved on to another counter with toys that didn't wind up. One was a little street car painted bright yellow. I studied it for some while, it reminded me so much of one we saw in a town we passed through on the wagon trip, but the girl who was waiting on me got the idea that I wanted to buy it, and before I realized what was happening, somehow I had bought it and was out in the street again.

A block away I came to my senses and, unwrapping the toy, turned it around in my hands. What was I doing with a yellow street car? The tears came bulging to my eyes and I ran back fast to the store. I didn't really imagine that the girl who'd made the sale would have forgotten me so soon after seeing such a lot of me, and I hated to face her again on that account, but I didn't want the little street car for my dime, all over me I didn't want it, and hastening past the other clerks who were going to wait on me, I found my girl and held out the package to her, and she understood and very kindly allowed me to start my shopping all over. What a relief after being so frightened! Once more I looked and looked, and presently I decided on a little cream pitcher, soft shiny gray in color, with pale pink roses painted on one side, and this time I had looked long enough and got what I actually wanted, and went homewards carrying it most carefully.

Back in the wagonyard it was the day for half-soling shoes. Papa'd got the iron jack and lasts from behind the door and selected the lasts that fitted our shoes, and Jennie was sitting with her stocking feet stretched towards the stove while he opened out his pocketknife and set each shoe in turn on a big piece of tough-looking brown leather and cut the soles to fit. The next step was to take the old worn-out soles off the shoes, place them upside down one after the other on the last and tack on the new soles. They were then ready for Jennie, and Sallie handed hers to Papa. After that it was time for me.

"I declare, I don't know whether Delphie's shoes are worth new soles or not, Papa," said Mama.

She held them up, and they did look pretty bad, the tops gray and wrinkled and the toes stubbed and peeling and even grayer in color so that every morning before going to school I had to hunt out the blackest coal in the ash bin and rub it over them. The laces were broken and tied together in so many places that they didn't quite reach to the tops any more.

"Delphie's hard on her shoes," said Papa, sounding not so much regretful about it, like Mama, as dangerous, like himself, "but these are goin' to have to last her out the winter." He drew the right one down on its last and regarded me sternly where I sat, feet to the fire and the beautiful little cream pitcher in my lap. " 'Pears to me sometimes like she don't try to take no care of 'em."

Had he seen me skipping? Or was the dime I'd so clearly wasted centering his attention on me? "I do, too, try," I said, almost weeping. "Last week I tried to win a new pair in a race."

"Oh, did you run in that race?" Sallie's shoes were on, and she was walking around the room to limber up their new soles. "I thought the sign in the store window said it was for girls in the third an' fourth grades."

"Well, I'm almost in the third, so I thought it would be all right."

"I'd a run myself," said Sallie, "only I was afraid they'd notice how tall I am an' find out I'm in the fifth."

"The girl who won was tall," I said. "That girl had awfully tall legs. They were tall enough for her to be in the fifth grade, but I believe she really was in the fourth."

"They sure were pretty shoes," said Sallie enviously.

I nodded, thinking of the shiny patent leather on their toes and in a band around their tops, and especially of the cute little red tassel which dangled in front of the buttons. For about two weeks the shoes had been in the window of the Buster Brown Shoe Store with a sign that announced the race. I used to pause going home from school and admire them and consider how it would be if they were mine. One thing I thought was that they wouldn't look like much with these old greenish black six-pairs-for-a-quarter mail-order stockings I was wearing. Women's stockings, they were far too big for me and had to be folded under at the heel and toe, and the way they were knitted, they stretched. Their stretching had no end, and you pulled them up tighter and tighter until they broke and became holes over your knees. The tops turned down inside barely disguised the holes. Then I was everlastingly falling down, tearing the holes larger and skinning my knees as well, and the stockings and underwear would stick to the sores. It nearly killed me to get myself loose at bedtime, however much I eased the stuck places by soaking them with a little water first.

My hope was, if I did win those shoes, that Mama'd buy me a pair of black stockings, the twenty-five cent kind with ribbing which children were supposed to wear, to mate with the shoes for nice. I knew I mightn't win the race, but I didn't see why not. Needing the shoes more than anybody else as I did, Jesus would naturally see to it that I ran the fastest. That was what Jesus was for.

But maybe I didn't ask Him properly and the prayer didn't get through. Or maybe somehow I didn't hold up my end of the thing like I should have done. Then again, maybe the store men were working too hard against us. For when the girls collected for the race after school one day, those men lined us up in the street in two rows one behind the other without the slightest heed to our size, and I was put into the back row, the girl with the awfully tall legs being exactly in front of me, so how was it possible for Jesus to stop her from winning?

"Get set, you girls!" came the call. "One-two-three, *go!*"

I did all I could, or thought I did, churning my knees up and down and trying to shove past the girl in front, but she struck me on the ear with her elbow, somebody else knocked off my cap and I had to pick it up, and still another girl stepped on my foot and caused it to hurt awfully. I'd scarcely raced at all, you might say, and the race was over. One of the men from the store was calling out, "Okay, now! Hold it, girls! Here's the winner!" and it wasn't me.

I wished so much I could tell that to Papa. But if I tried to, I'd cry, I knew I would, the tears would come along an easy road where the others had flowed as I went on home after the race, wiping my eyes when I thought no one was looking. Better to change the subject. "Are you goin' with me an' Sallie to the program at the church tonight?" I said to Jennie.

"Yes," said Jennie, "but not down to the tree for candy. I'm too big."

"Me an' Delphie'll have to go down twice then," said Sallie, "or there won't be enough for the whole family."

We planned it out, Sallie and I, on the way to church after supper, how we'd wear our coats on one trip to the tree and not on the next, in order to look like different kids. It had quit snowing and the street lamps shone on the puffy white trees and across the snowy ground, while in the darkness up above the cold seemed to be squeezing an extra sparkle out of the very stars. The church was warm and bright. We three girls sat at the back and feasted our eyes on the beautiful glittery evergreen and listened to the children singing, or reciting poems like

'Twas the night before Christmas and all through the house
Not a creature was stirring, not even a mouse,

and the Christmas shivers swooped out of my heart and went spinning all over my body, because in spite of Mama's and Papa's predictions and there not being any Santie Claus at all really nor any wonderful bulls to bend their ears to a whisper, how could you be absolutely sure, on a night like this mightn't something very unusual happen anyhow?

The candy and other goodies were in cheesecloth sacks, some red and some green, heaped under the tree down front. At the close of the program the man who was playing Santie began to hand them out to the children, and either he didn't notice that Sallie and I were the same kids who'd been down once already, or else he didn't care, and we got two sacks apiece all right. That made one apiece for each of us girls, and one extra. Papa said he didn't care for any, thank you just the same, and Bruce was too small to count, so the extra sack went to Mama.

She and Jennie set to and ate all of their goodies then and there, but not Sallie and not me. I divided mine exactly in half, and the half I didn't eat I left in the green cheesecloth sack beside my cream pitcher on the sewing machine close to my cot, where they made me a sort of special little Christmas. They were the last things I saw as I fell asleep, and the first when I awoke the next morning and opened my one eye that was uncovered, and I was glad about them before I remembered to be disappointed about not getting to set my cap. Just in case, I uncovered my second eye, but no, Santie hadn't paid us a visit after all, which gave me a chance to notice that I was drawn up so tight I hurt. I straightened myself a little, only to find that the cold was worse than the hurt, and I made an effort to get back into my warm spot, but I couldn't make myself fit it any more.

Why was everybody else so slow to wake up? Wasn't it time? I peeked at the windows. The panes had icy edges but through their centers a gray-speckled light was flowing. I listened towards the other beds. From the one across the room came some gentle nose whistlings, these were Papa's, and over against them some short heavy puffs, Mama's, while now and then among the puffs and whistlings I thought I could make out Bruce's tiny breathings. They weren't much more than the sighs you'd overhear from snowflakes in their fall.

"Quit your scrougin'."

That could be none but Sallie. I raised my head and saw Jennie's thrusting from beneath the quilts in the girls' bed in the corner close to my own. "Quit it your own self." Her voice was rusty from not being used all night, but her eyes opened to shine at me like two big blue beads—Christmas beads, naturally—and a little rise of mist went up from her gap.

"Now you girlies hush up an' act nice. Don't you know what day this is?"

Mama'd sat up in bed in her undershirt, and now she fell to hugging and kissing her baby. "He's the softest sweetest

66

little ol' thing just openin' them big brown eyes!" she told us, flushed with pleasure.

"Christmas gift, all o' yuns!"

Papa was sticking his long legs in their white union suit out from beneath the covers. His greeting brought the rest of us up, and we all began playing the game, laughing and calling from bed to bed, getting each other's Christmas gifts and becoming all mixed up as to who had got whose.

"Not that it matters," said Jennie. She meant that nobody ever received the gifts.

Soon the fire was popping and blustering in the stove, and Papa went into the kitchen to crack the ice frozen in the bucket and pour some water to wash his face. How stong Papa was! anyhow, for a skinny man. Mama was less strong, pulling on her corset cover and petticoat and as much else as possible as she sat in bed before making the lunge across to the heater. We girls were still half under our covers.

"I wish I'd a set my cap an' got a lot o' goodies an' playpretties this mornin'," said Sallie, producing her sack of leftover goodies from beneath her pillow where it had spent the night.

"I'd a took a pair o' shoes," said Jennie.

What a nuisance that girl was getting to be! First thing you knew, she'd have Papa stirred up again over how we should take care of our shoes, or Mama carrying on that we might as well wish a new outfit for the whole kit and bilin', weren't we all as naked as a jaybird in whistling time, might nigh it. The day would be ruined. I stretched out a hand to the special little Christmas I'd made myself on the sewing machine, placing the dainty pink and gray cream pitcher where I could see it better, and I said, "I'd a took a few more dishes to go with my cream pitcher, an' then I'd a had me a reg'lar little tea set. I've still got quite a bit of candy." I was lining it up piece by piece according to its kind on the countapin before me—five pieces of hard, ten and a half peanuts, two chocolate mounds and a chunk of peanut brittle.

"Well, we'll get some more candy at the Elks Hall this mornin'," said Sallie.

"Yuns ain't a-plannin' on goin' off up there this mornin', are yuns?" said Papa. He'd combed his hair and moustache and was sitting, arms folded, by the heater, waiting for Mama to get breakfast ready. "It's my understandin'," he told us gravely, "that that stuff is for the poor."

"We just as well have it, Papa," Sallie argued. "Nobody'll know who we are."

Overhearing us from the kitchen, Mama came to the door, floury hands in the air, to say that she'd saved up enough grease to make biscuits for our Christmas breakfast, they'd be delicious with molasses and a little hot grease on the side, and that with them and all the goodies we'd already had and still had, she didn't see any call for us to be running out in the cold this morning. Jennie appeared behind her, bearing a plateful of soda-and-molasses candy. Since yesterday when she and Sallie had pulled and twisted it and hung it to stiffen on nails around the kitchen walls, the stuff had stretched itself clear to the floor and hardened there in neat little heaps. "There's this, too," she said, and as Sallie and I hesitated about taking one of the solid pale brown coils she was offering us, she added crossly, "You know Mama's floors are clean. Ain't she allus scrubbin' 'em?"

"It ain't that," said Sallie, then declared straight out what was wrong for her. "If we get all that ol' homemade stuff piled up here, it'll look like we don't need to go to the Hall."

"Well, I'd a little ruther yuns didn't do it, childern," said Papa.

He didn't try to stop us, though, when we fixed to go in the middle of the morning. It was as cold outside as it looked, and setting in to snow again, not soft cool flakes that brushed your cheek sometimes like one of Mama's rare little kisses, as it had yesterday, but small sharp silver flecks which struck downwards in a steady silken swish. Mindful of what Papa'd said, we were glad to have them kind of conceal us as we waited in line with other kids outside the Hall. We were also wearing our toboggans to our eyebrows, and Sallie, observing that she was taller than most of the others, scrunched down under her coat as much as she could. And after we'd come out of the Hall and satisfied our curiosity by a peek into the brown paper pokes, we carried them under our coats so that nobody should guess where we'd been.

This time we had a banana apiece, besides some colored candy and niggertoes and two or three crinkledy English walnuts. "Ain't it a pity," said Sallie, as we scudded homewards, "that we couldn't get a banana for ever' member o' the family?" Her words whipped past on the wind. It had mounted while we were in the Hall, and across the slick icy crust of the old snow the new-fallen flakes were whirling, to sting our faces like grains of silver sand, only worse. And as we hurried, the cold was able to reach in under our coats. "I know I got my long underwear on," Sallie gasped, "but it don't feel like it." I knew I was running, too, but that wasn't what it felt like. It felt like two solid lumps, which should have been my feet, thumping against the snow. As to my hands, only the one hanging onto the candy bag beneath my coat had any life at all, and that was just sufficient to let me know it was aching. The other hand, on the outside, clutching my coat together at the neck, was too numb to ache. Thudding along so, I agreed with Sallie that this Christmas Day at Claremore, Oklahoma, was a day you'd call really cold.

It stayed disagreeable the whole vacation, Mama would scarcely let us children stir out of the house, and I got awfully tired of being cooped up, with nothing better to do than move from one window to another, looking out at the yellow and brown slush in the street and the dirty gray snow to either side. Gradually the snow sank down until only a few drifts, spotted with soot and pitted all over, remained close against the houses and fences, and on the morning when school reopened, the sun was actually shining. As I skipped along Main Street, I paused sometimes to look into the store windows, but in all of them the Christmas pretties were gone.

A lot of them had been given to the kids at school, to judge by the tales I heard at recess. You couldn't be sure, as so much of the stuff was at home, but it seemed likely. A girl named Eulalia had even got a beautiful bright blue bicycle which she rode up and down the walk, and you had to admire her although she was pudgy fat and white-colored in the face, and wobbled as she rode. Most of the girls were clustered together in bunches, giggling and bragging about what-all Santie'd brought them, and at the fringe of one of the bunches I knitted my brows over how to reply if anyone should inquire into my Christmas. There'd be no call to turn and walk away, as Jennie might, or to put up the kind of fight I'd seen out of Sallie, because these children weren't being sassy or mean. On the other hand, even to girls who were merely curious, I'd have to make some kind of answer, and without any big sisters around to back me up, or any Papa and Mama not too far off to sort of oversee what was happening to me. It was a problem. I certainly couldn't refer to colored candy or grocery-store chocolate mounds or even English walnuts and bananas in front of a girl who had a pair of shiny bran-new roller skates with ball bearings right here on her feet, and another girl who was wearing a solid gold locket on a chain around her neck, another with her hands tucked into the cutest little muff you ever saw, and yet another who'd made herself half-sick, she claimed, eating out of a big box of candy which must have been wonderful although homemade, as it was called divinity and she'd brought some of it to Miss Kitty. How would soda-and-molasses candy sound beside divinity, even if I called it taffy? All I had to work from really, in terms that would mean anything to them, was my little cream pitcher with the pale pink roses. So when someone finally did notice me and ask what I got, I grinned around the circle and lied as big as I could from that.

"I got a reg'lar little tea set," I said.

But something had happened as I spoke, either the girls had done some shrinking, or I was a little taller than before. Surely it couldn't be from handling my problem with a lie, which gave me no joy? Then was it that in that moment I stopped being quite so unthoughted about myself as, all by myself, I faced the world outside the family? Maybe that was it. At the time I was just amazed at a stretched feeling I had, as if I'd suddenly shot upward by a couple of inches.

BOOK TWO

Our Place in the World

CHAPTER I

Part of a Way

The whole winter at Claremore was cold, hard and cold. It wasn't over before I'd only one button left on my red flannel coat. After Christmas I did get promoted to the third grade, and just as I'd suspected, it was nicer in the second. Besides the difference between Miss Kitty and Miss Brady, there was that between the kids, those in the third knowing a lot more than those in the second, for one thing. Too, at recess the third-grade girls played a game called hopscotch, and nobody'd asked me to play as yet, so all I could do was to linger near, ready to be friendly if I was wanted, and independent if I wasn't.

To top all else, there was Arthur. He sat behind me in the new room and was always up to some trick, such as working his chewing gum into my pigtail so tight that Mama had to cut the gum and hair both out with the scissors. She was so provoked that she gave me a whack into the bargain while she had hold of me.

Another of Arthur's tricks was lists. He dearly loved making them, using a beautiful fresh sheet of paper for every list and never placing me on any of them, although I was always hoping. One list was of the pretty girls in the room. "Mama, am I pretty?" I said to her at home, and she answered no without even a glance to make sure, which put her and Arthur into agreement on one point at least. I studied myself in the looking glass, however, and after a while I got used to my looks and even seemed rather pretty, tilting my head now to one side and now to the other. I couldn't deny there was room for improvements. "Wouldn't bobbed hair help?" I said to Mama, and combed my hair flat to either side of my face to show her with the comb where I'd cut it off.

"You behave half as well as you look an' you'll be doin' well, little missie," she replied. "Never you mind about your hair. Looks don't signify. You think about bein' a good girl."

But Arthur never made any lists of good girls.

One day he wrote down the names of those who'd be promoted into the fourth grade when school let out in the spring. Name after name he called out, and came at last to his own.

"An' I'll pass," he announced, "'cause I'm smart, too."

The worst of that was, he really was smart after a fashion. For example, he could spell the names of all the states in the Union. At recess he'd have another kid give out states for him to spell, and he never missed one. He claimed he learned them off of railroad cars, and often and often in the evening I'd watch a freight train rolling past the wagonyard as if it had no end, and reading out the names of cities and states painted on the cars, marvel that Arthur could bear all their spellings in mind and attract so much attention to himself.

"Have I missed anybody?"

I didn't dare glance around, but I knew how he was sitting behind me, shining this way and that with those round black eyes and round red cheeks of his. Then Miss Brady walked into the room, and the list came to a sudden halt. I was still trying to tell myself that I might have got on if there'd been more time when I caught Arthur's whisper, so close that it tickled my ear.

"*You* won't pass!"

I stiffened my back and hunched my shoulders 'way up to give him to understand that he made me not one particle of difference, but I didn't really know how to get the better of him. Presently I had to pass him my spelling paper, while I took a paper from Muriel, the girl who sat in front of me. *One-two-three-four-five*, I heard him marking the wrong spellings as Miss Brady read out the right ones. From the sound of his pencil, the marks must be running clear across the page, heavy and black. I could hardly keep my mind on the paper I was correcting. There were five wrong spellings here, too, but I was checking them delicately to spare Muriel's feelings, and I wrote the 50 small and light. The 50 on my paper you could have seen a mile off. At last we had to read our own grades out to Miss Brady, and I said mine 60 for I was convinced that *r-i-s-t* couldn't be wrong when it looked so right, but Arthur said real loud, "She didn't neither get 60, she got 50," and Miss Brady told me to open my spel-

74

ler and see for myself, and there it was, against all common sense, *w-r-i-s-t*.

I didn't want 50 percent. I wouldn't have it. I pushed the paper off my desk, and dropped my head onto my arms.

"It's ridiculous for children in the third grade to cry," said Miss Brady.

"Cry baby!" said Arthur.

"What are *you* whispering about?" said Miss Brady. "Come here."

From under my arms I heard him go clumping past my seat and up the aisle.

"Take that gum out of your mouth and stick it on the end of your nose and stand over there until the bell rings."

Without a handkerchief to blow my nose on, nice and clean, in front of other people, I couldn't lift my head. I did steal a peek, to see what Arthur was like up there facing the room with a small gray wad on the end of his small round nose, and I thought he looked rather dismal for all his grinning and pretending to stand so easy with his hands on his hips and one foot out.

The sight gladdened me, and my cheeks dried off against my sleeves. My nose had to wait until the bell rang and all the other children marched out of the room, followed by Miss Brady. That left me free to clean up my face on my underskirt, to tighten my garter strings, and to pick up my 50 percent from the floor and hate it without anybody's reproving me. As to whether I'd have got my spelling and arithmetic and other subjects so well that Miss Brady would have promoted me in the spring, I never found out. Before spring came, Papa and Mama decided to move again.

But while the hard cold winter was still going on there at Claremore, and I was struggling along as best I could with one button on my coat and Arthur's lists and my garters and spelling and so on, Jennie got to the right age for beaux. I'd not been aware of its coming to pass, so it must have been gradual. I did know that she'd been in love several times, unsuccessfully, as you might say. The first boy was the big brother of some girls Jennie and Sallie chummed with at Allerton, Arkansas. A baby at the time, I'd heard later on about Goldie, Tessie and Brice. Brice was the boy. He had curly yellow hair which Jennie adored, and he died when he

75

was fourteen years old. Later, on the farm at Bonnot's Grove, there was Neal Edmiston, and he had dark curly hair, and Jennie adored it, too. Papa knew that this boy liked Jennie, and if she and Sallie went somewhere in the evening, to a spelling bee at school, say, Papa'd tell her she wasn't to walk home alone with Neal, so Sallie and Neal's sister Lacy always walked with them. Then during the period we were living at Claremore, Jennie was smitten for the third time, and once again it was by a fair-complected boy who had yellow curls, the only extraordinary part here being that a Jewish boy should have that coloring. Vasca Kovich was his name, a regular mouthful, and he couldn't see Jennie for dust, as she said it to Sallie, but she worshipped from some distance off, chiefly because of those curls.

For her to be so struck on boys with curls like that made it all the more peculiar about Frenchie, who wasn't a boy and who didn't have any curls at all. In fact, he had very little hair, and that little, straight as a stick, formed a half-circle around the back of a good-sized shiny bald spot. It must have been that by the time Papa and Mama thought Jennie was old enough to go with boys, there weren't any curly-haired ones around, which gave Frenchie his chance.

We'd left the wagonyard at Claremore and Papa'd traded Old Prince and Net on a piece of property at Bridgewater. The town was called that because it had a bridge over water, that is, over the Arkansas River, and it was the same town where we'd lived before. Our property was a pleasant brown house with six rooms, four downstairs and two up, in addition to a couple of porches, and it was located on the street leading up to the high school hill where we were living when Alma died. But since we'd made our home in Bridgewater the other time, they'd struck oil here, and oil wells had been drilled right in people's yards all over town.

There weren't any in our yard, however. Papa went to work with a road gang, and Mama, aided by Jennie and Sallie, took in washing. Jennie rubbed, Sallie ranched—or rinsed as she was beginning to say now—and starched and hung out, and Mama did a whole lot of everything except carry water from Miz Smiley's well across the draw, which was Sallie's special job if our well was low. They only got twenty cents a dozen for washing and the same for ironing, but Mama split everything with the girls and it gave them a little spending money all during our first summer back in Bridgewater.

Fall came, and Jennie hired herself out by the week to a woman who'd just had a little baby. The woman's husband was a barber, and Frenchie was a friend of the barber's and through him got his chance at Jennie. Mama and Papa said to each other that Jennie must have been seeing Frenchie at the barber's for some time before he began walking home from work with her in the afterooons and occasionally taking her out in the evenings. At all events, Jennie was evidently now the right age for beaux in the opinion of our parents as well as in her own. She was allowed to come and go pretty much as she pleased and nothing was said that I knew of even after Frenchie was showing up at our house almost every day and double-teaming it with Jennie in the rocker in the front room. Papa and Mama might not have known about the double-teaming, but I didn't see why not, as it looked to me like the bottom of our best rocking chair was going to be sat out quite soon.

Fully as queer was that two people could occupy that cane-bottomed rocker at the same time and not make any noise at all. It always screeked for me alone. I was also interested in how they managed just in general, Jennie being a little taller and heavier both than Frenchie, and one day after school I determined to satisfy my curiosity. I was reading in the kitchen and not making any racket myself, and in the front room there came one of those pauses which you really heard precisely because it wasn't a noise. Laying down my book, I quietly moved my chair to one side of the printed cotton curtain that hung across the doorway. In this position the legs of the chair didn't show beneath the bottom of the cloth, and I climbed softly onto the chair and bent sidewise a bit, to put one eye to a spy-hole somewhat higher up in the curtain than Jennie and Frenchie would be expecting anybody to look through, supposing they'd not forgotten all about my presence in the kitchen anyhow.

"What do you think you're doin', youngun?" said Mama, and I nearly fell off the chair. She'd gone into the back yard to gather her wash from the lines, and I hadn't heard her come in. "Get down from there!" Her expression was so aggravated that I went the other way around the table to my book. Struck by my arrangement, however, she dropped the clothes onto the table, stepped onto the chair and applied an eye to the same spy-hole I'd been using.

My book was *Little Prudy*, a loan from Miz Cole, our

neighbor across the street. I'd reached the last page, and behind it I waited for Mama to discover that the peek-hole wasn't quite in line with the rocker in the front room, and that to fix it she'd have to wiggle the curtain. Jennie and Frenchie had probably caught on in any case. There was a whisper, and at long last a screek from the rocker. Mama came to fold the laundry.

"Is Jennie goin' to marry Frenchie?" I whispered.

Again I thought she might be aiming to crack me over the noggin with her knuckles. "Now why should Jennie do that?" She sounded disgusted enough for anything, but again contented herself with a hard look in my direction. "An' don't call him Frenchie. Call him by his right name, Cecil. Or Mr. Dechere. It'd become a little girl like you better to say Mr. Dechere."

"Well, but," I said.

"Well, but nothin'," she replied, chin in air, very strong, to control me. And she sent me to borrow the little Cole boy's wagon, cautioning me to button my coat because what did I think, we were only in the month of Januwerry and it was cold enough to freeze molasses. I seized the chance to return Miz Cole's *Little Prudy* book and to borrow another entitled *Five Little Peppers and How They Grew*. Then with two dozen pieces of Mama's wash, neatly wrapped in newspaper, in the bottom of the wagon, I was ready to start across town to deliver them. "An' no foolin' around," said Mama, "or it'll be dark before you get back.

"Mr. Dechere'll be gone by then, I reckon," she added, with hope, and to remind me of my manners.

Mr. Dechere didn't sound a bit like Frenchie to me. Meeting him on my way home, however, I tried it out, and was rewarded with the flash of a smile across his nice white teeth.

"Would you like a nickel for some candy?"

"I'd ruther have it for *The Perils of Pauline* at the Nickelodeon, if you don't mind," I said politely, and explained that Pearl White was in the picture. "She'd just fell over a cliff the last time I got to go. That was two weeks back, so I expect she's been saved from that peril an' is in some other by now." Frenchie didn't care for the moving pictures, I'd heard him say there was too much reading matter in them for his taste. I wasn't talking to interest him in the picture but to make

78

conversation while he fished in the pocket of his good navy blue serge pants.

"I'll save it till this comin' Saturday afternoon," I enlarged, so he'd have all the facts, and went on home to find the rest of the family at supper in the kitchen. Crumbling a piece of cold corn pone into my glass of sweet milk, I was eating hungrily before it came to me that I was surrounded by a dead silence, the kind that can suddenly follow a lot of talk, especially excited talk. I glanced around the table.

"Mr. Dechere gave me a nickel," I said, to break the ice and get off on the right foot with Mama, but she replied, "Now why'd he have to do that?" so vexedly that I stared.

"Why shouldn't he?" Jennie flared, and turning to her, I noted what I'd missed earlier, that she was uncommonly red in the face.

"Listen, daughter."

This brought me around to Papa, who'd pushed away his empty glass and with one forefinger was drawing imaginary lines on the white oilcloth. He always drew imaginary lines when he was thinking, and the lines always made the letter *B*. Maybe it stood for *Brittie*.

"Me an' your maw's been studyin' about this thing." He was as solemn as Mama'd been edgy. I quit chewing, with my mouth full. "We don't know what you're figgerin' on, but we think you'd be makin' a mistake to marry this feller. We don't really know nothin' about him."

"Don't he look nice?" said Jennie. "Don't he act nice?"

"Appearances ain't ever'thing," said Papa.

"They're an indication."

"An indication o' what, daughter?"

My glance slid back and forth between them. Twice he'd called her *daughter*. He was in earnest, not little everyday threatening-earnest, like home, but big scary-earnest, like the world. With something of a gulp, I got my mouthful of milk and cornbread down.

"Maybe he's all right." Papa's eyes were on Jennie with an expression foreign to any I could remember. It was as if she was farther away from us than she had ever been, as if somehow she didn't quite belong to us as before. "It ain't like we knew anything about him beyond what he says, which ain't much."

"He says enough to satisfy me," said Jennie.

79

"He orter be a-sayin' it to me. Under the circumstances."

Jennie seemed to have no ready answer to that. Papa went on. "Does he say where he gets his money from? He ain't been workin' this winter, yet he 'pears to have ready cash. Where does it come from?"

"It comes from what he's got on hand. He ain't workin' 'cause he's lookin' for a location. He's a cook, Papa, you know that. He wants to get a little restaurant of his own to run."

"He may be tellin' the truth," said Papa, "an' then again he may be talkin' to hear his head roar."

"He ain't talkin' to hear his head roar."

She couldn't ordinarily contradict Papa like that. He'd say, "You keep a civil tongue in your head, my girlie," and reach for the leather strap. Now, he traced a few more imaginary lines, and spoke mildly, almost pleadingly. "Me an' your maw'd like awful well to see you back in school, honey. Wouldn't it suit you to let this feller go an' start in to school again?"

"You know I can't start in to school again, Papa. You know I don't possess the clothes to do it."

She'd softened up, too, in response, and her voice rose to a squeak. She was going to cry in a minute.

"I'll tell you what we'll do, honey."

Honey, now, for the second time. I gave up eating entirely, and sat back from the table.

"You go back to your books," he was saying, "an' we'll get you a complete new outfit, from the ground up. Don't worry about this here Frenchie causin' trouble on account o' your keepin' company with him kind o' steady. You say the word, an' I'll send that feller down the road a-talkin' to hisself."

"It wouldn't do no good to get clothes for me now, Papa. I been out o' school too long. I'm 'way behind where I orter be. I orter be up in high school, Papa. I got behind at Bonnot's Grove an' back there in Arkansas, an' it wasn't 'cause I wasn't smart in my books either. It was 'cause you don't learn nothin' in them ol' country schools, Papa. An' anyhow, you an' Mama moved around so much, me an' Sallie didn't stay in one school long enough to make our grades."

"Sallie's done all right," Mama broke in. "They let her go in the sixth here in Bridgewater last fall. Ain't the sixth all right for Sallie?"

"No, it ain't," said Sallie, darting a black look all around the table.

"You keep your oar out o' this, Sallie," Papa warned. "This ain't none o' your quarrel."

Jennie wasn't through. "Sallie's small for her age, an' I'm big for mine. I'm too big to be with a bunch o' little kids. Look. There's Delphie. She's in the fourth, an' she ain't quite ten. An' I'll be seventeen in another few weeks, an' even if I went back to school now, it's doubtful I'd pass the seventh this year."

"You orter gone to school when we come back to Bridgewater last spring, like Delphie done," said Mama. "You an' Sallie both orter. I told yuns so at the time, but no, yuns had your minds made up. They ain't no mortal reason to blame me an' your papa for that. Yuns had as many clothes as Delphie."

I wished they wouldn't go on about me. I hadn't done anything to be bragged about, I'd just reported to the third grade when we moved here from Claremore in the spring, and the teacher had liked me, I thought it was from my memorizing *The Raggedy Man* quicker than anybody else in the room, and at the end of the term she'd promoted me into the fourth along with most of the other children. There was no cause for me to feel guilty, and yet I did, with Jennie across from me, dobbing at her eyes, and I couldn't think what to do.

"It's no use to talk, I ain't goin' back." The last light of the wintry sunset shot through the window behind as she stood up. In that red blaze her hair seemed to throw out sparks, she might have been afire on the outside to match what she was within. "I tell you, I won't go back an' give nobody a chance to belittle me again. They was a time when you could a bought me a nice new outfit, Papa, an' it'd meant a lot to me, but you didn't do it."

"When was that, daughter?"

"At Bonnot's Grove. I'd been workin' in the cotton patch all summer, an' at the openin' o' school in September Mama said you had to buy me a few things. An' what'd you do? You took me with you into Bridgewater here an' bought three yards o' black an' white checked gingham to make me a dress, an' a little ol' felt hat that cost fifty cents, an' a fifty-cent corset. It was all cheap stuff, an' I didn't like none of it. You knew I'd earned it an' more, yet you was put out at havin' to buy it. An' I vowed to myself that as long as I lived I'd never ask you to buy me another rag. An' I never have. I know you've bought things for me since, but it's always been through Mama. An' now it's too late for you to offer."

She gave another swipe at the tears which were rolling all the while. It was so unlike her to talk so much at one time. And Papa and Mama neither one answered her a word. And she wasn't through yet.

"It's too late," she repeated, the fire flashing blue in her watery eyes. "Goin' to school don't mean nothin' to me no more. I'd ruther work for fifteen cents an hour cleanin' house for other people, or help to take in washin'. But I don't have to. I'm gettin' two dollars a week an' most o' my meals now. An' Cecil wants me to marry him. I don't see what you've got against him. He's as good as we are, I reckon. Him an' me'll get us a little restaurant to run. He'll do the cookin', an' I'll wait on tables. I know Cecil's a good cook. I've et his cookin'." A sob got away from her, a big sob that I thought was being wrenched out of me as well. "He makes the best tomater sauce for beans I ever et in my life."

With that she rushed for the back door. We heard her feet across the porch, then on the stairs to the loft. Sallie flew after. Papa didn't even see the hateful glance she flung him as she went. He was staring at Mama, and Mama at him, without a word between them. Surely somebody would do something helpful now, I thought desperately, but nobody did, and after a moment I slunk out of the kitchen and into the front room, where my eyes fell on my arithmetic book.

It chanced right then that Miss Maybelle, who taught the fourth grade, was reading *Pollyanna* out loud to us children in her room. I became quite interested, and noticing the book on her desk after school one day, I couldn't resist the temptation to find out what happened next. Unexpectedly Miss Maybelle reappeared, saying I should wait to hear the story with the rest of the class and that it wouldn't hurt to apply some of all that interest of mine to my schoolbooks. She recommended my arithmetic, or geography, or physiology, or all three, and in order to pacify her, I was having to tote one or two of them home every blessed afternoon.

In a chair by the stand-table, I thumbed through the arithmetic to the multiplication tables. As I whispered them over, it suddenly dawned on me that I wasn't having to force myself. This astonished me so much that I left off repeating the tables, and in the silence I heard Mama and Papa in the next room. Mama was saying that they'd made their mistake in letting Jennie quit school in the first place, if she hadn't gone to working out she'd never have met Cecil Dechere, and Papa replied that Jennie was a grown woman, prit nigh it, and very self-willed, and he didn't guess it would do any good to further oppose her.

Far from getting his walking papers then, Cecil fell into the habit of bringing Jennie home from the barber's every afternoon, and of staying later and later. One day he brought her a white rat. Of all things, for a present! On another day he and Jennie fixed to have their picture taken together. Jennie borrowed a green satin blouse from the barber's wife and put it on with her new green wool skirt. It was supposed to be a very stylish skirt, as it had a split on one side filled in with a pleated piece of roman-striped silk which showed when she walked. Cecil wore his blue serge suit. In the picture Jennie was standing beside his chair, one hand on his shoulder. Cecil looked bigger sitting down.

"That's why they taken it like that," said Papa to Mama, and couldn't hold back a grin.

He found it no grinning matter that Jennie'd spent a whole week's wages on her skirt. He felt she should have been saving her money for a wedding outfit. It was going to be mighty hard for him and Mama to buy it for her, the dollar and a half a day which he made digging ditches for the county didn't keep us in the necessaries of life hardly.

"I promised her a white satin weddin' dress an' the things that go with it," Mama made reply. "Jennie's mine and your first child to get married, Papa, an' if we could a scraped up the money for clothes to send her back to school in, I reckon we can get it together for her weddin' outfit." She explained that she'd saved up a little from washing, and said that if Papa'd see to the dress, she'd be responsible for the rest. Jennie had her heart set on white satin. But they'd make it so she could dye it and get some use out of it afterwards.

Mama and Jennie were sewing and trying on the white satin dress for days on end, it seemed to me. It took longer to finish on account of their having to be ready to whip it out of sight in case Miz Smiley or some other prying old neighbor woman came poking her nose in. The goods was glossy and soft, looking rather like the white rat's fur, but catching on the roughness of my fingers, which showed redder beside it. Jennie was rubbing Mentholatum on her hands every night at bedtime to make them nice enough for the dress.

The evening came when she put it on with her new high-button shoes, and combed her thick red hair out long and smooth, pinning it up again with her amber-colored hairpins into the big loose figure-eight she wore it on the back of her neck. Mama got Papa a clean shirt, and had me change my dress. Bruce was scrubbed and dressed in fresh rompers. Sallie didn't have to slick up special, she was doing that every day now that she thought she was such a young lady, though in truth she was the same scrawny little nubbin as always. Last of all, having seen to it that everybody else was ready, Mama donned her best dress. Then Cecil showed up, his shoes gleaming black as his eyes, and his blue serge pants pressed till you could have cut bread with the crease. On his heels came Preacher Maquiddy.

I saw this preacher every week at Sunday school, and once in a while I stayed to church and listened to him get all wrought-up pleading with sinners to come forward, join the church, and be saved. Mama and Papa were also acquainted with him, although they hadn't put their membership into his church and it was mighty seldom that they went to hear him preach. Very likely he'd been in our house once or twice, but it was in my absence, and as he followed Cecil into our front room, deposited his Bible beside my geography book on the stand-table, rubbed his hands together and smilingly said, "Good evening, folks," while his glance strayed—very inquisitively, it seemed to me—over us and the room, I found that my usual feeling about him was reviving in full strength. Chiefly this feeling was a simple wish not to get too close to him, and on Sundays I'd sidle past at the door of the church where he'd be stationed, so beaming and hearty as he shook hands with people going out that you could hardly believe he'd been pleading for their very souls the merest few minutes ago. Tonight, very softly, I slid to the far corner of the room and made myself small alongside the stove.

Meantime, with Jennie and Cecil facing him side by side, Preacher Maquiddy was reading from his Bible and saying some things to them. Back of his voice the room took on that special quiet which called attention to itself, and my eyes sought the others for something to go by in the extraordinary circumstances that had been allowed to develop around us.

Sallie'd flopped down on the rocker, her face black as a thundercloud, which I took to be the expression of her own uneasiness. In front of the organ—that old organ which we'd brought all the way from Arkansas and which Jennie could play so prettily by ear—Mama held Bruce by the hand and watched Jennie and Cecil with eyes that were too big and too full of gleam. Papa? He was quite close to me, on the opposite side of the stove, arms folded and moustache as combed and unlively as ever I'd seen it. Everything was unnatural and dispiriting, and while I was lost in that angle of the situation, Jennie and Cecil got to be man-and-wife. One minute they weren't, and the next they were, and now Jennie couldn't back out any more.

I didn't like its being so quick and yet so forever like that. All of my dislike seemed to come to a point, a sharp point, on the person who'd done the job, and it was several minutes after Preacher Maquiddy had congratulated the happy couple, as he called them, and said goodnight and left us to ourselves, that I perked up sufficiently to ask Cecil why he'd given the preacher that money. It was neither curiosity nor pure sociability so much as an effort to get back to normal.

Cecil replied that the money was to make the preacher feel good, like himself. The smile came and went across his white teeth, and leaning down to Jennie, sitting large and soft in her white dress that was so beautiful except for being a little puckery along the seams, he gave her a hard squeeze. Papa coughed. Mama began to unbutton Bruce's rompers, remarking that it was long past the little fel's bedtime. Sallie didn't stir, but her black eyes were boring a hole in the floor. I ran out to the middle of the room.

"Let's have that celebration we was talkin' about," I proposed, "with Cecil's bottle o' wine!"

"Nobody was talkin' about it but Cecil, I don't think," said Papa, half apologetic and half annoyed, as I understood him. Cecil, already on the way to the kitchen, must not have heard.

"Wait'll you taste this!"

Tipping a small portion of the pretty red liquid into one of our water glasses, Cecil held it out to me. A bare thimbleful it was, and I only meant to stick in the tip of my tongue to find out for the first time in my life what wine was like, but out came one of Papa's long arms.

"Pass that right over, my girlie!"

Such a glance he sent me, I almost felt it hit.

"Delphie's too young for any drinkin'," he said, again with that mixed tone, stern for me and polite for Cecil, who'd tilted a larger order of wine into the glass and was offering it around. Everyone refused except Jennie, and Papa felt called upon to speak again. "We don't none of us do no drinkin' around here, Cecil."

To my ear he was becoming much more grave than anything else, but this was something Cecil wouldn't know about. He gave us a wink with what I thought of as his winking eye, from the fact that it was a bit paralyzed and drooped in a sort of continuous half-wink, and said he'd show us how a fat old Catholic priest would swig the stuff down like buttermilk. Eyes shut, he held out one hand over his second good-sized pouring, mumbled some words, tapped his forehead, each shoulder and his stomach, spun on his heel, and threw back his head for the wine. It went down in a single long pull. "The old priest does it just to get the wine," he said, wheeling around to us again.

I was filled with wonder. "Are you a Catholic?"

Mama answered, sharply for her in company, that Cecil wasn't a practicing Catholic, to her knowledge.

"That's right, Mother," said Cecil.

I waited a moment to see how she was going to take that Mother business. She let it pass, and I asked Cecil what it was he'd said over the wine.

"That was Latin. Catholic priests always pray in Latin."

"They do? An' you know Latin?"

Cecil said he'd learned it from hearing the priests so often.

"It sounded crazy," I said, laughing. "Take some wine an' do it again."

Again, and yet again, he did it, so eager was he to oblige, while Jennie sipped her drink and we others looked on. I was growing tired from the long evening, though, and asked would he mind saying us some French for a change.

Wee-wee-mamzell-something-or-other, said he, and with the last bright glassful of wine in hand, dropped down with an arm around Jennie's shoulders. If he was going to recommence that nonsense here in front of us all where it was so embarrassing, I thought I'd better interrupt him quick. Had he ever been to France on a visit?

He replied that his father and mother had come from there to Louisiana when they were young, but that he himself had never been across the Big Pond.

The *Big Pond.* I reflected on this expression for a moment, then, as he seemed on the point of squeezing Jennie some more, possibly even of nuzzling her neck, I reached for my geography on the stand-table, opened it, and laid it on his knees.

"Show me on the map where your father an' mother use to live in France."

He gave the page such a queer slanting look that I glanced doubtfully at Mama. *Her* response was to get right up, take the geography from the two of us, snap it shut and put it back on the table.

"You heerd him say he's never been in France, youngun!"

"Well, but," I said, preparing to argue with her from some distance off. "That wouldn't keep him from showin' me on the map where his folks use to live in France, would it?"

She retorted that I was plaguing her out with my monkey-shines, and would I kindly stop hogging the whole show for a while. Cecil straightened the creases in the knees of his pants. He was just a sprucy little Louisiana Frenchman who could cook the best frog legs and the tastiest sweet taters that ever set your mouth watering. Oh, how he winked and smiled as he said that! glistened, too, for although the fire in the stove had been allowed to die down for the night, he was sweating a little. He was going hunting one of these days and shoot some rabbits, he declared. Or, he'd bring home some sowbelly from the market to fix with the sweet taters instead.

"Would you fix us some sowbelly, Mother, if I showed you how?"

"Why, sure, Cecil, I'll fix it. I don't think none of us here would care for it. But if you get it, I'll cook it for you, even if you're the only one to eat a smidgen of it."

"Okay, Mother."

Mama's hint was the one he'd missed this time, if you could call it that instead of something stronger, and maybe it would teach her a lesson. Cecil, at any rate, was still taken up with the subject of food, and describing a lip-smacking dish called slumgullion. This had to be put together in a hobo jungle for it to be good. Cecil had learned to make it when he used to ride the rods all over the country before his Jennie tamed him. With that he was fondling and feeling around on her again. If she didn't watch out, he'd have her lovely wedding dress all soiled and mussed before the wedding day was over.

In the midst of his yarnings, Sallie stalked off through Mama's and Papa's bedroom into the lean-to bedroom beyond, muttering something about yes, we killed a bear, didn't we. What did Mama and Papa think of these tales which we'd been hearing for the first time this evening? They weren't saying much, and sitting down on the far side of the stove, I prepared to follow Sallie to bed.

"Put them shoes right on again, missie," said Mama, peering around the stove, "till other folks are ready to take off theirn. Do you want to smell us out with your toe jam?"

"You don't need to go to excremes," I said coldly. "I ain't got no toe jam."

She'd made it excremely clear, in my opinion, how little she relished Cecil's stories, but wasn't it time she quit taking her feelings about him out on me? I was glad to hear her admit that after all it was nigh onto bedtime.

"It occurs to me you an' Jennie may want to take your clothes off in the kitchen, Cecil, it's pretty cold upstairs."

It occurred to me that it would be pretty cold for them to make the dive from the kitchen across the back porch to the stairs which led to the loft with nothing on but their night clothes. But I thought to myself, I thought, if people don't appreciate what occurs to me, I believe I'll just let them suffer. Besides, Papa, who'd been drawing *B's* on the knee of his pants, had cleared his throat and crossed his legs the other direction, and maybe we were going to get an inkling of how Cecil rated with him now. His remark, however, had to do with Cecil's and Jennie's plans for the future.

"I don't aim to be a-pressin' yuns," he said, smiling a little at Cecil, "but a feller would just like to know."

Cecil replied readily that now that he and Jennie were married, they wanted to get a little beanery of their own.

"What's a beanery?" I stumped out from behind the stove with my shoes on unbuttoned. It went without saying that I knew what he was talking about. I simply didn't care for the word.

"Where you been all your life to be so green, Sis? Down in the sticks?" A little beanery, he continued to Papa, was the very size for a young couple like him and Jennie to start out with, between them they could handle all the work of the place. And if not, then Big Sis could sling hash for them, and when she was some older, so could Little Sis.

"Sounds all right, don't it, Dad?"

Mother, Dad, Big Sis and Little Sis. He'd taken us all over pretty fast and thoroughly, hadn't he, I thought, and wondered what Sallie'd have to say to his big plans for her and me. I could imagine. In fact, I didn't need any imagination. Clumping over to the stand-table, I sat down below the lamp with my open geography on my lap.

"Hold on there a minute, though," said Papa. "Until you get this here beanery, as you call it, Cecil. You'll have to have a little stake for that. 'Course,"—and it was as if all in the world he wanted was to be as cheery as Cecil if only he could —"'course, yuns may be fixed to get it right now, I don't know nothin' to the contrary."

Well, right now Cecil and Jennie were only looking for work, the beanery was for later on. Like sunshine on a wintry day, the smile came and went across his white teeth. "Coffee, copper, sugar, wheat," I whispered to myself, "cattle, cocoa, nitrates, sheep." Divided up like that, the words were almost a rhyme. Diamonds and tapioca followed, one hard and one soft, one to wear and one to eat. If I could but remember these thoughts about the ten chief products of South America, they should be easy to name when Miss Maybelle asked me for them in class. From now on, I was thinking, as my lips of themselves went on forming the words, I'm going to bring home still more of my books, up to and including my physiology with its lists of bones—femur, tibia, tarsus and metatarsus, phalanges, and so on and on—and one of these days very soon Miss Maybelle is going to be surprised to find that I know every single list she can ask me for. Not that I was so ignorant as to suppose that memorizing such lists meant very much all by itself. It was part of a way. And the way wasn't to a beanery. For the more I studied about it, the more I found myself opposed to the idea of slinging hash in a beanery, and the more I was determined not to do it, not in Cecil's or in anybody else's. And while Sallie might be more violent about it than myself—she was always more violent than I was—it came to me that I'd turned my back on Cecil and everything Cecil stood for just as flatly and finally as ever she could, and presently would.

CHAPTER II

How? What? and Why?

As matters went, Papa needn't have worried about footing
the bills for Jennie and Cecil. A few days after the wedding
they went down to Sapulpa, and we didn't see hide nor hair
of them until another winter rolled around. Before then there
was a lot of time to be got through, including the stretch between school-out in June and school-taking-up-again in September. It was a long stretch. Once in a while Mama received
a letter from Jennie and I'd be reminded of her. I'd recall the
wedding, but more especially the day after, when she and
Cecil came down to breakfast and I had a chance to give
Preacher Maquiddy's happy couple a fresh morning once-
over. Cecil's winking eyelid was drooping more than common
and his cheeks seemed unusually white, at least in contrast to
the short black stubble they were sprouting. Jennie was even
more different from yesterday. She was eating much less than
was customary for herself, but what impressed me most was
the trouble she had looking anybody in the eye. I knew it had
to do with those funny bluish bruises on her neck, almost
they had the prints of teeth in them like those I left on
Sallie's leg one time when we got into an in-earnest fight and
I bit her there, that being all I was in position to do at the
moment. Sallie's marks didn't disturb me in the least either,
even after Mama'd made it clear that she was deeply disappointed in us two girls. The sight of Jennie's prints had another effect, and I went to stand staring from the window,
following Sallie's flight like that of a red-winged blackbird
down across the draw to tell her friend, Miz Smiley's
daughter Selmie, about the wedding.

Quicker than I expected, here she was flying back, her red
sweater aflap, and bursting in on Papa, Mama and me alone
in the kitchen, was blazing forth her story, that Miz Smiley'd
suspected what was going on at our place last night when she

saw the light on so late, as she knew we always went to bed with the chickens, and she'd watched from her window and prayed for Jennie and wished that this foreigner had never come into her life. She said she *prayed* for Jennie. And Sallie, not one little bit calmed down by Miz Smiley's also saying that Jennie was too good for Cecil, retorted that she didn't care if Cecil was a foreigner, kind of, she reckoned he was as good as Miz Smiley's husband who died last year, everybody knew he'd drunk himself to death. "You pray for your family, an' we'll pray for ours," she flashed, and snatching up her sweater to leave before anybody had a chance to answer back, she tacked on the clincher. "An' we don't allus go to bed with the chickens neither!"

She felt she'd got the better of Miz Smiley, and so did we all. Nevertheless, our neighbor's words hadn't made us any happier, and listening to Mama read from Jennie's latest letter from the ranch near Sapulpa, where Jennie did the cooking and Cecil acted as handyman, also getting in quite a bit of rabbit-shooting, I'd say to myself, things don't sound too bad for her, do they. I couldn't quite convince myself, and I might go to stand staring from a window, as a person would if things went wrong inside, as I'd done on that cold March morning after the wedding, watching the glint of snow as fine as needles through the windy sunshine and trying to master the uneasy lonesome feeling which Jennie aroused in me.

Mastery was less difficult at this distance from the wedding and from Sapulpa, and, in truth, I didn't miss Jennie very much after she was gone. Papa'd bought a pair of mules and a wagon, and early in the season he and Sallie drove off to western Kansas where they found work in the wheat fields. Sallie washed dishes in the cookshack for the same outfit that hired Papa to haul water.

"What's a cookshack?" I asked Mama.

She'd just had a letter from Papa. "Why, a cookshack's some sort o' little room out in the fields, handy for the threshers. This un Sallie works in is built on a wagon bed, an' they move it around to wherever the men are threshin'."

More than once Mama remarked that Sallie sure was finding out what hard work was this summer. It was a shame her and Papa'd had to go clear out to Great Bend, Kansas, but there'd been no jobs for them here in Bridgewater. Papa claimed those wheat fields were the hottest place he'd ever struck. It tickled Mama that the other hands called him Dad.

"Papa ain't as young as he once was," she added, with a little pleased laugh.

"You ain't either, Mama."

"Your papa's a way yonder older'n I am. He's twelve years older'n I am." She was pretty warm about it.

"He ain't old enough to die, is he?" I said anxiously.

"Well, I'll say he ain't. Papa's been imaginin' he was dyin' o' consumption for ten years now, all 'cause his own paw an' maw died from that complaint. But he ain't goin' to die from consumption or anything else in the near future, Papa ain't."

Alone in the brown house with only Bruce and me to keep her company, she missed Papa and Sallie the same as I did though, sending me to call for our mail at the post office much oftener than there was a chance of a letter from one of them, and being even more surprised and pleased than myself the day Sallie walked in on us with a new red straw hat sitting on the back of her head like. She'd taken some of her cookshack money and bought it for herself out of the mail-order catalogue, also paying her fare home on the train.

"You little heifer you!" Mama exclaimed, laughing, and hugging her.

This was in mid-August. Not long afterwards Papa rolled in behind his mules, and soon it was Labor Day. School reopened the day following. I was in the fifth grade now, and Sallie was in the seventh. During the summer it had seemed as if the weeks would never pass, but going to school I scarcely noticed time, whether or not anything was happening to it, and almost before you could shake a stick Hallowe'en whizzed by, then Thanksgiving, so fast you very nearly had to look over your shoulder in order to see it, and we ran smack-dab into Christmas vacation. And it was a Sunday morning, the very day before Christmas, and I was leaning on the table in the kitchen intent on a handful of pie dough which Mama was rolling out with a fruit jar on a floury piece of brown paper.

"Can I go to Sunday school now?"

"No. It ain't near time for Sunday school yet. An' take your fist out o' them apples." She knocked one of the slices out of my hand and back into the bowl. "I got just enough for a good pie as 'tis," she told me, adding didn't I have any duties to occupy me.

I was patient, knowing she had a lot to contend with.

There was this business of Christmas falling on a Monday this year, which meant a special dinner on each of two days right together—the mere last of what-all had piled up on her. Sallie'd come down with the tonsilitis she had so bad every winter, Bruce was worse sick with something else, and Jennie and Cecil were home for a visit, the first they'd paid us since they were married. It was entirely too cold for anybody to sleep off upstairs, however, and Papa brought the extra bed down from there and set it up for Sallie and me in the kitchen, turning our bed in the lean-to over to Jennie and Cecil. But as Sallie went hog-wild when I tried to take my usual place beside her, I ended up on a pallet in the front room.

I pointed out to Mama that one of the duties I'd accomplished was to fold my pallet neatly and place it on the stairway to the loft. I'd also stayed with Bruce for a while, until Papa relieved me. "An'—an'—" Nothing further came to mind, and at that moment Papa pushed aside the curtain to the front room, stooping to pass under it.

"I ain't real satisfied about Bruce this mornin'," he said to Mama, as he joined me near the stove. "Jennie an' me's been wonderin' if Doc Blaine rightly thinks he's got a touch o' ptomaine poisonin'."

"It stands to reason the cause is somethin' he et," said Mama. "Though I don't know what it could a been."

She sounded in a very ill humor, this being from anxiety, as I knew, and when she'd got her pie tucked into the oven, she washed her hands and went with Papa to look at Bruce.

In her absence I found a tin lid in the kitchen cabinet. The extra pieces of dough trimmed from the pie were still strewn over the brown rolling-out paper, and placing them on the lid, I sprinkled them with sugar and set them in the oven by the pie. Then I asked Sallie, in bed in the corner of the room, where my book was.

"What book?" she croaked, flouncing over on her back.

She knew very well what book. We just had one besides the Bible. Mine. The one she was always reading when I wanted it. The one I got last summer shortly after she came home on the train from Great Bend, Kansas, wearing that red hat like a sundown on the back of her dark head. To earn that book I'd gone up and down our street, knocking at doors and asking women if they wouldn't like to subscribe to *The Gentlewoman* for twenty-five cents a year, finally locating one who'd subscribe if I'd stay with her children for the afternoon. I studied the list of novels which I could pick from as my prize for the subscription, and decided on *The Homestead on the Hillside* by Mary J. Holmes, partly because of the pretty repeating sounds of the words, and I mailed the subscription quarter to Augusta, Maine. The book took a long time to come and still longer to reach my hands, as Sallie happened to get it at the post office and didn't hand it over till she'd read it through. And now she could say, what book.

"Where is it?" I insisted, and would have kept on at her but that Mama came rushing in to snatch her pie from the oven. It was dangerous to try to claim my crusts at such a moment, and they got somewhat too brown as a result, but they tasted good. I had a sort of knack for fixing them.

Now it honestly was late, and at last Mama said I should go on to Sunday school and quit pestering her, among us all we had her running around like a chicken with its head off. Away I sped.

She'd made me tardy, however, and the other girls in my class were already seated in their semicircle. They were talking about boxes of food which the church was giving away for Christmas, and Miss Smoot, the teacher, was asking if the class knew of any worthy poor people who might need them. There was a poor family named Reed living across the draw down back of us at home, and I imagined they were worthy and suggested them, but Miss Smoot wasn't sure they were poor enough. Then we discussed the Christmas program, and she said that we must be at the church at seven o'clock this evening with our white dresses on, and I had to tell her that my mother wouldn't let me wear mine. Miss Smoot was quite put out.

"But didn't you give her my note last Sunday, asking her especially to let you wear it?"

"She's stubborn," I said regretfully.

That seemed to cover it, and without more words we went on to the lesson, the usual Christmas one about the little Lord Jesus, born in a manger, and the star that stood over His head. It was a gentle story, and walking home afterwards I moved along slowly so as not to jar the sweetness and softness it always roused in my heart.

"Delpha!"

94

One of the girls in our class was running after me. Her name was Dorabel—Dorable Ames, as I remembered—and I wasn't very well acquainted with her.

"Miss Smoot says I can ask you something."

I examined her curiously, wondering why she should suddenly turn shy and mumble so badly that it took me a minute or two to make out what she was saying. When I did understand, it took another minute or two for all my gentle feelings to drain away.

"Didn't you hear me say I've *got* a white dress?" To clear up any possible doubts, I sketched in some more details. My white dress was put away for the winter, and my mother said she wasn't getting it out for any little old goings-on at the church. "She wouldn't let me wear anybody else's even if I didn't have one of my own," I ended up, and chin in air, very strong, like Mama with me sometimes, I stamped off home.

Once there, I paused by the front steps to make sure Miss Smoot's note remained safely hidden under a rock in a pile of old snow. If Mama saw it, her response would be that I didn't have to take part in any program, I could stay home with the rest of the family on Christmas Eve. She might even blurt it out in front of someone like Dorabel Ames that I didn't possess a white dress, and Miss Smoot, or Coot, or Poot, whatever her name was, could go to grass and eat mullen for all Mama cared.

The dress I did possess was heavy green wool. Maybe it looked funny in among the white dresses of the other girls that evening, but nobody said anything, and the whole matter dimmed in my mind, it was such fun to be in a Christmas program for the first time in my life and to wind around the platform with the group, singing about up on the housetop, click, click, click, down the chimley, good St. Nick. And it was a very good warm dress to be wearing on a night of so much black rain, and silver mist, and wind that rushed around the yellow shining street lamps, whirling and swirling the wetness and silver and gold all together. With those big yellow lights above my head, each one gleaming hazy but steady like a mighty Christmas candle to guide me home, how could I be otherwise than grateful and gay? Young though I was, I knew already that you must never turn your back on any happy moment. Sometime, I supposed, I'd have to think further about Dorabel's offer to lend me a white dress, how she'd come to do such an outlandish thing, but not tonight, no, surely, not tonight. Skipping, I passed along the street among neighbors and other people who were leaving the church to go on with Christmas Eve at home.

At our house everybody except Bruce and Sallie was in the front room—Jennie tatting, Cecil rocking, Papa bringing in some chunks of icy wood to dry out in the wood box, and Mama handing around a dishpanful of popcorn, popped in a skillet from some she'd raised last summer. Even on the burnt side and lacking butter, it tasted delicious, and scooping up a handful, I threw myself down on the floor alongside the stove.

"Listen to that stove pop snow," said Mama delightedly, as Papa dropped in a stick of ice-coated wood. "That's a sure sign o' snow tomorrer."

"I hope it snows tonight," I cried. "Then Santie can get here easier!"

"Now you know Santie won't bring you nothin'," said Papa, scratching his ear as he would when cracking a small joke. He knew that I knew all about the Santa business, but it made a nice little understanding between us, and his saying anything at all showed that I was sure to receive a bit of something.

"You wouldn't know what to do if you had the kind o' Christmas we use to at home, with hardly ever a boughten present," said Mama. Altogether overlooking a recent Christmas which wasn't much better, she began telling about one when she and her sister Rosie and brother Albert set their caps and didn't get a solitary thing in them. On Christmas morning their mother told them they could run over to their Granny and Granpap McNabb's and play the Christmas-gift game on them. "She thought maybe they'd give us somethin'," she said, laughing to recall how their mother had felt sorry for her little old younguns.

What a beautiful morning it had been! the ground hard underfoot, the dead brown oak leaves rustling, and everything so bright and sunny as the three children cut across the fields together, all full of their hopes. Into the house they tiptoed, and there was their Granny McNabb, pulling her best black silk dress down over her head, getting ready to go over to Mama's Uncle Hy's place for Christmas dinner. Her and Granpap McNabb liked Uncle Hy the best of their in-laws,

son or daughter, because he was the best-off, Mama reckoned.

"So us younguns called out, 'Christmas gift, Granny!
Christmas gift, Granpap!' An' when Granny'd got her dress
on an' her hair fixed, she was wearin' it in a roach, that was
the style then, why then she said, 'Yuns can get yourselves an
apple apiece out o' that bucket in the corner.'" Mama'd
never forget going over to the bucket with Rosie and Albert
and hunting through for the best apples. They were the ones
their Granpap McNabb had culled out of his barrels in the
cellar. "I declare that sure did beat me," said Mama. "Granpap had worlds an' worlds of apples."

"Your other granpap wasn't close like that," said Papa, tilting his chair more comfortably against the wall, "an' he had
cents where your Granpap McNabb had dollars."

"Yes," said Mama, "an' the McNabbs allus thought Paw
chose beneath him in marryin' a Broadbent. They never did
like Maw."

Papa crossed his legs the other direction and cleared his
throat. I reached for more popcorn and settled back against
the woodbox. If all went well, we might expect some fine old-
timey stories this evening, particularly from Mama, who was
so very good at them but needed Papa to spur her on, with
questions like his present one, that her Granpapa McNabb
was one of them fought the Yankees, wasn't he?

Sure he was, Mama replied, didn't he have every reason
to? Together with Granny McNabb, he still owned those two
slaves her pappy'd given her for a wedding present.

"Father was on the Union side," said Papa gravely.

"Granpap McNabb fought in two wars," was Mama's stout
retort. 'The other'n was the War against Mexico. 1846-48.
James Claiburne McNabb. That was before he moved to Arkansas. Him an' Granny McNabb, she was a Maness before
she married, what was called Welsh, they use to live six miles
from Nashville, Tennessee." Fixing Papa straight in the eye,
she added on another little item. Her Granpap McNabb had
fallen dead in the hogpen when he was eighty-eight years
old.

Somewhat like me with Dorabel Ames, Mama seemed to
be developing a whole picture in order to prove her point.
But what was her point exactly—the justice of fighting on the
side of slavery, or the difference between the military records
of the two families, Doud and McNabb? It often took me a

while to wind my way among Mama's accumulations of small facts, although it was pretty safe to say that somewhere along the line they really would sum up to an answer.

Papa stuck to slavery, and one big main point at a time. His father had got a pension after the war was over and the slaves were freed. He was making Mama pretty hot.

"James C. McNabb's father was Jack McNabb. That was my great-grandfather on Paw's side. He was borned in Scotland. He come over with three o' his brothers an' fought in the War of 1812. Once they was a military election for commander-in-chief o' the army, an' he lost by one vote to General Andrew Jackson. If he'd a got two more votes, he'd a been president o' the United States."

I was overwhelmed. "You mean one of our own kin would a been the real president o' the United States?"

"I don't mean nothin' else. Captain Jack McNabb. He liked just two votes o' bein' president, too."

How interesting all this was! Even if the argument came down to no more than a standing disagreement between Mama and Papa for some underneath hidden reason, he was going to have a rough time getting around a triumph like Captain Jack McNabb's.

He did so by pointing out that the captain lacked just two votes of being commander-in-chief, which wouldn't have made him president.

"It'd a come mighty nigh it. You take General Andrew Jackson. I've heerd Paw recount that many's the time, Papa."

"I ain't questionin' the fact, Mama. I'm just sayin' you don't know he'd a been president."

"Well, maybe I don't know it. But I got a pretty good notion," she added, flashing him a look.

Papa took up a little time rearranging his knees. He was remembering his father and this here pension he received, twenty-five dollars every three months, because of a wound in his knee at the battle of Shiloh.

His mother didn't collect the pension after his father died, though, Mama said promptly, calling them paw and maw to indicate they were the same plain folks as her own.

"No, but Father left her pretty well-fixed," said Papa, and mentioned the three farms at the junction of Bear Creek and Buffalo River, all good bottom land, and other smaller things, like a year's supply of hog meat. He started to tell more about this, how his father had always done a right smart butchering and they'd round up the hogs in the woods, the Doud brand being easy to recognize, smooth crop and underbit on the right and a swaller fork on the left, he meant left year, of course, child, but Cecil came out from underneath the popcorn pan, which somehow or other had wound up in his lap, and opening out a neatly folded but rather soiled white handkerchief to wipe his hands on, sighed and remarked that people sure had to work hard in them days, didn't they.

Was that all he was capable of taking out of an evening with well-to-do and important kinfolks, Doud and McNabb?

"Maybe they didn't have nobody to fall back on if they didn't work hard," said Jennie, from the bedroom. She'd gone in there to sit beside Bruce's cot, and since that room was to the back of the front room while the kitchen was to one side, Sallie from her bed couldn't catch what Jennie'd said.

"We can't talk no louder, Sis," said Cecil. "We'll disturb Bruce."

"I ain't addressin' you, sir. An' I ain't no sister o' yourn!"

Cecil laughed. "So Big Sis is on her high horse tonight." Winking at us with the eyelid that was partly paralyzed, and heedless of Bruce, he imitated Sallie's hoarse cracked voice. "I ain't feelin' so well, Sis. Maybe I caught your sore throat when I kissed you."

"You didn't kiss me! I wouldn't let an ol' buzzard like you touch me!"

"Then it was you kissed me. An' you want me to come let you kiss me again, don't you, sweetheart?"

I thought Sallie'd go crazy. "You come near me an' I'll knock your block off!"

"She'll burst one o' them swole tonsils in a minute," said Mama.

Papa made a move to get up.

"I want you to hush, Sallie, or I'm goin' to take the razor strop to you. Why must you allus be on the rule o' contrariness?"

It was only a threat, he wouldn't have laid a hand on her, sick, and even as he spoke he was letting himself back down in his chair. Anybody but Cecil would have known that he was the one Papa was really laying the law down to, but Papa had to say to him, with a direct glance, as he, too, seemed on the point of leaving his chair, "Now don't go out there, Cecil. They ain't no need of eggin' a sick girl on."

"I think Cecil'd better go to bed," said Jennie.

"Are you goin' to ree-tire, Cecil?" Mama's little homemade joke was to ease things over. "That's what rich folks would say, they was goin' to ree-tire."

Cecil grinned and gapped and stretched. "My nice big corn-fed Arkansas gal says it's time for little Frenchie to rip an' tear, so that's what little Frenchie has to do." I didn't like his applying those terms to Jennie, and I didn't think he was being very funny saying rip-and-tear instead of retire, but Jennie didn't answer him back, at least not in our presence, and only followed him into the lean-to bedroom and closed the door behind them.

Then the rest of us went to bed. There was a double door-way, without doors or curtaining, between the front room and Mama's and Papa's bedroom, and from my pallet near the stove I could listen to Mama and Papa in their bed mulling over the happenings of the day, as was their wont the last thing at night. Naturally, it was Cecil and Jennie they were whispering about tonight. Papa said he'd always be glad to have Jennie, he wanted to do all he could for her now especially because of her condition, but it was a bad time for Cecil to be bringing himself home as well, to lay around the house on the flat of his back all day, complaining about his health, without any thought for the fact that we had two sick children in bed already. Mama said it was a God's pity that Jenny'd ever married him in the first place. Maybe she'd thought she was showing her and Papa something, but she was only biting off her nose to spite her own face. Life hadn't been no bed of roses for that girl around those old cat-tle ranches. Cecil would get a job that included them both. He claimed that he supervised her cooking, but she did the real work in the kitchen as well as part of his as outdoor handyman whenever he disappeared on one of his rabbit-shooting excursions, leaving her to put up with things from the boss on this last ranch which Mama hated to pass on to Papa.

Here they talked so low that I couldn't make out their words, though trying hard. Then I heard Papa whispering that Jennie sure had turned out to be a fine-looking woman, and people liked her and felt sorry for her married to that jackrabbit. Mama had to laugh a little, because Jennie herself had referred to him as a runt.

"Somethin' else you don't know yet," she said. "That feller

100

can't read nor write. He can sign his name, the priests taught him that, but he has to get Jennie to read an' write his letters for him."

I was as shocked as Papa. Now I understood why Cecil didn't enjoy the moving pictures because of what he called their reading matter, and why he'd acted so queer and embarrassed when I showed him the map the evening he and Jennie were married, and asked him to point out the place where his folks used to live in France. He couldn't read and write. Never in my life had I known anybody else so ignorant, and yet here he was, right in among us, a member of the family. How could such a thing have happened to us? How could Jennie have been so careless? We were good people, nice people, weren't we? Look at all those kinfolks Mama and Papa had been telling about this very evening, ancestors who'd owned slaves and a lot of good bottom land, who'd been wounded at Shiloh on the Union side and almost become president of the United States on Mama's. And now we'd come down to the level of a man who couldn't read and write. No wonder Miz Smiley had prayed for Jennie. I couldn't blame the woman as much as before.

". . . little better than a hobo."

What was that? Papa was whispering, and in reply Mama said something which I thought was, "Sooner or later, it's my guess she'll leave him."

"One thing sure," said Papa, "he ain't a-goin' to peddle booze from our place. I told him after I come across that shipment o' beer he'd slipped into the woodshed, he could just get it out. First thing you know, he'll have the law down on us."

All by myself down below on the dark drafty floor, I hugged the quilts around me. Outside it was blowing and raining, washing away the last of the old snow, just such a night as an awful Law might swoop down with the wind and find the beer still in our woodshed.

"He orter be ashamed," said Mama, "an' Jennie in her condition."

I stopped shivering for a minute.

"Just what is her condition, Mama?" I whispered.

"I swear to God!" said Mama. "Ain't you gone to sleep yet? Then get to work doin' it!"

Again she and Papa talked so softly that I couldn't follow, and soon I wasn't hearing anything at all except the wind, which shook and rattled at the doors and windows as though it was the very Law itself trying to get in and catch us. With that sound in my ears, and my eyes on the stove, glowing round and red from a few sticks Papa'd dropped in the last thing, unexpectedly I fell sound asleep.

A scream woke me. Dazed with sleep, I sat up. Where was I? The room was strange, and queerly, palely lit.

"Mama!" I cried.

"Hush your mouth," said a voice, strained and peevish, which I knew instantly, and in a dim light entering from beneath the curtain to the front room I recognized the kitchen around me. I was on the floor beside Sallie's bed, and the warmth I was feeling came from a fire in the cookstove.

"How'd I get in here?" I was almost as out of sorts as Sallie.

"They carried you in on your pallet. Keep still. I can't hear."

"Hear what?"

"Jennie's baby gettin' born, o' course."

"Baby?" That jarred the ill humor out of me for sure. "Did you know it was comin'?"

"Not exactly. I just knew it's somethin' you've got to look out for after people've been married for about nine months."

Three rooms away, in the lean-to, Jennie sobbed. I could identify her voice now. "She won't die, will she?" I got out, swallowing hard.

"'Course not." Sallie was scornful. She was actually half-sitting up in bed, I saw. "All the same," she added, getting mad, "it's ever' bit Cecil Dechere's fault."

For a few seconds everything was quiet. I was just beginning to breathe more easily when Jennie gave another of those long screams, ending in a sob. What were they doing to her? "I hope you an' me don't ever have any babies," I whispered tightly.

"We won't if we've got the sense we was born with. Mama told Jennie not to either, at least not right off, but you can see for yourself what happened. Now hush. I don't think it's here yet, but if it is, I want to hear when Doc Blaine spanks it."

"He wouldn't do that to a bran-new baby!"

"Oh, you're so ignorant! It has to be spanked, to make the blood circalate."

102

Together with Sallie, I waited and listened for this new thing, and heard only those sobs and cries from Jennie. Why did it take so long for a baby to get born? "Make 'em stop hurtin' her, dear Jesus," I prayed in my mind. "*Please* make 'em stop hurtin' her!" I was crying myself by this time. "Let her alone, Cecil Dechere!" I whispered fiercely, clenching my fists and wishing I could use their strength on him. "You leave my sister alone!"

There came another quiet spell, and Sallie suggested that I could go into the front room and maybe get a peek into Jennie's room from there. If I got caught, I could pretend I'd come to see what Santie'd left in my cap.

"Why, it *is* Christmas!" I was flabbergasted to have forgotten it so totally. "Maybe I got roller skates, after all!"

"No, you didn't. You got a green glass bowl an' some candy, just like me."

So I had. I couldn't help looking first to make sure, which was a good thing, as our neighbor, Miz Fivecoat, who had the telephone we used if we had to call the doctor, say, chose that moment to come out of the lean-to. Lamp in hand, she was on her way to the kitchen to fetch hot water from one of the kettles steaming on the stove, and gently but firmly she returned me to my pallet there.

The next morning there was a new baby in bed with Jennie. I went into Papa's and Mama's room and strolled past the door of the lean-to several times, not letting on I knew the baby was there, just stealing side-glances now and then so as not to remind Jennie that she'd got it only last night and made a lot of noise about it. Presently some of the strangeness had worn off, and I found an excuse to enter the lean-to. The baby looked worse close up, very wrinkled and red and with its eyes screwed shut, but Jennie seemed right down attracted to it, saying it was a good little creature not to cry, and referring to it as Master Francis Dechere.

Now that Jennie wasn't being hurt any more, it would have been interesting to discuss the baby with Sallie. Sallie, however, didn't even wish to see it. "I know it's the spittin' image o' Cecil Dechere," she grated, and rolled over with her face to the wall. "Leave me alone. I'm sick."

Reminded of Cecil, I went to the back window of the kitchen to study the woodshed, wondering if he'd got his beer out of there yet. Mama was in the chicken pen alongside, winding up to wring the neck of an old red hen. It was dreadful to see the chicken flopping about on the ground with her head off, and I squeezed my eyes shut to give her time to stop it and become dead. When I opened them, Mama was hurrying up the garden path, puffing and blowing, and carrying the old hen by the legs. I didn't suppose I'd be allowed to go outdoors to play, but asked anyhow, and was told certainly not, couldn't I see it was setting in to sleet. Mama's idea was that I should go in and entertain Bruce.

"I don't think he acts like he wants to be entertained," I said.

"Well, maybe you can get him to want to." Mama was unusually cranky because she hated to wring the necks of old hens fully as much as I hated to see it done, though she had it to do. Laying the chicken in the dishpan, she poured a kettleful of scalding water over it, and a steamy feathery disagreeable smell rose up around our noses. I removed mine to the window facing the street, and saw Papa approaching.

Although it was Christmas Day, a couple of grocery stores were open until noon, and Papa was bringing us a good-sized brown paper sack filled with food of one sort or another, mostly the necessaries of life, I imagined, and nothing to get excited about. At the same moment, a delivery wagon was pulling up in the street and a boy was lifting down a box of groceries. I expected him to cross the street to the Coles' place, as they were people who always had a lot to eat, and was very much surprised to see him head towards our own back porch.

"Ain't you got the wrong place, son?" Mama was opening the door for him.

"I don't think so, ma'am." He set the box on the table and hurried out as fast as he'd come in.

Mama began sorting out the collection. There were sweet potatoes and a chicken ready-dressed, various cans and packages, as well as certain items never on our board, such as oranges, celery and cranberries. What had come over Papa to order all this stuff? Mama met him with the question as he walked in.

"I didn't order it. I've got my groceries right here."

"Then that boy had the wrong place, after all," said Mama vexedly, and started to pile the food back into its box. But I had spied an envelope in the bottom, and dug it out for her.

104

"Why, it's got our name on it!" Dumbfounded, Mama raised her eyes to Papa.

"Look inside."

Instead, she passed the envelope to him, and he drew out a card, holding it at arm's length as he didn't have on his spectacles. "Christmas greetings," he read out slowly, "from the Christian church."

"They were sendin' boxes to poor people," I said, uncertainly.

Sallie was sitting up in bed. "It's a charity box," she croaked.

We stared around at each other. All at once Mama gave a jab with her finger to the scrawny little blue hen. "Look at it!" she said disgustedly. "It gags me to see. Ourn is twice as big an' fat."

"Well, I'll say it is," said Papa. "I'd like to know what Preacher Maquiddy means sendin' that stuff down here. He knows we don't stand in need o' no help."

With a great deal less respect than before, Mama finished cramming the groceries into their box. "I tell you what you do, Papa. You take this stuff down to the Reeds. Them folks really do need it. Then the next time you see Preacher Maquiddy, you can tell him exactly what you done. An' tell him from me that his church people didn't show a grain o' sense in their givin' or they'd a done it thataway theirselves."

From the back window I watched Papa angle towards the draw, balancing the box on one shoulder and setting his feet down carefully on the frozen slippery old vines of last year's garden, and disappear in the direction of the Reeds' place. I felt very confused. I'd known that we were poor, of course, but not that we were so poor that other people could get together and look down on us publicly—first Dorabel Ames with me, and now the whole church with us. How had they dared! I didn't know whether I was more mad or humiliated. Behind me in the room Mama was cutting up our chicken and getting it into the pot. Somehow at this point I couldn't bring myself to face her. I waited for Papa.

Presently he came, in no rush as he slipped off the outside jacket which covered his old red sweater, and warmed himself at the stove. I supposed he was organizing his thoughts about whatever he had to tell, but such little patience as Mama had at her disposal wore out.

"Well, Papa, ain't you comfortable yet?"

"I run into Preacher Maquiddy as I was goin' yon way," said Papa, gravely.

This was more than Mama'd banked on. "What'd he have to say for hisself?" she said, a little weakly.

"I had the groceries on my shoulder at the time. He said, 'I told them people not to be sendin' no box to you folks. I knew yuns wouldn't appreciate no such gift.' Or words to that effect," said Papa.

"An' what'd you say to him?" Mama was plucking up courage as she began to understand that Papa'd been equal to the preacher.

"I said, 'I'm takin' these groceries to some people that really need 'em, Mr. Maquiddy.'" Papa was stern. "He said, 'That's exactly what you should do, Mr. Doud.' An' I said, 'Yuns must a been awful short on poor folks to be sendin' stuff our way.'" Papa brushed at his moustache, first its one side, then the other. "I think he realized his mistake, all right."

I felt a good deal better. Yet there were questions in my upset mind, produced by the shock of learning we were so poor that people could see it and insult us because of it, and as I gazed at Papa, rubbing together the long bony hands on which I'd seldom seen a pair of gloves, even in the coldest weather, and as I noticed—saw, really for the first time—that his red sweater was out at the elbows and that there was a patch on both knees of his old gray trousers, suddenly I found myself asking: *why* were we so poor? what was the matter with us? how did it happen that we were so much less well-off than people around us, who, so far as I could see, had no better qualities than ourselves for making a pretty good living? Only last night, in my bewilderment over Cecil, I'd recalled the evening's talk about the people we came from, surely I had the right to be proud of some of them, and as for the others, not talked about last night, weren't they as good as or better than most families I knew? Even in the case of Granpa McNabb, who was lazy, and his father and mother, who were stingy, I knew from other discussions that there were explanations, like the war which freed the McNabb slaves and put Granpa, who wasn't used to it however fair it might be, at work in the fields, and which, I supposed, made his parents careful of what they still possessed. As for Little Dave Doud, who was a gambler by profession and who'd been shot to death by Wild Bill Hickok at Springfield, Missouri, he was a brave man though misguided, and in any event only second cousin to Papa, his namesake. There was my half brother Frank, I realized he didn't amount to much, but he'd been left half an orphan at an early age, and wouldn't this help to account for if not to excuse what he was? I knew other facts which went to prove that we were perfectly all-right people. Papa'd taught school, an honorable though poorly paid job which nobody could look down on, he'd run a flour mill prosperously in partnership with his father, and later on, with Mama's help, owned and operated a good hotel at Allerton, Arkansas, where I was born and where, as I'd heard Jennie sigh and say many times, we'd been so very happy. But at that point all the good times for us had come to an end, and we'd been poor ever since—so poor that we'd become objects of public charity. What had gone wrong? How could we have become so run-down like? Why? I didn't understand, and with all my wonderings and searchings still throbbing and hurting within, not as clear questions but rather as feelings too deep for me to see into at the time, I sat down to Christmas dinner with Mama and Papa.

We were the only members of the household at table, and it was only now that we were struck by Cecil's absence. He'd left the house soon after breakfast, and Papa guessed he was off some place with those barber friends of his, bragging about being a father. Mama didn't doubt he'd be back when he got hungry, and set aside a big bowlful of chicken and dumplings. It would keep warm in the oven until he got in.

Nobody had any real concern about him yet. That built up as the afternoon wore on and the sleet changed to snow, piling up on the windowsills, weighting down the thin old cedar in the side yard, and bringing evening on so early that by three o'clock it was already threatening dusk. Seeing this happen, Papa went to look for Cecil.

From my post at the kitchen window, I kept tab on the alley. Between me and it lay the wintry garden, its row of old yellow cornstalks marching stiff and ragged across the smooth new white, and as my eyes roved the gloom, half of falling snow and half of coming night, I wondered why I was so sure the two men would return by the back way. The question was part and parcel of all the other painful doubts and uncertainties of the day, hovering in that darkness of their own around the outskirts of my brain. The first inkling I had of a difference inside the house was a summons from Mama.

The window beyond Bruce's cot gave me a view of her, shawl caught up over head and shoulders, as she hastened from our back porch past the house next dooor, which belonged to some rather unfriendly people, and on towards the Fivecoats' and their telephone. I bent over Bruce. "Listen, honey."

> *I know something I won't tell,*
> *Three little niggers in a peanut shell . . .*

Don't you hear me, Bruce? Wake up, honey. I'll dance a jig for you. I'll get Mama's ol' red petticoat an' tie it under my arms an' dance with the broomstick. Wouldn't you enjoy that? You did the other day. Say, Brucie. Please, pretty please!"

Oddly, I was whispering so as not to disturb him, after all, and he never stirred. Yet he wasn't asleep. I'd often looked at him when he napped, and his hands and mouth would give little twitches and sometimes his legs would jerk so hard that he'd wake himself. He was never still like this, and I didn't dare touch him, and couldn't think what to do or say. Only lines from the rhyme I'd been saying kept running through my head:

> *Three little niggers in a peanut shell,*
> *One can read and one can write . . .*

The whole house was so unnaturally quiet. Were Jennie and her baby and Sallie all asleep?

> *And one can smoke his pappy's pipe.*

At last these words, too, died away in my thoughts, and I just waited, staring now at Bruce and now through the bedroom window. Would Mama never get back? Then through the snow Papa took shape alongside the woodshed, half-carrying, half-hauling Cecil, and my first feeling was of gratefulness for the near-twilight and the fact that beneath his jacket the redness of Papa's sweater didn't call attention to itself. The two men approached my window, and I saw that Cecil's nice blue

108

overcoat had straw all over it and that he himself looked white, at least where he didn't look yellow. Were our unfriendly neighbors next door peering from their windows? Could Miz Smiley, always on the alert across the draw, make out anything from there? Oh, if night would but instantly fall, or Papa make a little more speed! All at once Mama was there, and helping Papa with Cecil up the steps and along the porch. From underneath I heard them lurch up the stairs and across the loft.

"They're puttin' him on that ol' mattress up there, I reckon."

Jennie spoke from the lean-to. Somehow she seemed to know what was going on.

Mama and Papa came in, Sallie also, her shoes on unlaced and a blanket around her shoulders, and beside me at the foot of the cot fixed her black eyes on Bruce.

"How is he, Mama?" Jennie again.

"We covered him up warm an' give him a pot, honey. He's sicker'n a dog, but he'll be all right by mornin'."

"I didn't mean him."

Mama opened her mouth to reply, it jerked, and she shut it without a sound. Bruce hadn't moved. He lay on his back, eyes closed and lips drawn away from a row of little white teeth. Only the lips were cracked and black, and between the eyelids, top and bottom, gleamed a streak of white eyeball.

Was he breathing? Mama whispered the question, and Papa shook his head. No, or be quiet—what did he mean? He was in the chair by the cot, with one of Bruce's little hands in his own, and as I gazed, two tears spilled from his eyes and made a slow track down either cheek.

I tiptoed fast into the front room and to the window overlooking the street. Outside, darkness was creeping in, over the snow and around the house. Doc Blaine's horse and buggy were nowhere in sight. "Dear Jesus," I was praying all the while in my mind, and I hurried on through the kitchen and across the back porch, and opened the door to the loft, shutting it behind me and kneeling on the bottom step. My folded pallet lay to one side on the steps above, and on it I rested my arms. A mixture of thoughts swelled and whirled in my head. I wanted to confess, not just my faults, whether they were little ones like having for a moment, the merest moment, wished I could keep an orange out of the charity box this morning, or more important lapses like taking my attention from Bruce a few minutes ago to worry about the neighbors' seeing Cecil, but something big enough to count, like my whole life. I wanted to promise to be good, and to say that Bruce was the only boy we had, and if anybody had to die, why couldn't it be Cecil? But only to have had such a thought as that about Cecil frightened me, and the rest of it I couldn't say either. My heart was in my throat, stuck tight there, and all I could do was to hold my hands clasped before me and my prayer close around me, trusting that Jesus would understand and that somehow my being here in the cold and dark would help, like an offering, too.

How long I stayed on the stairs I didn't know. Above me, Cecil moaned and groaned, and sometimes threw up. When I was so cold and stiff I couldn't stand it any more, I went back into the house downstairs. Lamplight shone from the bedroom, and Doc Blaine, already in the act of snapping together the two sides of his worn black bag, was in the chair by Bruce. More than ever in the past, I was aware of the doctor, what a big heavyset man he was, dark and slow-moving, who had little to say but that little carried weight, and who was always nice. He'd been saying something to Mama, and whatever it was, her face declared that it was good to hear. Papa was getting out his thin old leather wallet, so much too long for all it ever held, and after he'd fished around in it unsuccessfully for a couple of minutes, he poured its contents into the palm of one hand and carefully counted out enough dimes, nickels and quarters to make a dollar. Doc Blaine without a glance dropped the loose coins into a side pocket.

"We're mightily obliged to you, sir," said Papa.

The doctor shrugged into his overcoat, he and Papa shook hands, and Papa opened the door for him. Again, and for the last time that day, I was drawn to a window, from where I watched the doctor amble across the snowy yard and heave himself up into his buggy in the street. What a day it had been! or rather two days, I thought, with so much happening in them that it was hard to remember everything—Sallie sick and grumbling, Jennie hurt, and Bruce almost dying, Cecil drunk, and a charity box from those unthoughted church people, not to mention a white dress, also charity, offered to me —and when it did begin to come back, it was so mixed and jumbled as well as overshadowed by its most recent part that for the time being I could feel nothing but happiness and relief so great that I could hardly bear them.

CHAPTER III

A Child with a Past

I strained my eyes after the doctor until his horse and buggy became one single great black shape blurring into the night, and the sound of wheels and hooves on snow fading in my ears, I began to hear in the room behind the clank of wood on iron as Papa built up the fire. So also did I find, during the wintry weeks which followed, that the hurt and press of all my unspoken *why's* and *what's* and *how's* were sinking ever more deeply into the shapeless twilight fringes around that part of myself which wanted so much to be happy; and as spring came on, day after bright blue day so shining and beautiful as seemed impossible to be true, but was, I found myself feeling little besides its joy, plus, of course, my usual keen interest in the fifth grade at school.

One special friend I had there, Edna Deed by name, and I loved her very much. She lived on a farm at the edge of town, and her father brought her to school in their buggy, her lunch neatly done up in a paper bag. Occasionally it consisted of a banana and a box of graham crackers, and when I got back from home, we'd spend the rest of the noon hour strolling about the schoolyard arm-in-arm, munching on a few of the crackers she'd saved back. Once in a while we'd glance at each other and say, "The firm of Deed and Doud. Behold!" Sometimes we said only, "Behold!" Either way, it tickled us mightily.

Both Edna and I were getting rather stringy, like bean poles. But where my hair was red, hers was black, and her eyes, although brown like mine, had a black look. I didn't know the reason, unless it was that the look came from so deep inside her. Edna's leading quality was smartness. Among the various smart things she could do was to sing a song in French and another in German. She'd learned them from her big sisters. They were off somewhere going to college, and one afternoon Edna and I were walking along the street and met Mr. Hansen, who was superintendent of schools at Bridgewater, and he stopped Edna, and regarding her with his clear blue eyes, inquired how her sisters were getting along towards their degrees. That was how important the Deed family was. But it hadn't given Edna the big head. I could have chatted with Mr. Hansen much like Edna, could have smiled and said, "Yes, sir," very politely, because Papa had taught me, insisting, "Yes, what?" if I answered him *yes* without the *sir*. Of course, there wasn't any reason why Mr. Hansen should talk to me, except that I was as smart as Edna, though lacking kinfolks in college.

Another pleasant interest which I had in the fifth grade that beautiful spring at Bridgewater had to do with Snuffy. Snuffy Snyder. His real name was Ellis, and his father was a Socialist. I knew that, Mr. Snyder being a man who made no secret of his politics, so that Papa with his own ears had heard him say that Teddy Roosevelt was a demagogue. He'd brought it out in front of a whole bunch of people in his shoe repair shop, which was an awful thing to do as Teddy Roosevelt was one of the most wonderful Republicans who'd ever lived. I didn't think Snuffy deserved a black mark on account of his father, though, and his stiff sandy shock of hair sticking up in front of me at school appealed to me even before the day he twisted around in his seat and laid a flower on my desk. It was a big yellow wildflower, and I smelled at it off and on the rest of the morning to show how pleased I was, afterwards pressing it in my geography. And it was still there, although it had turned black.

This was the first time that a boy had ever given me anything, as well as I could recall. Could it be that maybe I was prettier than I thought? I did have pretty hair, at least our neighbor, Miz Fivecoat, had said so very recently, at Easter. She'd taken her girl, Mary May, and gone on a visit of a few days, asking me to look after the chickens in her absence. I did this very dependably, and hoped she'd reward me with a pair of roller skates—not the two-fifty kind, I was well aware that I hadn't earned them in what Mama was always referring to as this root-pig-or-die-poor old world, but the seventy-five cent kind, without ball bearings—or, if even that was too much, then with a book, possibly one in the William Green Hill series, cost fifty cents. What she brought me, however, was hair ribbons. Hair ribbons!

"They go with your hair and eyes, which are almost exactly the same color," she told me kindly, coupling this with the remark that I had very pretty hair but didn't do it right for my age. Now I could wear it like Mary May's.

I was so disappointed, as well as mortified because my hopes had been so far beyond my prospects, that it took several days for me to make up my mind to change, even partly. For if a braided roll pinned behind either ear was too old for me, a braid hanging over either shoulder was too young, as I felt. I made a single pleat at the back and tied it with one of the silky-new rusty red ribbons. Used one at a time like that, they lasted well through spring, when school paused for the summer, the hum of busy days slowed to a drone, and Sallie got a half-time job at the telephone office.

She and I no longer talked play-people. Instead we wrote stories, withdrawing to the privacy of the loft, where she did the actual writing and I helped invent what happened. She was less available for this activity after she got on at the telephone office, and less inclined to agree to my inventions. She was harder to get along with in general, and growing prouder by the minute as she improved herself with one little bought item after another. One item was white tennis shoes, accompanied by the advice that they cost only fifty cents a pair and Mama'd do well to get some for herself instead of going barefoot. Mama retorted that she never went barefoot except in hot weather and not even then if anybody outside the family was around, but Sallie'd hurt her feelings a little.

Sallie paid no heed. "*Farthermore,*" she said to Mama, "I'm afraid somebody at the office'll find out about you takin' in washin'." She forgot that she'd been glad to do it herself not long since. About that time Jennie came home to stay while Cecil went off to Texas to see if he could rustle them up a job in the oilfields that would pay better than the cattle ranches, and with her Sallie went still further.

"I didn't say she wasn't welcome at home herself," Sallie defended her action to Mama later on. "I said she wasn't welcome to bring that whiny kid o' Cecil Dechere's around here."

"Well, she can't come without him," said Mama, "so it amounts to the same thing."

And Papa said, "It's a mighty poor way to act, regardless, for a girl o' Sallie's pretensions."

But Jennie'd had her feelings hurt, too, and spent her time with Mama rather than with Sallie. This threw Sallie back onto me, and I was delighted to make up stories with her not-withstanding her tendency to disagree with my ideas. It could be more than a tendency, of course. Such was the case one hot morning in the loft when we were writing a story called *Emmeline Devereaux*, which Sallie ruled should be pronounced *Deverex*, and having consented to a southern plantation, dripping with gray moss and overrun with darky servants, I went on to propose ghosts. *No.* You didn't know what to do with ghosts in the last chapter.

"You can let 'em go back into the walls," I argued.

No. We had plenty to work with in this story without putting in ghosts. Emmeline had just finished finishing school —the kind of school, in Sallie's unnecessary explanation to me, where you didn't have to study, you merely learned how to enjoy yourself in a refined way—and was unpacking her grips while her parents watched her lovingly.

"They were waitin' for her to unpack their presents," I suggested hopefully.

No. Sallie was describing Emmeline's bedroom, fixed over by her parents in pink and white.

"So as to hide the blood," I interrupted, with a horrid shudder. "While Emmeline was away, somebody was murdered there."

Again, *no.* Emmeline's family was *respectable*. Nobody had ever been murdered in it. *Farthermore*, said Sallie, the pleasure and the excitement in this story were refined love affairs. Emmeline was to have several.

"Not for me, she ain't," I said, and leaving Sallie to invent her story to suit herself, I tiptoed down the stairs and across the back porch, trying not to attract Mama's attention from the kitchen.

The breakfast dishes would have been finished by now, but Mama could very well have some other work arranged for me.

"Actually an' canally, you've fell away till you look worse'n a summer possum," I heard her saying to Jennie as I passed. "It's funny you still have so much milk."

Actually and candidly, it was funny she hadn't caught sight of me, but she gave no special sign, and I tiptoed softly on down the steps and went around the corner of the house to the honeysuckle trellis. Between it and the back window of Mama's bedroom was a shadowy green space, very cool and private and quiet. I crawled in and made myself comfortable. Patches of faded blue August sky gleamed through my broken green roof here and there, the scent of honeysuckle hung thick and sweet around me, and from outside and all about came the drowsy hum of summer. I smelled, and listened, and planned. As soon as Sallie left for the telephone office, I'd go up to the loft and write an *Emmeline Deverex* of my own, spelling it *e-x* to start with instead of a fancy old *e-a-u-x*. Also, there'd be a mortgage on the plantation, so that Emmeline would be forced towards marriage with a certain rich old guy, who was after her in spite of knowing there was a handsome poor boy she loved with all her heart. Mary J. Holmes used this setup a lot in her stories. The fellow after Emmeline was Horance J. Blackmire. What a villain! His very name, said aloud, brought a curl to the lip and a snurl to the nose—*Horance*. As for the hero, his name was romantic: Cyril Glendenning. He was the poor boy, as you'd expect.

"Delphie! O-oo-oh, Delphie! Where are you? Why don't you answer me, Delphie?"

With that voice going up and down and all around from the back steps, fit to scare the neighbors out of their wits, at last I did have to answer, and let Mama send me uptown with a bucketful of big red ripe tomatoes from her garden which I was to sell for two and a half cents a pound. It was hot work, lugging that load all the way up our long street, and in the grocery stores nobody would pay more than two and a fourth cents. Tired out, I sank down on a bench on the shady side of the street, presently Sallie went past on her way to work, stepping along very pertly in her white tennis shoes and pretending she wasn't acquainted with me as she was ashamed of my peddling tomatoes, and after another while one of the grocery-store men happened by. "Haven't you sold those tomatoes yet?" he demanded. "Well, take 'em back to my store and tell the clerk I said to give you two and a half cents a pound!"

A little success was all I needed for me to go bounding homewards, gleefully reflecting how smart I'd sound reporting the story of those tomatoes. The man coming towards me along our street had repeated my name twice before I actually heard it.

"Don't you know me, Delphie?"

I quit swinging the empty bucket, and stared. He was a kind of young man, in a dusty brownish suit and an old brown felt hat, and he was smiling at me in the friendliest manner imaginable.

"I'm your half brother Frank."

"I rather thought that's who it was." This wasn't true, to be sure, I hadn't laid eyes on Frank since we lived on the farm at Bonnot's Grove and he and his sassy-walking wife Vannie that Mama called Brollium to make fun of her had stayed for a few weeks in the tenant house across the creek. I wouldn't have known him from Adam if I hadn't beeen told.

"How you come on?" I said, and all at once I reached up and gave him a hug and a kiss. Why I did that I wasn't sure. I knew Mama was opposed to him, it was coming back to me how she said his wife Brollium was lazy and no-'count, and wouldn't let me and Sallie associate with her and her younguns there at Bonnot's Grove, and now that I was getting a close view of Frank I could see for myself that Brollium didn't keep him in the good condition that Mama did Papa. His sun-browned skin seemed on the oily side for one thing, and his shirt could have been fresher. Yet he also looked a little timid under his dusty felt hat with the sweat stains going up into the crown, as though he needed something from me and had really almost pulled it out of me, to help him, in spite of my disliking in general to touch anything that might be ready for washing.

"Do you think your mother'd mind if you walked back uptown with me?"

He wanted to buy me a little something, a nice ten-cent poke of candy it turned out to be, and we sat on the curb around the corner from Main Street and ate some of it, and talked. He was asking about Father—Papa to me—and time passed and got to the point where I just about had to invite him to come home with me to dinner.

"You're the only one that's mentioned it, so fur," he said. I couldn't think of the right answer to that, and was glad to have him get to his feet, brush the sugar from his hands, and add that he had to catch the train as soon as he'd been to the feed store and seen Father.

"Goin' back to Tulsie, Delphie. Don't you wish you was comin' along?"

"I sure do," I lied as hearty as I could, and even sent my regards to Brollium, being careful to refer to her as Vannie. I didn't see that this sociability would hurt Mama if she didn't know about it. "Are you catchin' Oil Johnny?" I went on, and

116

mentioned that Granpa and Granma McNabb had moved away from Arkansas and were living at the little town of Gisper at present. "We go down on that little ol' train Oil Johnny to visit them sometimes. I ride half fare for 'leven cents."

"You won't do that for long," said Frank, shaking hands in goodbye. "You're shootin' up like a briar."

This time as I went homewards I was debating which to tell about first, Frank or the two and a half cents. I decided on the money. I thought it would put Mama into a better mood to receive my word of Frank.

During the interval she and Jennie had moved from the kitchen to the front room. There, with the sewing machine pushed out into the double doorway to the bedroom, Jennie could keep an eye on Francis on Mama's bed and work a little away from the dust which Mama with her broom was stirring up to a fare-ye-well.

"I don't know what Frank wants this time, but you can mark my words he wouldn't a showed up here if he wasn't after somethin'."

Mama's words greeted me as I opened the screen door. "I got you two and a half cents for your tomaters," I announced, loud enough to attract attention but failing to get it.

"I wonder how he knew where you an' Papa was at," said Jennie, pedalling the machine to run up a seam in the dress she was making. "I didn't think Papa'd heard from him for a long time."

"No, Papa hadn't heard," said Mama, with the grimness so unusual in her, "'cause I seen to Frank's letters, that's why. But him an' Papa knowed where each other was, all right."

I tried my other piece of news, and had no trouble at all in catching Mama's ear.

"You met Frank a-comin' home? What'd he have to say for hisself?"

She was so hot and quick that she drove all else from my mind except what he'd said about not being invited to dinner, and I didn't think I'd better bring that up. Handing her the tomato money, I went into the bedroom. Somebody had fixed Francis a play-pretty of used sewing-thread spools on a string, and he was gnawing on them and not whining at all the way Sallie was always claiming he did. Mama was speaking again, as much to herself as to Jennie, it seemed to me, as the dust flew up around her broom.

"I don't much think Papa'd go another note for him. I don't think Papa's yet forgot that time at Bonnot's Grove when we went Frank's note for a hun'erd an' fifty dollars an' had it to pay, ever' last red cent, to the bank right here in Bridgewater. We paid that note out o' what we made grubbin' that ol' farm for a year an' a half, we did, you younguns workin' an' sweatin' an' dirtyin' yourselves up in the cotton patch like any ol' field hand, an' Papa willin' for yuns to do it, too, while Frank's woman laid around the house like a lady o' leisure."

"I remember," said Jennie. She sat very still at the sewing machine for a moment to gaze into her remembering. "I worked myself half to death on that ol' cotton farm, choppin' cotton, an' pickin' it, milkin' cows an' pitchin' alfalfa hay, which no woman should have to do. An' when my menstral periods came around, many's the time I've laid down between the cotton rows an' rolled on the ground with the pain. Then Papa'd come along an' tell me to get back to work. Even after Bruce was born, he wouldn't let me stay in the house to help you except the first two or three days, before he made me go back to the field. Then you had to crawl out an' do the cookin' an washin' an' other housework as usual. Either Papa was dumb, or else he didn't care. At the time I never thought o' criticizin' Papa, I loved Papa an' thought we had to slave like that or starve, but I understand better now, an' it makes me feel awful bad to think o' you havin' to get up so soon like you was an animal o' some sort." As she gazed across at Mama and remembered, a small bright tear gathered and trembled at the very edge of each clear blue eye.

It was all terribly disturbing, first the fact that somebody else was laying around the house like a lady of leisure while I was one of those out in the field, dirty and sweating, then that Papa'd made Jennie slave during her menstral periods, whatever those were, and treated Mama like an animal of some sort. A little more and I'd join my tears to Jennie's over her and Mama, if I wasn't too mad about myself, that is, like Mama over Frank's note.

We were still paying on it during the winter we ran the wagonyard at Claremore, and that, Mama said, was the reason we came so near starving to death. We younguns went to school half naked, and she had to pinch and scrape to feed us. Many was the day she couldn't make bread because she didn't have any grease, and we never had any gravy that wasn't white livered. Then Frank's woman was telling it

118

around Gisper that Mama didn't set a good table. She said Mama didn't even give her younguns enough to eat.

"Sister Rosie told me Vannie done that very thing while we was payin' off Frank's note. An' I swore to myself that I was goin' to get shut o' Frank an' his woman in our neighborhood if it was the last thing I ever done. So I took care o' Frank's letters, an' I did think maybe we'd seen the last o' him till he come knockin' at our door this mornin'.'"

She swept the dust and fuzz into a pile, pausing to say something and then sweeping again, and prepared to brush the pile onto a newspaper she spread out on the floor. Nobody spoke for a couple of minutes while she did this, then, wadding up the paper with the dirt inside, carried it to the kitchen to stuff into the cookstove for burning. On her return she brought a damp rag to wipe up the dust she'd been scattering over the furniture and windowsills, and that job done, wrapped another rag around the broom and went after some cobwebs on the ceiling. Our house never got such a good cleaning as when Mama was on fire about something. Finally she did sit down. I couldn't see her from the bed, where I'd sunk down, too, near Francis, but I could hear the small quick squeals from her rocker. They went with her argument.

"It looks like Papa would a learned his lesson, but Papa can be awful soft where Frank's concerned. 'Pears like he allus thought more o' that first wife o' his'n an' them two younguns o' hern than he ever did o' me an' mine. It use to be after me an' him was first married, he'd never come back from town without a nickel's worth o' candy for Frank an' Gordon, but later on when yuns came along, he never brought yuns nothin'."

"He was tryin' to make up to the boys for their mother bein' dead, I guess," said Jennie, with a sigh.

"Maybe he was, an' I don't know as I held it against him, but I couldn't help noticin' the difference, Jennie. An' one thing I saw from the start, he'd let me work my fingers to the bone for them two boys if I'd only but do it. Work wasn't the worst of it. Frank an' Gordon never would mind me, an' their Granma Doud was responsible. She taken care of 'em after their mother died till me an' Papa was married, an' before she sent 'em to live with us she told 'em I wasn't their real mother an' they didn't have to obey me. If I tried to make 'em do somethin', they'd get out in the yard an' throw rocks at me. Till one day, I was carryin' Sallie at the time, Jennie, they hit me in the forehead with one o' the rocks, an' Papa happened to come in an' found me in the cookroom, washin' off the blood an' cryin'. He whipped 'em both that time," said Mama. "That put an end to the rock-throwin'. But in general Papa never would get after 'em like he orter, though he wasn't slow about makin' you younguns toe the mark right enough. Add on that Frank was lazy an' dirty, an' that Gordon was allus ailin', while at the same time I was havin' one baby after another'n, an' losin' the first two, an' you can see what I had to contend with."

"I could cry my eyes out, thinkin' about you then, married so young an' little more'n a girl yourself," said Jennie. "It's a hard thing to say, but I wonder if Gordon's dyin' wasn't a blessin' to you in disguise."

I knew about Gordon's dying. Sometimes Papa'd talk about it if Mama wasn't around, and he was sitting by the stove in the front room, say, in a remembering position, his chair tilted against the wall while with his forefinger he traced out *B's* on the knee of his pants. Gordon had died at the age of twelve. He'd been a pretty good boy, according to Papa, he'd never given much trouble. "What did he die of?" I once asked softly, as I stood by Papa's chair. "He was taken down, just got under the weather, Delphie," was the reply. "Gordon allus was a puny boy. But we didn't know he was anything like bad sick till he just died, almost before you knowed it." "He was my half brother, wasn't he?" I said, to be certain, and because claiming kin with him made me feel gentle and sad, like his dying, and very close to Papa. His gaze was on me as he spoke, but it was almost as if he didn't see me. "Gordon was my oldest son by my first wife. Her name was Betsy, short for Elizabeth. She was an Osborne before she married." So now I knew what the *B's* stood for which in thoughtful moments he was used to drawing—not *B* for *Brittie* but for *Betsy*—and I was curious as to what Betsy had looked like, but he said it'd be hard for him to describe, except that she was a little woman with big blue eyes. "I use to have her picture," he said, "but I don't know what's become of it."

This was something else I knew. Mama'd taken care of the picture, the same as Frank's letters. In the stove.

Responding to my questions, Papa went on to relate, in the short plain words he always used, how Betsy had died, like

120

Gordon later on. "She'd been sick for quite a while. We'd been out to her father's. I'd had the doctor an' he'd stayed all night. Next mornin' he give her some medicine before he left, an' I was fixin' to go help Mr. Osborne haul some wood. She said, 'Dave, I don't feel very well. I'd ruther you didn't go.' I said, 'All right.' An' the first thing you knowed, she was gone." I looked into his eyes, trying to realize how it had been, but it was hidden from me by a mist. "We'd been married for six years," he said, "since 'eighty-four. Her an' Gordon's buried in Osborne cemetery down on Dry Creek. It's an old landmark. I ain't been there since the day o' Gordon's buryin'."

Close by his knee that day, I'd longed to tell him I could cry about Betsy and Gordon, too, but more about him, because he'd loved them and now he didn't have them any more. You could never say those things, but I hoped he'd guess my feeling, and waited in silence. But the telling was over, and presently he began to sing.

> "Yes, we shall gather at the river,
> The beautiful, the beautiful river,
> Gather with the saints at the river . . ."

There were other times when he sang that song and seemed a great distance off like that, winter evenings in the front room, with the stove popping, and Mama and Sallie tatting, and himself speaking of the old days, of his father, Frank Standifer Doud, who'd been sheriff of Searcy and Monroe Counties before they were divided, and who'd owned all that fine bottom land at the junction of Bear Creek and Buffalo River.

"When I was married the first time," I'd heard him say, "Father give me twenty-five good acres an' I bought twenty-five more. Me an' him also run the flour mill together. It'd be right interestin' for me to go back there."

"Not for me it wouldn't," said Mama. "I don't never want to lay eyes on that ol' Arkansas again."

"I'm not sayin' what it'd be for you, Mama," he replied, and continued with stories of his growing-up, until he'd charmed his thoughts clear away from us, and he'd get up to thrust another stick of wood into the fire and, as with me before, start humming and singing to himself.

> *"Yes, we shall gather at the river*
> *That flows by the throne of God."*

Mama's mouth would go down at the corners, and when she had a chance out of his hearing, she'd say to me and Sallie, "He's studyin' about that first wife o' his'n, it ain't nothin' under the shinin' sun but that. He thinks he's gettin' ready to die, I reckon." And it was true that he had made out his will, leaving everything to Mama except a dollar apiece to us children, including Frank, but the will itself declared him to be in good health, only sensible of the uncertainty of life. Papa, on the other hand, never remarked to us children anything at all concerning Mama, and more than once it had occurred to me that for some special reasons of her own she had it in for him.

Now today in Mama's telling I was learning of those special reasons, and only a few minutes ago I'd near united my tears with Jennie's, over her and Mama in the past. It was almost impossible to bear in mind the way I'd felt towards Papa on that other occasion as I went on listening to Mama squeak to and fro in the rocker in the next room, so excited and worried, declaring that she had never wished Gordon any harm and had always done everything she humanly could for the boy and been glad to do it, she'd a done might nigh anything to please Papa in those days, and she'd do a lot for him yet, so far as that went. She'd used to love Papa when they were first married, but she'd cooled off a lot seeing how he done her. At the time they were living on the farm on Dry Creek, he used to get mad at her and hitch up the horses to the wagon, get Gordon and Frank in there with him and pull out and be gone the livelong day. "When'll you be back, Dave?" she'd ask. "I may not be back," would be his answer. "You an' me's just about to the partin' o' the ways." And there she'd be, scared to death he'd left her for good. Those were the days that had seen her tears shed, Jennie, she felt so lonesome and miserable, but he always did come back, and after a while she got over being so scared. She'd never thought Papa loved her like he orter, and she couldn't a stood him if she hadn't respected him, though the time had come, as Jennie knew, when she hadn't been able to do that either.

"But as for Gordon's dyin' bein' a blessin' to me," she said, getting back to that, "they ain't no denyin' they was less work

122

afterwards, an' it made for more peace in the family. Seemed like Papa could better get his mind on me an' you younguns after that. An' more specially after all the trouble that come to us in the hotel at Allerton, startin' off with Frank an' endin' up with Lutie Elder."

"It was because you stuck by him," said Jennie, "through thick an' thin. Not ever' woman would a done it."

"You can bet your sweet life they wouldn't," said Mama. "His lawyer over at the county seat wasn't none too sure o' me neither when Lutie brought suit. 'What's that redheaded wife o' yourn goin' to say to all this?' he said to Papa. 'She already knows all about it,' Papa told him. 'I've seen to that,' he said. He had, too, Jennie, an' I'd give him my bounden word."

She was silent for so long that I thought she mightn't be aiming to tell anything else, but she'd only broken off to consider whether or not she'd had a choice in spite of her bond and word. By then there were three of us children to be looked after. How could she have made a living for us all? If she'd gone back down to our Granpa McNabb's, we'd just have been knocked from pillar to post among those ten or twelve younguns of his own. Whatever his shortcomings, Papa'd been a lots better provider than she ever could have been by herself.

"Yet me an' him together's never been able really to get back on our feet," she said. "It looks like all that misfortune comin' at one time was too much for Papa."

"Yes," said Jennie. "What Frank started, ol' Lutie finished. Between 'em they ruined our lives an' happiness."

In the hush that followed I seemed to hear the words echo, and reecho. Leaving the bed, I went to stand by Jennie in the doorway. The machine whirred, halted, and whirred again. Mama's lips were clamped down tight over her thoughts.

"What about ol' Lutie, Jennie?" I said softly.

With that I got myself scatted from the house. Mama wasn't talking any stuff for younguns' ears, and anyhow, she added, coming further out of the distance to immediate problems—anyhow, I wouldn't stay with her and Jennie this morning when there were dishes to be done, I could just go on out and leave them alone now.

She sounded so everyday like that for the moment I too came away from that far-off frightening place of ruin and unhappiness, and much as I wanted to stay, admitted to myself the justice of her remarks. So easy was it at that point still to be like usual that as I passed through the kitchen and saw the salt on the table, I naturally reached for a pinch, the idea of those big red ripe tomatoes of Mama's rising naturally to mind. There were plenty of them, firm and cool under the matted green vines in the garden, which in their turn promptly suggested my own cool green hideaway beneath the honeysuckle trellis. Sweeter than ever, almost stifling under the hot noon sun, was the smell of the yellow and white blossoms. I breathed it in while I rubbed a tomato clean against my skirt and broke it in two.

"Papa hired him three of the able-est lawyers in the state. The Face brothers, from Williams. They charged plenty."

Mama's voice, low but clear, struck on my ears through the open window of her bedroom just above my head. Startled, I stopped sprinkling salt in among the little yellow seeds of the juicy red tomato halves.

"After takin' care o' Frank, then payin' the lawyers, they wasn't much left over from the sale o' the hotel. Under the circumstances we couldn't get what it was worth nohow. Papa was all for leavin' them parts, but I said no, we'd stay an' live it down, ever'thing connected with Lutie Elder an' Frank both. I didn't realize what-all we was up against. Them sure was hard times that follered. Do you remember that ol' forty-acre farm up above Allerton, Jennie?"

"I couldn't forget it," came Jennie's voice, in the pause of her machine, and a little closer above my head than Mama's, "if I lived to be a hun'erd."

"It didn't have no house. We put up a two-room shack. The first summer the kitchen only had a floor halfway across, the rest was packed dirt. They wasn't no well neither. You an' Sallie carried us drinkin' water in your little tin pails from a spring at the foot o' the hill."

This didn't sound like anything I oughtn't to listen to. I already knew something about that old farm anyhow, and as Mama's tone had moderated considerably, too, as she went on to say that there was a lot of timber on the forty acres, I carried a half of the tomato the rest of the way to my mouth and bit into it. Mama was dwelling on how Papa cut down the trees and she helped him saw them up into railroad ties. It was back-breaking work. We'd moved from the hotel too late for her to put in a regular garden, but she and Jennie and

Sallie picked wild berries along the lane, and she also had twelve hills of sweet potatoes.

"Them sweet taters!" said Jennie. "When school took up at Allerton in September, all me an' Sallie had in our dinner pails was a couple o' them boiled taters an' a few cold biscuits. At noon we'd sneak off by ourselves among the rocks in the schoolyard, an' eat where nobody could see us."

They were laughing together, Mama and Jennie, thinking how they'd got through those hard times, but the laughter had an edge rather like crying. In the fixedness of my attention I'd failed to suck at the tomato, and its juice was dribbling down my wrist. I wiped it away. The machine stayed quiet. Jennie must be sewing on her fingers now. She was saying that she and Sallie didn't have any stockings, and Mama took an old suit of long underwear which somebody had gone off and left in the hotel, dyed it black, and fashioned them some. "They wasn't much to look at," she said, "but they covered your younguns' little bare legs." Mama reminded Jennie about a trip which the whole family made into the woods that first fall, gathering enough black walnuts to heap the wagon bed. Back at the house, Papa lowered the wagon's tailgate and spilled the walnuts into the yard, and all during the winter, if anyone was hungry, he'd go out and sit down at the walnut pile, crack the nuts on a handy stone, and eat his fill. Papa was sick that winter. Mama scarcely knew how we'd got by. But the second summer was better. She had a garden, and Papa made a crop. After the corn was ripe, he'd bring it in from the field and Mama'd grate it for bread. Did Jennie recollect that old grater? It was a surrup bucket, split open and flattened out and driven full of nail holes, then fastened onto a board with the rough side out. It made awful coarse meal, though.

Jennie protested that she'd loved bread made from that meal, but then she guessed almost anything would have tasted good to her. It was the first time in her life she could remember of being actually hungry. "I hate to tell it on myself, but at school in the afternoon I'd get so hungry after recess I'd hold up my hand to be excused an' sneak past the other kids' dinner pails in the hall an' swipe somethin' that'd been left over in them an' go on out to the toilet an' eat it. All my life since then it's seemed to me I ain't ever really got filled up from that time o' bein' empty. I don't have to do nothin' but remember those days an' I feel myself gettin' hungry. An' to this day the thought of anybody else or even of an animal bein' hungry makes me choke up an' hurts my heart."

"I didn't know yuns was that hungry, Jennie," said Mama, so softly that it was unnatural. There were no more noises from her chair.

She couldn't be crying herself, could she? I didn't want Mama to cry, and I listened hard to be sure about it. The only sounds from inside were small rustles and scrapings of dress material and the click of scissors as they were picked up or laid down on the arm of the sewing machine. Reassured, though less than I'd have liked, I looked at the piece of tomato in my hand. Somehow I'd lost all appetite for it. Knowing I should avoid waste, however, after a moment I ate it anyhow. It might help stave off hunger later on. Mama's voice was stronger again, she'd gone back to all that she'd been up against after the trial, such as lots of people not having any use for her.

"I don't see why," said Jennie. "You hadn't done nothin'. Papa was the guilty one."

That was how it was, all the same. Take that Miz Shipman, for example. She used to come visit Mama real often. A few weeks after the trial Mama met her down by the river at a baptizing and preaching and church picnic. She spoke howdy all right, but then she said, "They's somebody over there I want to see," and went off and left Mama standing there by herself. It sure did cure her of going into public places again right soon. Then it wasn't a year afterwards that Miz Shipman's own daughter was flat on her back in the same fix as Lutie Elder'd been. Miz Shipman run across Mama one day, and she said, "Brittie, I never imagined anything like this would happen in my own family." She was ready enough to be friendly when she was the one who was kind of down and out.

Closer home was the case of Mama's Sister Hat. She sided with Lutie in the suit for main-tainance of the child. "I knowed in my own mind she would," said Mama, "though you'd a thought the sister she growed up with would a meant more to her than a sister-in-law."

"It wasn't on account o' Lutie," said Jennie. "It was Uncle Ben."

Mama knew. Ben Elder never had liked her, even before him and Hat were married. He thought his family was better than ours. Those Elders held their heads mighty high, or tried to, without much reason, so far as Mama could see. "When the trial was over, he told Hat she wasn't ever to set foot in our house again, an' she never did. If Maw'd come to see us, I'd meet her at the depot in Allerton, she'd stay a few days, then Hat'd drive over in her buggy an' stop in the road where the lane turned off to our house, an' Maw'd walk that far an' go home with her."

There were other bad things in connection with the Elders, worse things. While the trial was still going on, it was told around Allerton that Ben Elder'd said he was going to horse-whip Papa. "After we moved onto the farm, we use to turn the horses out to graze along the lane at night. Papa went to get 'em one mornin' early, an' somebody follered him behind the bushes an' trees along the fence the whole way back. Papa allus thought it was Ben. When daylight come, we found a buggy whip fastened to our gate."

Cold prickles had risen up all along my arms. If I had been there, and Ben Elder'd *dared* to lay a finger on Papa, I guessed I'd have killed the fellow.

Of course, I had been there, but too little to do any good. It was this same Aunt Hat who'd stayed with us for a week after I was born in that same hotel at Allerton, Arkansas, so that Mama'd felt called upon to put her name off on me. To Mama at the time it'd been a way of speaking her thank-you.

"A lot I had to thank her for, as matters went," Mama was saying. "Hat was the one interduced Lutie into our house, she sent her to help out in the hotel when she left. Lutie slept upstairs. More'n once I've waked up in the middle o' the night an' found myself alone in bed. Dave'd say he'd had to go outdoors. After a while nothin'd do him but he must sleep off upstairs, too. Delphie had the colic, an' he claimed she cried an' kept him awake."

As I followed the tale she was lifting light and clear out of those bygone days, I'd forgotten to worry about eavesdropping. Now with the talk of myself, uneasiness returned. Jennie was asking if Mama hadn't suspected Papa at the time.

"Yes, Jennie, I did. But I never tried to find out for sure. Maybe it was because I didn't care like I once did. I'd been feelin' pretty independent about Papa. He hadn't used me very well, an' I knowed it. I allus thought," Mama went on, stern justice yielding to something milder in her tone, "that my feelin' like that while I was carryin' Delphie is the reason she's got the disposition she has. She's just as independent as they make 'em, that kid is."

Independent, was I? Against all other feelings, I couldn't help being interested in myself, and at its mention the independence in me seemed to be swelling right up, too, so that I had to sit up straighter in order to accommodate it. In that position my eyes were above the level of the windowsill, and through the screen I watched Mama take Jennie's place at the sewing machine. However, as Jennie lay down on the bed to nurse Francis and the nursing embarrassed me, even to see it unbeknownst to others, I let myself back on my heels below the window.

"I never could abide that Lutie Elder from the start," Mama was going on. "The mealy-mouthed little slut, smilin' an' actin' so nice around me in the kitchen in the daytime, an' layin' out upstairs with him o' nights."

This really was talk not meant for younguns' ears. It bothered me, too, to hear Mama use a word like that one beginning with *s*. I might have taken myself away at once, except for the fact that if I moved, either she'd see me from the sewing machine or else Jennie'd hear me from the bed. Instead, I went on picturing almost in spite of myself the scene Jennie was sketching in, of the trial. It took place in the office of our hotel, she used to slip in and sit on the stairs, and every time she did, someone would see her and run her out. She didn't understand what was being said and done except she thought all those strangers were against Papa, and she wanted to stay by his side. One thing she hadn't any doubts about, looking back on it all, it was because Mama stood by Papa and made everybody believe she had faith in him that he beat the case.

It came down to being Lutie's word against his, according to Mama. "It wasn't her first slip, Lutie was thirty years old at the time an' she'd already had a child by somebody else, it wasn't known who. The defense tried to prove they was others could a been the guilty one this time instead o' Papa. Another thing helped him, he was a Mason in good standin'. Them Masons sure stuck by him. Papa had awful good character testimony, an' that in spite o' the disgrace Frank'd brought on us such a short time back."

"That says a lot for Papa," said Jennie, and after a moment asked if Mama'd ever seen Lutie's little woods colt.

"Yes, Jennie, once. It was the spittin' image o' Sallie when she was a baby."

"It was a little girl then, wasn't it?" Jennie mused, and gave a sigh which, from what I knew of Jennie, might have been for the little girl as much as for anybody else. "Whatever become o' them, I wonder."

"Oh, Lutie went off down to her paw's for a year or two, an' I never made no effort to find out about her after we left them parts. The youngun died, though. Sister Idy wrote me that."

There wasn't any sighing from Mama. I couldn't remember ever having heard any. In the quiet I listened to Francis as he nursed. Sometimes he grunted like a contented little pig, and sometimes he glupped and burbled because Jennie had so much milk. What good familiar homey sounds they were! like a shield against those desperate far-off events which I was hearing about for the first time—but which weren't so far off after all that they hadn't exploded into our present lives this very morning in the form of Frank. Then Mama said she knew she orter forgive Papa, and she had forgive him, too, in a way, but you couldn't forget just by telling yourself it was for the best.

" 'Course, I'm glad I've got ever' one o' you younguns now I've got you, an' I don't love one o' you any better'n another. But me an' your papa ortn't to a had seven childern, Jennie. That's plumb out o' reason, the way families run now, an' in view of our circumstances. But he never would leave me alone, Papa wouldn't. He thought he had so blame much self-control," she wound up disgustedly, "an' he didn't have none."

Ignorant of the precise meaning of these last words, still, after a general fashion, I knew what she was talking about, it seemed furtive and ugly, and what I felt was not embarrassment but shame. I was tired also from the strain of so much listening and sympathizing, and my heels hurt from being bent backwards and sat on. Could I creep guiltily away? At that moment a bug bit me right where I was sitting, and I shot upward, stirring the greenery above my head and striking my nose against the screen.

"My God A'mighty!" Almost as fast as myself from below

the window, Mama rose up behind the machine. "Have you been there all this while?"

She had to laugh a little, though, probably out of nervousness and surprise, combined with seeing me rub my nose where it hurt.

"Scoot around to the back an' wash the prints o' that screen wire off the end o' your nose. Yes, I can, too, see 'em from here, or anyhow I'd know they was there from what you been doin'. Then you come on in here to me."

Did she have a swat saved up for me? Just in case, I established myself on a chair a good stretch across from her in the front room. For the sewing she was wearing her spectacles. Papa'd bought them for both him and her really, paying fifty cents for them at the notion store, and the stems were too long for her, so that the seeing part would slide down to the tip of her nose and sort of dangle there. It made it convenient for her to regard me over their tops when she continued, as if she hadn't left off several minutes before, "An' if I catch you eavesdroppin' again, I'm a-goin' to tan you within an inch o' your life, Delphie."

Calling me Delphie showed how serious she was. Otherwise it would have been something like you-little-good-for-nothing-heifer-you. On another level also, a childish half-comical everyday level that belonged with her laughter over my bumped nose, I could have explained that I was merely sitting in my private green bower and had merely happened to eavesdrop, so to speak. Or I might have pointed out that the chances were I'd find out everything she and Jennie were talking about in due course anyhow, since it belonged in the family and there were few secrets among us. This would have been a plain direct grown-up statement, and would have thrown me wide open to a thorough swatting, or maybe, after I'd been backed into a corner, a pecking over the head with the broomstick, very undignified, as I wasn't supposed to be that direct and grown-up as yet. It didn't occur to me somehow to try to tell the exact in-between truth, which was that I'd been pretty unhappy about the eavesdropping as well as about what I'd overheard. Casting about in my mind, I produced instead, at random, something I'd held back earlier, that she hadn't asked Frank to stay to dinner.

"No, I didn't ask him to stay, an' they's plenty reason why, as you know if you been listenin' to me all mornin'."

Between her teeth she broke off the sewing threads from

the dress, eyeing me so sternly over the spectacles as she did so that I could remember nothing but the guilty remains of Frank's candy in my pocket. Then either she figured I knew so much already that a little more wouldn't hurt me, or else she couldn't quit talking once she was well wound-up, for now I heard precisely why and how it was that Frank had brought disgrace on himself and on us all, and this time Mama was addressing me rather than Jennie.

It had happened at Allerton, before I was born. Frank was about twelve or thirteen years old, and he'd always been a troublemaker of one sort or another. Well, he was at the poultry house one day, and the train whistled off in the distance. That was a sign for everybody to go down to the depot. The poultry man, a Mr. Moore, would Mama ever forget the name, went off and left Frank alone in the store, and he stole sixty dollars from the till. The man missed it at once, and lost no time sicking the marshal onto Frank. Oh, they caught him red-handed. He'd run off up the railroad tracks to the stock pens, and the marshal found him there and brought him back to the hotel. He told Frank he'd give him time to change his clothes, so while Papa talked to the marshal in the office, Mama tore a screen off a back window and Frank crawled out and took to the hills.

My heart nearly stopped beating for her. "But didn't it scare you?"

"It like to scared the liver out o' me. But I knew Papa an' the marshal had it fixed up between 'em that Frank was to get away. The marshal made a pretence o' searchin' for Frank, but he didn't search very hard. Him an' Papa had knowed each other for a long time."

I imagined Frank out in the hills, living wild in caves for years until people had forgotten him, but it appeared that wasn't the way of it at all. He'd gone off up to Missouri, and this old bachelor cousin of Papa's had taken him in.

"An' that was the last we saw o' Frank till after we left Arkansas," said Mama, "but we hadn't no more'n moved over into Oklahoma an' got settled here at Bridgewater the first time than he was at our door again, only a grown man now, might nigh it, askin' favors like he'd never left home, an' gettin' 'em, too, then an' later, even though it took the bread out o' our own mouths."

Something was burning me through my pocket, Frank's candy, of course, and I held it out to Mama.

"I don't want none o' his candy, thank you."

"I don't reckon I do either," I said, and I set it on one of the organ shelves, where Bruce ran onto it presently and ate it all up. But then Bruce was still young and innocent, while I—what had happened, what had been done to me, during this endless stirred-up morning? It used to be that I'd fall into dreams and drowsiness whenever Papa and Mama talked of the old days. How far away the possibility of that seemed to me now! I recalled that, as I crouched beneath the honey-suckle trellis a little while ago and bit into a tomato half, the strong green smell of the tomato vine stains on my hands had driven away the perfume of the deep gold-hearted blossoms all around. Like that, the hard sober facts which Mama related had overcome any disposition on my part towards soft and sleepy dreaming. Their connection with me was too near, it tied right into what I myself could almost remember about that hotel at Allerton where I was born, and I was beginning to see into old puzzles and half mysteries which had vaguely tantalized me for years. I saw why Mama was so dead set against Frank, why we'd left our nice hotel and had so much starving and struggle ever since, and why, coming still closer, as close as last Christmas, there could be people who'd dare to send us charity food and to offer me a charity dress.

I felt heavy and strange. It came back to me how, on that dreadful Christmas day when Bruce had so nearly died, I'd peered into the snowy night after good Doc Blaine, only half-conscious that deep within me there was seething and struggling a whole series of questions which I'd been shocked into asking. Already then, in my enormous relief over Bruce, they'd been pushed down below the surface of my mind, and during the months that followed—more than half a year of months—that was where they'd quietly remained, allowing me to be happy, or almost happy, at home and at school. But they were still with me, every one of those questions and all the feeling that went with them, biding their time. And today I'd had their answers. I'd had them with a vengeance, hadn't I? All at once I'd been given the reasons for our being a very great deal of what we were. I understood why Papa and Mama kept so much to themselves, why they didn't join the church here in Bridgewater, for example, or go on picnics and such with other people but were always on the outside of

132

things, so that was where we children were, too, for the most part, all of us as a family forever looking on at other people's activities but never really sharing in them. I understood also, I thought, why Jennie'd always seemed to feel we didn't amount to much as a family, and could stoop so low as to marry a man who was little better than a tramp.—Wasn't that exactly what Papa'd said of Cecil once?

All of this had been explained to me in the course of one single morning. And what was I to do with all I now knew and felt? Like the knowing and the feeling, which were there but not thought-through, I couldn't even put the question, not then. I was merely aware that I'd been through a bruising battering event, between an early morning when I planned a story called *Emmeline Deverex* and the late end of the same morning when in a flash I realized how silly that story was and thereafter lost all interest in it. I was on the other side of something. It was as though I'd been standing all morning long on a bridge, watching a pent-up heaving murky flood from farther away as it surged and sucked and whirled below, and as though now I'd stepped off on the shore across from where I'd come. What it would be like on this side was still hidden from me. But without being able at the time to search out and speak the truth of things within myself, I knew after a misty fashion that something had come to a head in my life, a stage that had been growing for several years really, as our place in the world was brought home to me and I began to feel its pressure, seeing what it had done to Jennie, how Sallie was fighting against it in her pride, and that it was a threat to me. And if, long afterwards, I was to remember the story *Emmeline Deverex*, it would be as a souvenir of this important day when I'd had to cross over from being just a child to being a child with a past, not a good past. That was the way I felt it.

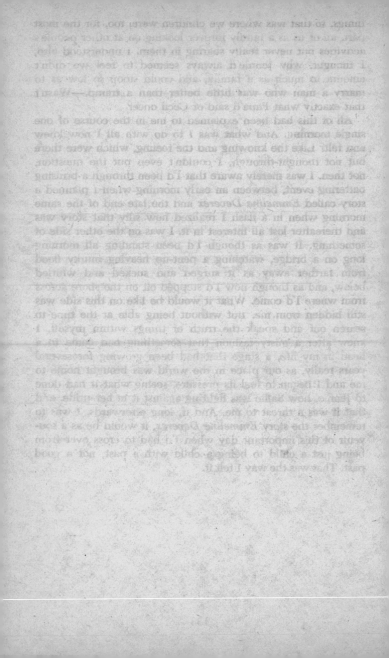

BOOK THREE

Where I Didn't Belong,
and Where I Did

CHAPTER I

With Shoes on My Feet

Frank never came back. Probably it was because Papa hadn't
gone another note for him. Mama was mightily relieved, and
after warning me that under no circumstance was I ever to
repeat in front of Papa any of what I'd heard that morning—
which I'd not have done in any case—after that in my hearing she never again referred to it. It would have been unusual
for Papa to speak of such matters to me, and all he ever let
fall that had to do with them I'd already heard several times
in the past, that sometimes a feller did things he hadn't orter.
Even that I was a long while in relating to the remote events
described by Mama and Jennie. For quite some time, however, I couldn't forget the story itself, or dismiss thoughts of
Papa—poor Papa, who'd been tried in public like a criminal,
threatened with a horsewhip, and sick most of the winter following—and my heart hurt for him as Jennie's did for people
and animals who might be hungry.

Then school reopened and fresh interests and other problems came to the fore. The most important problem was
shoes. It was far from the first time for that particular problem, but it was the first time I'd had to drop out of school
and go to pick cotton at Uncle Berry Broadbent's in order to
buy the shoes. Lucky Sallie didn't have to go. She was
staying with a chum and wouldn't miss any school.

"Why can't I do that?" I protested. "Maybe I could stay
with Edna Deed."

"An' maybe you couldn't, too," said Mama, and Papa
ended all discussion by saying that Sallie was paying for her
clothes by working in the telephone office on Saturdays and
Sundays. "If you don't want to go to school barefoot," he told
me, "you'll be happy to pick cotton for some shoes."

That got me back to my customary feelings about Papa,

and I was just glad that the kids at school knew nothing about the cotton-picking or about my Uncle Berry. I knew very little about him myself, except that he was my great-uncle, one of Granma McNabb's brothers, along with Price, Clay and 'Poleon, short for Napoleon, and that about the same time when Granma and her family were moving away from Arkansas to a farm down near Gisper, Uncle Berry was bringing his own to live on this cotton farm where we were to work. It was about ten miles from Bridgewater, on the far side of the Arkansas River.

In addition, I knew that like Granpa and Granma McNabb, Uncle Berry and his wife had a big family and that the older children were married and gone from home. One further thing was known to me: that if Uncle Berry brought a load of cotton to the gin at Bridgewater, he was apt to spend some of his money on whiskey, and that once he'd drunk so much that he went to sleep in the empty wagon and got home only because the horses went there of their own accord. It was a cold night, too, it was in November, and the next morning Aunt Siller saw them, poor old things, with their heads hanging down over the gate into the barnyard, where they'd been standing for nobody knew how many hours, with Uncle Berry stretched out in the wagon behind, almost frozen to death.

" 'Pears like a feller does things he hadn't orter," said Papa. "He regrets 'em afterwards."

Mama wasn't sure about Berry's regretting, anyhow he didn't mend his ways. Siller had a lot to put up with from Berry, first and last.

"Is her name Siller?" I said to Mama, in wonderment.

"Well, it's Prisciller, Siller for short. It's all the same thing."

"No, it isn't, Mama. You orter call her Prisciller. It'd sound better, if that's her name."

"It'd sound better if you didn't say nothin' at all, my little lady," said Mama, and she reached back to crack me over the head with her knuckles, but I was too far away, so I gazed at her calmly.

We were in the wagon driving out to Uncle Berry's—Papa and Mama on the seat in front, and me, back of them with Bruce, cushioned on the folded tent and bedding we were to use during our stay there. Papa waited until he judged Mama and I were through looking at each other, then, flicking the reins over our mules' smooth brown behinds, remarked that the worst of Uncle Berry was, he couldn't resist that old tanglefoot. And couldn't you just rely on him to get religious about it afterwards! Berry was strong on Scripture anyhow, and could reason about the Bible until he was blue in the face.

"Will I get to hear him reason about the Bible?" I put in, interesting myself as much as possible in the situation ahead.

Papa laughed. "I don't reckon you'll be able to help yourself, if you're goin' to be around him in the cotton patch."

Where else I had a chance to be for the next several weeks, I'd have been pleased to hear. Leaving out Sundays and occasional wet days, every day found me just there, hemmed in on a row between Mama on hers and Papa on his, with Bruce larking freely around, and Uncle Berry on the farther side of Papa, his long canvas bag drawn out behind him, his tall back bent over the cotton stalks, arguing as he picked and picking so fast that nobody but Papa was able to stay even with him. But as they went past, I might hear him asking Papa what he made of something or other in the Bible, such as in Revelations, where it read that there should be hail and fire mingled with blood, and the third part of the trees should be burnt up and all the green grass.

I shuddered, and Papa replied that he hadn't studied into it much of late, but he guessed that must foretell the approaching end of the world.

"Verily," said Uncle Berry. "Hit'll be a terrible an' wonderful time."

It came to me that this strange, rather wild-looking old man, with the ragged black beard and small deep-set eyes, was relishing the prospect of the terror as well as of the wonder.

"Think of hit," he said. "A great mountain burnin' with fire cast into the sea, an' a third part o' the sea become blood, an' a star fallin' from heaven upon the third part o' the rivers an' makin' 'em like wormwood."

But Papa preferred to dwell on the world to come after this present one was past, and wondered how Berry thought it'd be in heaven. "Do you reckon them walls'll really be jasper, an' the city itself pure gold? Will the foundations all be garnished with precious stones an' each o' them gates all o' one big pearl, just like St. John says?"

"That's sure what hit leads us to expect, Dave," said Uncle Berry, reasonably and politely.

"The eternal city," said Papa, straightening up from his work in order to meditate on the idea. "It'll be a beautiful place, won't it?"

To me his voice sounded beautiful, too, speaking of heaven out here under the blue sky which was just this side of the eternal city, as we were taught, but then he stooped over and went on towards the end of the field, and I didn't hear him again until he and Uncle Berry on their new rows met and passed me and Mama still heading the other direction on our old ones. Papa was asking if Berry thought the resurrection would take place for every person at the hour of his death, or would each of us have to wait for the end of the world, when the graves would reopen and all the dead people rise and stand facing to the east?

What a horrible notion *that* was! I thought with another shiver, and how surprising to hear it from Papa! Halting for a moment, I searched his face, but his eyes remained as I knew them, mild and a little far away, as if they dreamed of what was fair and lovely to behold, and I concluded that rather than reflecting his own thinking, Papa in his turn was being polite and here on Uncle Berry's home ground was accommodating himself to Uncle Berry's special lines of reasoning.

At the moment this reasoning had it that your spirit couldn't stay in your body after you died, since examination proved that the worms ate your flesh and it went back to dust. "Well, where is yore spirit then?" said Uncle Berry. "Where does hit go an' stay if the resurrection ain't for ever' person at the hour o' his death? We know hit's got to be somewhere. Yea, verily."

As I stood peering up into his face, he spat some tobacco juice onto the ground. A few drops failed to clear his beard and hung there trembling, very offensive to my eyes, and suddenly I remembered something I'd forgotten before, something else I knew about Uncle Berry. He was the person who'd taught Mama to chew tobacco.

Yes, Mama chewed. Or at least she'd hold a piece of chewing tobacco in her cheek. It was a family secret. Papa bought her ten-cent plugs of Granger Twist for her, or if it was necessary to send one of us children to the store, she'd have us tell the clerk we were buying it for our papa. She was very careful about the whole thing, never spitting at all but just swallowing the juice, I guessed. Her teeth she kept clean with a tiny ellum twig chewed brushy, and it was a rare occasion when I'd glimpse a little brown dab at one corner of her mouth. I used to wonder what there was about the stuff that was so attractive, and chancing one day on the wadded-up paper poke where she kept her plug stowed away, I nipped off a small corner. Naturally I got caught—before I'd made any discoveries about the tobacco, too—and I was afraid that this time I'd really gone too far and was going to be rewarded with more than a little old slap or broom-handle pecking. This time, however, I'd gone so far I'd turned Mama deeply serious.

"I want you to promise me you won't get into that stuff no more, Delphie."

She was so sweet and earnest that I loved promising, explaining that I'd only done it anyhow out of curiosity. And hadn't I heard her say that to chew tobacco wasn't any sin?

"Well, it ain't no sin, but it don't do me no good either."

"Why do you do it then?"

"'Cause I've got the habit." She hadn't been much older than me when Uncle Berry began letting her and her brother Albert have a chew of his tobacco. They'd be out in the field with him, working. They didn't know any better than to take the stuff. It tasted kind of sweet to them like candy. In those days they didn't have any sweetening hardly, except for sorghum and a little honey from a bee-tree now and again. Granma tried to break her and Albert of the chewing as soon as she learned of it, but they already had the habit.

With this freshly recalled fact threading into my knowledge of Uncle Berry, I listened to him say that the matter which puzzled him, and he wanted to put it to Papa, was whereabouts in yore body did yore spirit reside? Was hit in yore head or was hit in yore heart? Papa maintained that the seat of the soul was in your breath, and once again he'd gone so far along his row that his voice came back thin and light in the sunshine.

"Is all that in the Bible?" I said to Mama, after the two men had passed out of hearing.

"The main part of hit is."

141

"You don't have to say *hit* simply because Uncle Berry does, do you?"

"I ain't a-sayin' it for that reason."

"Yes, you are, Mama." Noting that she'd left off saying *hit* in any case, I pressed my point. "You've started sayin' *hit* an' *yore* an' *pore* an' other words like that ever since we've been out here."

She knew I was right, but she wouldn't admit it. This was because usually she was the one who did the correcting, and she liked it better that way. "You 'tend to your speakin' an' I'll 'tend to mine," said she. "Just you remember you're still in your goslin days."

"All I'm doin' is tellin' you," I protested. "Don't you want to talk nice?"

"I talk nice enough for folks like us. If I want any suggestions from you, my little missie, I'll ask for 'em."

That was how she'd do, act like we weren't as good as everybody else, when you made her mad trying to get her to spruce up a smidgen. Yet I knew for a fact that Mama in the bottom of her heart held us to be as good as the best and could fancy herself quite at home among the very nicest people, say bankers' wives. And how many times had I heard her brag about her great-grandfather, Captain Jack McNabb, who'd almost been president of the United States? or speak with pleasure of her Uncle Hy Shelby, who'd educated those children of his to amount to something? She was just a mite mixed-up, in my opinion. Furthermore, it wasn't like her at all to overlook such a point as whether or not people were clean, like the difference between Papa and Uncle Berry, which really you couldn't help noticing with the two men side by side here before you. That difference was the big one between the two families, to my mind, it was still plainer inside Uncle Berry's house, and I wondered whether Mama didn't know about this because she never went to see Aunt Siller, or whether she never went because she did know about it.

It certainly didn't charm me, but on Sundays and those rare rainy days which kept us out of the cotton patch, I could find very little to occupy me, and as Mama hadn't absolutely forbidden me the house, I did frequently visit there, simply closing my eyes to anything objectionable, such as flies sitting so thick on top of a white coconut cake that at first glance I thought it'd been sprinkled over with raisins. If Cousin Pussy hadn't gone to school, we'd play together; otherwise, I'd stand around watching Aunt Siller and Cousin Vinita card cotton bats and sew blocks for one of Vinita's getting-married quilts. Vinita was the youngest of what you might refer to as Uncle Berry's first crop of younguns, and the oldest of the children remaining at home. After her was a gap, then came Pussy, who was my age and the oldest of the second crop, followed by Little Berry, just old enough to start school this fall, and then by two or three quite little ones not much in evidence outside the house.

A favorite game with me and Pussy was to try on each other's hats, posing before the tall looking glass in her front room. Pussy's hat, a pale yellow straw with daisies around the brim, was better than mine, but if I wasn't mistaken it was more becoming to me, from my having a kind of city look about me. In the mirror we could view almost all of us both at one time.

"You are really the prettier," I'd say, to test what I thought I was seeing, and watching my grammar so as to impress her.

"No, you are the prettier," said Pussy, who didn't know that much grammar but was willing to take my word for it, and as she repeated for the second time, no, I was the prettier, I could tell she realized it was so.

This was gratifying, and after several weeks away from school and Sunday school, town and home—all the places where I longed to be—it bolstered me up. It seemed to establish that I had no real kinship with life at Uncle Berry Broadbent's, and I'd have sought the looking glass with Pussy even more frequently if Vinita hadn't so often been planted there, primping and prettying herself up, and combing the long hollow curls which she wore flopping about her head. One day she showed me how I could make my own hair into such curls, and as soon as I was at home and could get hold of some of the long strips of cloth needed for the purpose, I meant to try it. Meanwhile, Pussy and I might desert Vinita and the front room in favor of Aunt Siller and the cookroom.

It was in a shack out behind the main part of the house, and you got to it through a covered passageway. My understanding was that both the cookroom and the passageway had been knocked together by Aunt Siller and her girls after they moved here from Arkansas, which no doubt accounted for their being so flimsy and slaunchwise. In the cookroom Pussy and I would get in among the littlest Broadbents, who were lined up around the range, with their eyes glued to the skillets. Ordinarily I had no appetite for food from the Broadbent table, but whatever came out of these vessels would have been purified by cooking, and occasionally Aunt Siller would reach right into a sizzling hot pan with one knotty brown hand, lift out a few slices of the sweet potatoes she was frying, and distribute them among us. The other big iron skillet was apt to contain cut-up pieces of two or three squirrels which Uncle Berry had brought down with his shotgun, and I wasn't offered anything from that pan, as it was too much for Aunt Siller to give away.

Vinita and Aunt Siller took no part in the cotton-picking, but on Saturdays Pussy and Little Berry might come to the field for a dab of work. Uncle Berry didn't make them, and for the rest, on picking days, there were only Papa and Mama, Bruce and me, in the patch with him, and I continued to overhear a good deal of his reasoning about the Bible. The discussion one morning centered on faith. According to Uncle Berry, it could move mountains, cure a man of any disease, and give him power to work miracles, such as walking on the face of the waters, even as Jesus done—*did*, I meant.

"Could I do that, Uncle Berry?" I said. "Walk on water, I mean?"

He came out from the inside of his head to stare at me as if he hadn't actually seen me before, finally answering yes, he didn't doubt hit, child, providing I had faith without any holes in hit.

"You'd have to be filled up with faith till you was light as a feather," he said, "an' then the waters would bear you up. Verily."

We'd reached the end of the field and all religious argument broke off while we weighed in. Uncle Berry and Papa heaved their sacks in turn up onto the hook of the scales which dangled from the limb of a cottonwood, and Papa, producing his stump of a pencil and a midget-sized notebook, added the amount he'd picked this morning to what was down for his other days. Mama's sack wasn't full, and mine was less so, but Uncle Berry weighed them anyhow and their amounts were entered both in his notebook and in Papa's. Then we shook the cotton out onto the great loose white pile

144

growing up beside the scales, placed the canvas straps of our sacks across our shoulders again, and recommenced our work.

Well, the others recommenced theirs. I loitered behind. It wasn't so much that I hated the work as that I just seemed to feel I'd get along all right if I didn't do it. Up ahead the long empty bags of the others went twitching along, held down only by their own weight and that of the slick damp black earth which clung to their undersides. Gradually I was falling behind.

"Oh, Beulah land, sweet Beulah land,"

I sang, gazing across the field towards the woods which, from having a sprig of yellow with a prick of orange or red to surprise you here and there, had fattened up all over in all of those colors and were starting to edge towards purple and brown and deadness. Just what was a Beulah land, anyhow? I wondered idly, singing on,

"As on thy highest mount I stand,"

while I pondered further this business of walking on water.

Maybe I'd try it one of these days. I'd use a tub of Aunt Siller's rain water, one that was off by itself under the eaves at the back of the house, pausing for a moment in front of it and thinking about Jesus, so kind and loving, who died on a cross, until my throat hurt and I got tears in my eyes, and then, before anything else could enter my head to make a hole in my faith with inattention, I'd step out onto the water. How would it feel, all that browny clearness beneath my feet, bearing me up? I'd call to Little Berry and Pussy to come look at me. Simply that. "Look at me." I'd do it once and then step off on the ground and gaze at them. No need to tax Jesus with too much walking just to show some stringy little second cousins. Later I'd have to perform in church. The big square container under the pulpit where the baptizing was done would be opened up and filled for my special use, and I'd set my clean bare feet onto the water, and stand there, and walk around with a holy feeling. Everyone, including Preacher Maquiddy, would look at me as if I was wonderful. It'd be hard for the preacher, being so important himself, but he'd have it to do, because I really would be wonderful, although for Jesus' sake, to be sure.

I picked an easy handful of cotton, and laughed, to imagine all that. I couldn't walk on water. Uncle Berry couldn't. Nobody could. It was the influence of Uncle Berry's cotton patch which was bringing such fancies into my head. And yet . . . and yet . . . it wasn't that alone. It was that mixed with something else already strong within me. And just as Papa'd been directed towards his own inner thoughts of heaven, and Mama'd begun using language which must have belonged to her in some long-ago time before my own, so after the same fashion I'd turned inwards to a belief that maybe I wasn't a plain ordinary person after all and that something splendid was in store for me. Often it seemed to me that I was absolutely bound to turn out wonderful, for there was that about me, going round inside me, which made me different from Pussy and Little Berry and other kids I knew. It wouldn't matter very much whether they were here or others in their place, but it couldn't be the same if I were missing, and it would boil inside me that this was how it had to be whatever I must do in order to bring it to pass. I couldn't stand it any other way. It wasn't enough to know how different I was myself. It had to come out so that people would see it and talk about it. In all good sense, I couldn't suppose it would show itself through my walking on water, but if you were going to be wonderful, and didn't as yet know how, it was natural that any idea, however playful, might suggest itself to you while you were still a child, especially if you happened to be located where those ideas were floating around, like me here in Uncle Berry's cotton patch. It was all part of your feeling that you had to explore every opening that came along until you hit on the right one. At the same time I knew very well that any line I took must be turned to some good purpose. Above all, faith ought to be employed like that, and instead of trying to walk on water, a master thing that was mostly for show, however you looked at it, I should be trying to have faith at some point where I truly needed help. Truly I had such a point, which had developed out here at Uncle Berry's, and which worried me and was so horrid that I could hardly bear to think of it, much less to mention it to Mama, though I'd have to do both, sooner or later, if there wasn't some improvement.

"Get to work there, young lady!"

Mama, now halfway between me and the men, had glanced around and seen me dawdling. I picked a few more handfuls, to pacify her. But my thoughts were still on myself, on how I absolutely had to amount to something, and I seemed to understand why I found myself this morning a little more opposed than usual to the job I was doing. It wasn't from laziness, real laziness. It was because I knew that nothing I wished to befall me ever would, at least directly, as a result of my being a good field hand. It was the same feeling I'd had when Cecil once proposed that I could sling hash in his and Jennie's beanery, which proposal had had the effect of facing me more ardently towards my books than ever before. So now, in this cotton patch. I was here for one reason, and one reason only, and up to the present morning I hadn't as a matter of fact slowed down very much but had a good while since picked enough, and more than enough, to send me back to school with shoes on my feet. And if this morning I'd fooled around a little with Uncle Berry's notions, it was only that I was entertaining myself, filling in time as best I could, while I waited for the hour of my escape.

It came sooner than I expected, swept in by wind that shook the clouds across the sky, ripped leaves from the trees, and snatched up dust from the ground to fling in our faces as we sat at supper around our campfire that evening. Behind the wind came the rain. All through the night it beat on our canvas roof, and half-asleep on my cot, I felt it in a fine mist over my face. Once I waked altogether, to hear a thick gurgling in the drain ditches which Papa'd dug around our tent, and in the morning I saw that the water had run in anyhow, leaving queer dark paths across the hard-packed dirt of our floor.

It wasn't easy to get a breakfast fire started out of wet wood, and by the time Papa succeeded, he and Mama had made up their minds to bring our stay at Uncle Berry Broadbent's to an end. The wind and rain meant further change, according to Papa, there'd be heavy frost from now on, and Mama, bidding me and Bruce to put on our shoes, remarked that there'd be no sense in wearing out those we had picking cotton for more. We two children helped gather our stuff together, Mama and Papa let down the tent, folding and stacking it with the cots, bedding and all in our wagon, Uncle Berry paid us for our last week's work, and we pulled away along the muddy road towards Bridgewater.

Oh, it was good to get back to our clean warm dry house at last! Sallie was joyful at sight of us, too, and before bedtime found some strips of cloth for me to make my curls with. Following Cousin Vinita's instructions, I wetted and combed my hair and divided it equally into sections. The next step was to tie a strip of cloth to the top of each section, wrap the hair around the strip and roll it into a tight wad which was tied again at the top. Altogether, I had ten wads. They punched against my head and ears the livelong night, but the next morning, sure enough, each wad unwrapped in a beautiful curl, or what would be a beautiful curl once it was loosened and combed. That flock of curls flopping this way and that around my head would change my looks entirely. I could just see myself coming in as pretty as a peach to Sunday school tomorrow and to regular school the day after.

"Want me to comb your curls for you?" said Sallie.

She'd been so very agreeable since we got home, scarcely herself at all, that I said all right, but be careful.

On the sheltered back porch, in the warm soft sunshine, I sat on the steps and Sallie fell to her operations. I was pretty nervous at first. But seeing how cleverly she ran the comb through the long heavy hollow tubes of hair, shaping and smoothing them one by one around her finger, I was able to relax and sing a little tune.

> "Oh, Beulah land, sweet Beulah land,
> Tra-la-la-la-la-la-la-la. . . ."

"Ee-ee-ee!"

Sallie's frightful screech shattered my song, she slung the comb from her, it clattered down the steps, and in one bound, so it seemed to me, she was across the porch to the well.

"What is it?" Thoroughly alarmed, I'd started to my feet.

"Ee-ee-ee!"

She was hauling away at a bucketful of water. From inside the kitchen Mama heard the commotion and stuck out her head.

"Quick, Mama, the soap!" cried Sallie, sloshing water into the pan and scrubbing violently at her hands.

148

"What ails you?" I begged to know, still on the steps in the sunshine with my beautiful curls indeed flapping this way and that about my shoulders but not counting for anything any more, and Mama, rushing out with the soap, put the question with more authority.

"Not me. *Her!*" Such a shudder ran through Sallie I could almost feel myself turning pale. "Ee-ee-ee! I wouldn't touch her again with a ten-foot pole!"

"Well, all right, don't touch her. But tell me what's wrong with her!"

"Lice! Nits!" It came out in a regular hiss. "Behind her ears! All over her head! One critter in the comb, wigglin'! Ee-ee-ee!"

"Well, I swear to God!" Before I could move, Mama reached out and caught me by the curls so tightly I could feel my eyebrows being pulled upward. "I told you not to wear them younguns' hats out there!"

"You didn't give me no reason," I blurted, sort of dangling there with my nits and lice at the end of her arm, helpless, and trying hard not to cry.

"Do you have to have a reason for ever' blessed thing you do? Can't you take nothin' on faith?"

"I tried to have faith," I whispered, "but it didn't work out on the worms."

"On the *what?*" said Mama, glaring, but she'd understood all right, and I just didn't know what would happen next. A terrible whanging, probably. After a moment she quietened down, however, and sent Sallie for the coal oil jug, saying, "Now pour it on for me, a few drops at a time."

She worked in the oil with her stout fingers until my hair was soaked to the roots, and after that, wrapping a towel around my head, she ordered me indoors. Papa'd already gone to town to buy me some medicine. Our new shoes, sent for some time back from the mail-order house, had arrived at the post office, and he brought them home as well. Wearing my towel, swallowing my medicine, and breaking in my new shoes, I spent the day. I also slept with the towel on. Then in the morning Mama lathered my head with some of her harsh homemade yellow soap and scrubbed and rubbed, and all the dead boogers came floating out in the panfuls of water she used. I thought she'd take every last piece of hide off my head before she finally allowed me to sit down on the floor in a warm corner by the stove. Presently my tangled thatch was

149

dry enough to comb and pleat, and buttoning on my new shoes, I set off for Sunday school.

We'd have no dreadful talk *there* of fire and blood and wormwood and graves opening up at the end of the world, as we sat in a semicircle, all us nice little girls in our Sunday best, in the small warm church with the familiar dust specks aswim in great bars of sunshine slanting down through tall bare windows, and what a pleasure it would be after the threats and drudgery and lonely farawayness of that cotton patch beside the Arkansas River! Yea, verily. I didn't have any curls, not unless you counted the pigtail coil which began halfway down my braid where the little black ribbon was tied, my scalp was tender, and I still smelled a smidgen of coal oil and must remember not to get too close to other people for a while. Moreover, my middle was extremely lean and hollow from the medicine I'd been dosed with, not to mention a soreness in a special spot which I felt when I sat down. But the worms weren't going to take my body before I'd even died, that was a cinch. And none of it was too much to bear if by bearing it I could rid myself of all traces of my late connection with that scary old man, Uncle Berry Broadbent, and his dirty backwoods family.

CHAPTER II

The Summer I Was Twelve

After that came the winter. Papa sold the mules and went to work again digging ditches for the county at a dollar and a half a day until the rheumatism in his toes returned. Then we rented our house in town to some people, and ourselves moved out onto Ol' Man Abel's farm.

This pleased Bruce, if neither Sallie nor myself. But he wasn't in school, he wasn't five years old yet, and what could you expect him to know about anything? Encouraged by Papa, he was forever talking about being a farmer when he grew up, insisting on referring to Oklahoma corn bread as Arkansas corn dodger, and saying you could eat hog meat and drink buttermilk and save the grocery bill when you were a farmer. And although I'd tried to impress him with the fact that living on a farm might very well interfere with a person's schooling, which you absolutely had to have in order to amount to something in life, it wasn't much use with Papa so firm on the farming side.

I only gave heartfelt thanks that Ol' Man Abel's farm was one for raising corn, not cotton, and that Sallie and I were able to foot the two miles in to school in Bridgewater. We carried our lunch, which consisted usually of two thick slices of Mama's crumbly homemade lightbread stuck together with peanut butter. The farm was stocked with chickens and several cows, and while Papa was to raise his crop on the shares, Ol' Man Abel allowed Mama to keep what she made selling eggs and butter. They were bringing good money that winter, and it paid her to sell them and buy peanut butter, which in bulk was very cheap, for my and Sallie's sandwiches. In the spring, as her garden came on, she replaced the peanut butter with a few green lettuce leaves. If we were careful about our eating, nobody could be sure that we didn't have something else between the slices as well.

Towards the end of May school was over for the summer. Sallie continued to go back and forth to the telephone office every day, but as a night operator she went into town in the evening and came home in the morning. Her job was full-time now, and every two weeks she got a good-sized check which she spent on herself, mostly for shoes and the goods for middy suits. She'd learned how to sew at school, and with a bit of help from Mama made herself several beautiful outfits. Mama forecast that in due course one of them would be passed on to me, but I was afraid Sallie might be as stingy with her clothes as with her fondant candy.

Like sewing, cooking was an outcome of her training in domestic science at school. She bought the ingredients for the fondant herself, so nobody expected her to pass it around at home, but I'd willingly have helped myself to a piece behind her back if I'd had a chance. One midsummer afternoon she'd laid out a batch on a piece of paraffin paper on the windowsill of her and my bedroom, where it was hardening slowly owing to the heat, and outside the window I was considering how I might coax a small hole into the screen wire and so obtain the chance. I might have risked it, trusting to the talk in the front room to cover up my noise, but for Sallie's entrance from the kitchen. I went on around the house and into the front room.

Mama was in there with Mrs. Steam Tuling and her sister-in-law, Miss Shaddy Tuling. Mrs. Steam was a neighbor, and Miss Shaddy was visiting her, from Tulsa. Both of them were big, but Miss Shaddy was the pinker. Mrs. Steam was showing her off with great pleasure, explaining that she'd been in the same hospital that Granma McNabb had been sent to down in Tulsa, only Miss Shaddy had been there ever so much longer. Another difference which she could have mentioned was that today Granma was on the bed in the corner of the room, her eyes on the ceiling and not a sound out of her, while Miss Shaddy was spilling over the sides of her chair, smiling and pink and eager, and sweating a little as she related to Mama how she'd spent all those months in the hospital but now, would you believe it, she didn't have an ache or a pain.

> *"Come away with me, Lucille,*
> *In my merry automobile,"*

sang Sallie, as she minced through the room on her way to town with her fondant box under one arm. I slid out of my chair and into our bedroom.

Disappointment. Sallie hadn't missed so much as a dripping of chocolate on the paraffin paper. Raising my eyes, I found myself staring into a pair of big brown ones in a rather dirty little face below a crop of red hair. Bruce was peering in from the other side of the window, where I'd been earlier, and with the same hopes, no doubt. After a moment he suggested that I should come play with him and his oil derrick. He and Granpa had built it.

"Then go get Granpa to play with you," I said. "You think he's so wonderful."

It used to be that Granpa would refer to me as his favorite grandchild, but of late, in fact ever since he'd brought Granma to stay with us so she could be closer to a doctor than was possible on the farm at Gisper, Bruce was the one he'd taken up with. It tickled him to hear the little tyke bring out something like, "Come on, Granpa, let's go chop the wood. We've got to be dodging that job now."

That was amusing, certainly, for something said by mistake. I had reached the stage where I was more able to be clever on purpose. For instance, very recently I'd written a letter describing some baby ground sparrows which I'd stumbled onto in a nest at the bottom of an old peach tree and fed with bits of potato and bread, then, begging a stamp from Mama, I sent the letter to a contest in *The Farm and Home Magazine*. It won third prize, that is, twelve post cards with color pictures of flowers and birds, and the letter was printed in the *Children's Corner*, issue of June 29, 1916, with a line at the top saying, *by Delpha Doud, aged 12*. The clever part was that I'd made the whole occurrence up out of my head.

Still, it was only third prize. I'd have liked first better. Humped over in a thinking position on the edge of the bed in the little lean-to room which belonged to me and Sallie, I thought whether I mightn't just turn out to be pretty after all when I grew up, like the ugly duckling. It might be easier than cleverness, if possible. The question was, what were the chances?

I got up and studied myself in the mirror, and my face seemed almost all right except for the nose. It was squarish at the tip, like Granpa's. If that was the reason I'd used to be his favorite grandchild, it seemed like a high price to pay, especially as it wasn't even working any more. Maybe in the end I'd have to compromise and grow up partly pretty and partly clever. Then possibly I could at least turn out to be an interesting person. That would be an all-over kind of look as I imagined it, and my nose would more or less blend into it. Surveying myself in the mirror again, this time at a distance so as to get in everything, I concluded that the main trouble was my middle.

Mama had a corset to confine herself in when she went places, and so had Sallie, though not possessing anything really important to confine, Sallie seldom wore hers. It had been hanging from a nail on the wall of our bedroom all summer. Tucking my dress up under my armpits, I put Sallie's little article around me. It wasn't easy, but I tugged and pulled and sucked myself in, and one by one I got the hooks fastened clear to the top. Then I lowered my skirt.

The corset made a difference, all right. I wasn't round and soft in the middle now, I was round and hard, and the extra of me that there wasn't room for under the corset was pinched up over the top, changing my loose belt into a very tight one. Had I been improved or not? Bruce passed the window, and I said to him would he care to come in and tell me how I looked.

He examined me about as long as I had myself, finally deciding that he liked me better in the corset. "I think you look good in it," he said.

He was a nice little fellow at heart, I thought, and asked would he care to help me out of the corset. By now it had worked up higher around my central part, and I was simply hanging over the top. "You untie the laces," I said, turning my back to him while I struggled with the hooks in front, and sweated.

"They ain't no ends to these laces," he announced, after a minute of fumbling around back there where I couldn't see him.

"'Course, they's ends to the laces. If they was a snake, they'd bite you."

Still he couldn't locate them, and getting desperate, I sent him to the kitchen for a sharp knife and had him cut the laces. Then I could undo the hooks, and my sides rushed out and my stomach heaved a big sigh and settled back into its rightful place, looking bad but feeling like a great relief.

"You can come see Papa chop my cat's head off pretty soon if you want to."

I was pulling my drawers loose where they'd stuck to me under the corset. I thought I hadn't heard right.

"Papa's goin' to chop my cat's head off so he won't be eatin' no more o' Mama's little ducks an' chickens," Bruce explained, very matter-of-fact and friendly.

"You don't mean he'll use the axe an' really cut your cat's head off?"

"Yes, I do."

"You aren't goin' to let him do that!"

"Sure I am. I want him to."

He didn't know what he was doing, that was all. He was too little. I'd have to make him feel sorry. That was the only way. You couldn't force him to do anything. He was too stubborn. I got a big breath.

"No, you don't want him to, Bruce. That's awful. You wouldn't do that to your little kitten that came out o' the same litter with my Inky-Cat-Cat an' Sallie's Muff an' Mitten. Don't you remember how cute they all looked, the four o' them all together in the hay, an' Sallie claimed the two grays, 'cause she saw 'em first, an' that left the black one for me an' the yellow one for you. An' Mother Cat was so proud, an' she's such a good cat, a wonderful mouser, an' this is her little kitten."

"I don't care if he is. He ain't very little nohow. I want Papa to chop his head off. I got him to do it. I seen my cat carryin' one o' Mama's little yeller ducks under the porch a while ago, an' Granpa said we orter chop his head off at the woodpile, so I went an' asked Papa to do it, an' when he's through down at the barn, he's goin' to do it."

I hadn't been strong enough. I was still too relieved at getting out of the corset to work myself up good and proper. I'd have to take a bigger breath and begin again. Then it occurred to me that Bruce might be mistaken about Papa's intentions, though if he wasn't and Papa had his mind set, it was doubtful whether he'd listen to me. I didn't have much influence with Papa. Still, I could see, and try. I ran out of the room, through the kitchen and across the yard and cow lot to the barn.

Papa was in the feedway. At the door I waited a moment to let my breathing quieten down so that I could sound natural, as if there was nothing to make a fuss about. "You aren't goin' to chop the head off o' Bruce's cat, are you, Papa?" I said then.

He also waited a little, throwing another bucketful of corn into the trough for the horses. Was he considering his reply? Or was he only finishing a job? I couldn't tell. But when he set the bucket down and faced me, I knew the answer before he spoke. He was going to do it.

I wanted to say, "Please, Papa, I wish you wouldn't," but I was so near to crying that I couldn't bring out a sound.

"It's my cat," said Bruce, shoving in under my elbow to the feedway. "I got a right to have his head chopped off if I want to."

"Well, we've got to do somethin' or your maw soon won't have no little ducks an' chickens, that's a foregone conclusion," said Papa. "I swear, that yeller cat's worse'n a skunk. I don't know how he got started, but they ain't no breakin' him now that he's got a taste for 'em."

I found my tongue at last. "Couldn't you let me an' Sallie carry him a long ways off instead?"

The answer to this was already known to me, too. For Sallie and I had carried the yellow cat off twice before. Once we left him at the edge of town, and once, when Jennie was home on a visit and willing to go with us, we tied him up in a gunny sack and took him to the river. We were supposed to put a rock into the sack with him and throw it into the water, but it was so piteous to see the sack twisting and jumping with a live cat in it that wanted to stay alive the same as we ourselves did, and the water was so dark and fearsome and ran so heavy and deep, that we thought how it would be if someone tied us up in a sack and tossed us in rather than the cat, and we looked at one another and didn't have the heart to do it to Yeller-Feller. That was what Papa'd named him, for Bruce. And both times Yeller-Feller showed up at the house two or three days later and went on helping himself to the young ducks and chickens.

So once again I knew in advance what Papa was going to say. But hearing him say it, and watching him go clambering up the ladder to the loft, and understanding that nothing I could do or say would make any difference to him, I hated him exactly as much as if there wasn't justice in his words, and I said, while I tried to swallow down the lump that was in my throat, caught tight there, I said, "You're just as mean as Bruce!"

I didn't aim to say it, actually, but my voice got away from me and came crying out, and I took to my heels before he had to admit that he'd heard, and do something about it.

Out in the open, I paused to take thought. Granpa was no-where in sight. Besides, he had put Bruce up to the whole business in the first place, and would naturally side against me. I ran back to the house and into the front room, which was empty except for Granma on the bed in one corner, her hands like two yellow claws on the quilt, and her eyes, which had become so hazy and sunk in her head, fixed on the ceiling.

"Where's Mama, Granma?"

Her gaze came down from the ceiling and wandered over the room, as if to find me. By the time it reached me at the foot of the bed, she'd forgotten the question, and her eyes travelled upwards once more.

"Say, Granma," I repeated, as urgently as I dared with a person who looked like her. "Where's Mama?"

It seemed minutes before her lips twitched. "I think your maw went down the road a piece," she got out.

I couldn't choke back a sob. The time was so short. Granma's gaze, lifting towards its usual spot on the ceiling, made a slow return to my face, and I saw that the thin lips in her shrunk yellow face were trying to say something else. I halted for any aid they might yet give.

"You've had a backset, child," she whispered. "You better go back to bed."

She was only out of her head when she talked that way, Mama said, and she was still the same Granma and wouldn't hurt a fly. But she always made me uneasy, and in any case she didn't know what was the matter and she couldn't help me now. I ran out again and across the porch and down the broken brick walk to the gate, to peer up and down the road. Nobody was to be seen in either direction. I ran back into the yard. Under one of the rusty cedars Bruce, undisturbed, was building around his little wooden oil derrick a wall of broken bricks taken from the walk. What I ought to have done was to get after him for ruining our walk and to try to stop him. Instead, I crouched alongside and laid a few pieces of brick myself.

"Where is your cat, Bruce?" I said, as offhand as I could manage.

He wasn't to be fooled so readily. "I don't aim to tell you. You'd go an' let him out."

I should have said, "No, I wouldn't, Bruce," and begged and persuaded him further and let him see that he was making me cry. Only when I was so close to crying really I could never use it like that. And all of a sudden I couldn't stand to have him so little and his mind so made up, with myself, way yonder the bigger and knowing what was wrong for him to do, unable to budge him a bit more than I had Papa.

"All right for you, you mean, mean boy you! I'll find him anyhow an' hide him where you'll *never* think to look!"

I began hunting everywhere, in the smokehouse and empty rain barrel, in the storm cellar and the attic, and while I was hunting as fast as I could, trying to locate him before Papa was through with his work, I glanced towards the barn lot and there were Papa, Granpa and Bruce moving towards the woodpile with Bruce carrying the yellow cat.

In Sallie's and my room, under the bed as far as I could go, I put my fingers in my ears and let the crying loose. No one would hear except Granma, it wouldn't mean anything to her, and it would drown out any sound from outside. "They're choppin' his head off," I prayed through the tears, and the dust beneath the bed. "Dear Jesus, hurry an' stop 'em, please, if You love me. Can't You please do it quick, before it's too late? Please, Jesus, please!" I pleaded and prayed, because that was all there was left to do, but I didn't dare take my fingers from my ears for fear I'd hear something, oh, I couldn't think quite what, but something terrible that I'd never be able to forget, the sound of the axe coming down on the log maybe, or of the cat screaming as he saw what they were going to do to him. Only a miracle could save him, and there'd be no miracle. God was everywhere and knew everything, but He didn't seem to do anything about a lot of it, not unless He had a great deal more help than I could give Him now.

So after a long while I knew that the yellow cat was dead. Then I heard Mama in the kitchen, straining milk and fixing supper. The others came up to the wash bench outside, and Granpa was saying, "Bruce was awful set on doin' it, but after you put your foot on the cat an' got ready to bring down the axe, he looked mighty funny, an' I thought for a minute there he was goin' to back out on us."

Papa laughed, not a merry sound. I heard it through the splash of water in the pan.

"Then the head flew over in his direction," said Granpa, chuckling, "an' he looked up to you just as wild-eyed!"

"I don't reckon he realized what it was goin' to be like. Did you, son?" Mama was speaking from inside the kitchen door.

"Yes, I did," said Bruce. "I wanted that ol' cat's head chopped off."

If he'd been upset, he'd never admit it, he'd never go back on his deed. I put my hands over my ears again and didn't take them off till Mama set in to whoop me up for supper. From the back door she hollered down towards the orchard, and in between hollers she wondered where that rabbity kid was hiding out anyhow. At length I crawled from beneath the bed and sat on the side of it, and when she'd pretty nearly hollered herself hoarse, I said coldly, "You don't need to yell your head off. I'm right here in the bedroom."

"Well, if you ain't the limit!" She came to the door, and she would have got after me for not answering to her call, but she took a look at my face and said instead, "Come on out now an' eat your supper, kid."

"I don't want no supper."

"Sure you do. You want your supper. Now come on out. What ails you, anyhow? Do any o' yuns know what ails that youngun?"

"I know what's the matter with her," said Papa. "An' she just as well quit her sullin' an' come on an' eat."

"Well, I ain't a-comin'."

"Well, you are a-comin', or I'm goin' to take the leather strop to you."

"He means what he says, Delphie," said Mama. "You'll come on now if you know what's good for you." I went to my place at the table, and she poured my milk and handed me a piece of cold corn pone. "Go on an' eat. You'll be hungry after a while if you don't eat."

"It's over an' done with," said Papa, "an' it ain't a-goin' to do her a lick o' good to cut her didoes around here this evenin'."

"What's over an' done with?" said Mama.

"Why, choppin' that cat's head off, that's what. Delphie knew as well as anybody we couldn't have that cat around here."

"You didn't have to chop his head off," I said. I didn't look at Papa.

"We had to do somethin'. You an' Sallie hadn't got shut o' him. He didn't know what was happenin' to him, an' he didn't suffer. He's just as dead one way as another'n, an' they ain't no use takin' on over it. Set up there now, an' let me see you eatin' your supper."

But I couldn't eat. My face was swelled up, my throat was set tight, and the food didn't look good.

"I'll make it look good," said Papa, and he jumped up and grabbed his razor strap from the wall and laid it across my shoulders.

"Don't, Papa," I begged, all the tears streaming again. "I'll eat."

"Let's see you a-doin' it then."

I broke some bread into the milk and put a spoonful into my mouth. It would hardly go down with the biggest swallow. The tears running down my face got into my mouth, too, and made the food salty. I couldn't stop them. They just kept coming strong and quiet while I pushed in the food. But I hadn't given in to Papa. I hadn't given in one inch. My shoulders burnt and my head ached and I was worn out, but everything was exactly the same as it had been before he got the leather strap from the wall.

"I don't believe she orter eat if she don't want nothin', Papa," said Mama, after a while. "It stands to reason she can't have much appetite, the way she's feelin'. It may upset her stomach."

"She ain't obliged to feel like that. She can straighten up an' enjoy her food if she wants to."

"I don't know whether she can or not, Dave. To tell the God's truth, the thought o' that cat has kind o' turned my stomach, too."

"I don't see why it should, Brittie. You been wantin' to get shut o' him more'n anybody."

"I ain't denyin' it, Dave, but I can't say I had in mind this partic'lar way o' doin' it. Anyhow, it ain't hardly a fitten subject for mealtime."

"Well, it wasn't no intention o' mine to bring it up. As for Delphie there, let her go on to bed without her supper if that's her wish. But I want to remind her o' one thing. I don't reckon Bruce's cat died anywhere near as hard a death as hern done. An' sure won't cause the stink an' trouble afterwards."

It was true, too. My cat had died in torment. And he hadn't done anything at all to deserve to die. He'd just been a little wild and hard to catch, and I wanted to tame and pet him. So I coaxed him with food and put a cord around his neck and tied the cord to the chimney that went up through the middle of the attic. I intended to feed and water him every day and keep him there until he loved me and would let me do anything I wanted to with him. But I had forgotten him. In bed in my and Sallie's room, I stared up at the ceiling, watching the smoky dark thicken in its corners, and I remembered the night when a wild screaming broke out from somewhere and Papa called from the front room, "Which one o' you younguns knows where that cat is an' what's the matter with it?" My heart had nearly stopped beating, for I knew it was Inky Cat-Cat and that he was screaming because he hadn't had anything to eat or drink for days. I didn't see how I could have forgotten him, but I had, and he'd borne it as long as he could, and then begun to scream. Up in the attic all by himself he was screaming, and I couldn't think what to do.

Bruce came awake, and denied all knowledge of a cat.

"Delphie?"

Papa knew I must be awake, too, by this time, and at last I had to admit that it was my cat and that I'd tied him to the chimney upstairs.

"Then you can just go untie him," said Papa.

But he didn't make me go alone through the dark kitchen and out and around the side of the house to the attic stairs. Getting out of bed and lighting a lamp, he led the way up the steep narrow steps and through the low attic door.

The cat was at the other end of the room, pulled as far away from us as he could get, and between us and him was the dry dirty saucer which had held his water. He wasn't Inky Cat-Cat now, or any of the other pet names I'd had for him. He was a black cat, and he was mad. As we neared, he strained farther and farther back against the cord cutting into the mangy fur on his neck, and opened his mouth and hissed. And his mouth wasn't red any more, it was pale, it was almost white, and his eyes, that had been only eyes in the past, had turned to fire burning in two hollows in his head.

"Hold the lamp," said Papa, and taking his pocketknife, stooped and cut the cord as close as possible to the cat, which gave a wild leap and disappeared through a hole in the eaves. He never screamed again, and he never came out. When we smelled the odor downstairs, Papa went up and pried the floorboards loose and got him out.

So it was nothing but fair that he should remind me of it. I had been thoughtless and cruel, and had run around laughing and playing, while up in the attic my cat was waiting for me, thirsting and starving beside his empty saucer, struggling against the cord which he had let me—yes, let me—tie around his neck, for how many days and nights I couldn't even recall, but until it was beyond endurance, and he was mad and hated us. I couldn't excuse myself because I had forgotten. I wanted to, but I couldn't. I wanted to believe that everything was right in the world, and feel good, and go to sleep, but it wasn't right, and I wasn't allowed to sleep. It didn't make the black cat alive and take away his screaming in the night because I was sorry. There wasn't anything I could do about it, not ever, all my life long. That was how I'd been. I had to stand myself that way. And I had to stand Papa and Bruce the way they were, and the yellow cat dead with his head off some place out in the pasture where they'd thrown him, to stink and to rot, for the buzzards to pick at and the worms to crawl over, until at last the rain and wind and sun had wiped everything away except clean white bones in the grass. It hurt to have it all over for Yeller-Feller like that, but it was.

I lay in bed, alone and remembering, and the night flowed in thicker and faster, and clouded the ceiling and sank down over me. Then it was bedtime for the others, for Papa, Mama and Bruce in the dining room, and for Granpa in the front room, which had been given over to him and Granma. His lamp on the stand-table threw a band of yellow light across the foot of my bed. Strong at first, it dimmed and flickered with its lowered wick. For a while I heard the springs of his cot fretting and complaining as he settled himself, but soon no one was awake in the house except me. I drew the sheet over my shoulders and watched the dark on all sides so that nothing should sneak up and get me, from the penned-up night in the room or the big blowing night outooors, and even after I fell asleep at long last, I didn't forget in sleep that the night was there nor that my cat was dead the same as Bruce's and I was guilty, too.

There came another night and yet another day that summer I was twelve which would never be forgotten. Sallie'd gone to town to work night shift as usual, and I was alone in our room and sound asleep. Then I began to hear someone crying and awoke to find it was Mama, sitting beside me on the bed, blowing her nose and saying to Granpa, "We'll have to wait till the boys get here to make final plans for the buryin', Paw, but we're goin' to have to have some new black stockin's for her, that's one thing."

I knew what had happened. Granma was dead. We'd been waiting for the hour to come. "It'll be a God's blessin' to her," said Papa, "sufferin' like she does, an' no relief except through morphine." Mama agreed that it was an awful expense to the boys, who'd sent Granma to the hospital at Tulsa only to be told that she couldn't get well, and who were paying for her doctor and medicine since she'd been at our house. It wasn't that Mama minded taking care of Granma, she didn't mind that one smidgen. "Maw's done a heap more for me than I ever can for her," she said. "Seems like she's had more'n her fair share o' work an' trouble. A woman can't have thirteen younguns an' raise a round dozen of 'em in that ol' backwoods section of Arkansas without knowin' what it is to go through the mill. She never had no conveniences to lighten her load, not one. An' though Paw's allus 'peared to think a lot o' her in his way, it was his way, an' he'd let her keep house an' make garden an' work in the fields till she was ready to drop. Maybe it'd been better if she hadn't been so willin', 'cept that Paw never was no kind o' provider, he'd been brought up in a home where darkies did the work an' he didn't know how to take hold, or else it was just laziness, an' if it hadn't been for her they's many a time we mightn't have et at all. I can remember back to the years when he was still a circuit rider for the Babtists an' goin' off on those preachin' sprees to preach hellfire an' damnation, which he may have believed in, I don't say he didn't, but while he was gone it was up to Maw an' Brother Albert an' me to make the crops an' try to lay by a little food for the winter months. None o' Paw's folks ever come to our aid, either. They had the idy he'd married beneath him. But if anybody ever went to seed around our place, it wasn't Maw, believe me. It sure makes me feel bad to think how little rest an' pleasure she's had in her life."

Her words came back to me tonight as I listened to her and Granpa through the sleepy fog in my head, and I'd have liked to feel sad about Granma. But Granma had never paid much attention to me. It was the consequence of her having so many children of her own, Mama explained, but then Granpa had the same number and he'd always noticed me, up to a point. For another thing, Granma was older than Mama seemed to think. She was fifty-five. Wasn't that old enough to die? Of course, I knew it was sad for her to die, even at fifty-five and looking older, but I simply couldn't feel it.

It was another matter to have Mama there close beside me, crying. I forced myself to wake up a little more and said, "You can have my new black stockin's for her if you want 'em, Mama."

"No, honey, we can't use your stockin's." I hadn't really supposed she could, but I'd wanted to comfort her, and it was so sweet to have her lay her hand on my shoulder and softly call me *honey*. "You go on back to sleep now," she said. "It's a long time till mornin'."

I yielded again to the hazy sleep that was dragging down at me, and my next awakening was to funeral arrangements already well advanced, and several neighbor women arriving to offer their services. Among them was Mrs. Steam Tuling, this time without her big pink sister-in-law, and a certain Widder Jones, who in Papa's words had a face as sour as vinegar but was mighty good to help out if there was sickness in a family or someone laying a corpse, like Granma in the front room.

These two women and a couple of others were on our front porch, and I went past them and on to the gate to wait for Sallie. The women had got the news from listening in on Papa's telephone calls over the country line, one of these being to Sallie, but there was a peculiar circumstance which I was eager to pass on to her privately. I didn't get a chance to open my mouth.

"I know all about it already," she said, shouldering past me.

I hurried along the rough brick walk beside her. "You don't know *all* about it," I whispered.

"I know all I care to know." Sallie didn't lower her voice, and according to her wont sailed past the neighbor women without so much as a nod.

"I don't think that girl's got nothin' in her veins but water," said the Widder Jones, glaring after her and paying no more heed to my presence on the porch than Sallie had to hers.

"Well, I don't know. Sallie's been at work all night." Mrs. Steam cast a vague sort of glance in my direction as if to take me into account without making too much point of it. "It may not be her nature to show her feelin's as much as other people nohow. Sallie's feelin's may be deep, for all I know."

I liked Mrs. Steam for sticking up for Sallie and for understanding that I too had feelings even though a child. On the other hand, so far as Granma's dying was concerned, I knew very well that it didn't mean much to either of us girls, and all I'd had in mind to relate to Sallie, and to ask her to explain if she could, was the strange fact that Granma's bowels had moved after she was dead. The one real distinction between us was what seemed a stronger interest on my part.

It would have been interesting, for example, to go with Papa to meet the train which was bringing Uncle Will, the twins Ras and Bras, and Myrtle and Troy up from Gisper. To that Papa said no, the surrey would be filled to overflowing without me. During his absence I gave my interest to Granpa. He'd borrowed my tablet and was writing down the names of all of his and Granma's children, headed by Britia Martia, born August 2, 1876, and closing with Troy Duglas, who'd been born in 1901, just three years before myself, and who was Granma's baby. The name of the thirteenth child, who had died, was included in its proper place in the list.

"You got my name spelled so fancy I don't hardly recognize it, Paw," said Mama, who always signed herself Brittie Martie.

Reading over his shoulder with me, she counted names. "Albert won't be able to make it, I know he ain't well, an' Rosie's too fur away to get here even if she had the train fare, which I doubt she has, an' as for Hat, I don't reckon Ben Elder'd let her set foot in our house to this day, whatever the call for it."

The other married children in Mama's naming were Annie, Idy and Linnie, recorded by Granpa as Anna Pawhatten, Ida Deliah, and Malinda Linn. These three lived on farms in the neighborhood of Gisper, and receiving word at once from the children who were still at home, could surely be depended on for the burying. With their husbands and kids, a few of our neighbors and all the rest of us, we made a sizable crowd the next afternoon as we climbed into our buggies, surreys and wagons, and followed the big black hearse out of the yard, past the dusty cedars and over the long hot road towards Bridgewater. The graveyard was near the river on the opposite side of the town, which we skirted among scattered houses and a sprinkling of oil wells. Sometimes the derricks had been taken down and only the pumps remained, hammering up and down, never ceasing by day or night to bring the thick black oil up out of the earth. Although it was Sunday, the pumps went on hammering, and it was the only sound you heard, save for that the town had gone to sleep as always on Sunday afternoon in summer, under a sun as hot as the one we had today.

Papa halted our surrey in the shade of some cottonwoods outside the graveyard, and tied up the horses. He and some of the other men slid Granma's coffin from the hearse, carried it along the path to the new grave which had been dug, and set it on the ground. There, at its head, Preacher Maquiddy opened his Bible. Before he began to read, however, he looked up at us and all around, to be sure we all had our eyes on him. In the outdoors, with no walls to keep his voice from spreading away, it was hard to catch what he was reading, but as in church it was like a song you spoke instead of singing, and besides seeming more distant, the sleepy drone might almost have been melting into the hot yellow sunshine over the graves.

Presently I quit trying to get a grip on his words, and after his fashion allowed my eyes to rove the circle of people, to see what we were like gathered close by that long black box and the deep damp hole which would receive it. Right off, I was struck by how much better we Douds showed up than the other families of our kin, who were awfully poor and seedy-looking. They were all from the same drawer, so to speak, the men in their best serge suits that were still out of press and dusty-like, as if they'd been hanging on a nail behind the door all summer—and they certainly had—the women in long black skirts with thin starched white lawn blouses, the little girls in dresses made from the same sleazy white lawn and much too long for them, and the boys, several of them barefoot, in tacky homemade pants and shirts. How grateful I was that none of these people lived very near to us, and that none of my friends and acquaintances from town were here this afternoon to get a glimpse of them!

As I went on gazing, however, it was borne in on me how sorrowful Granpa was looking. Ras and Bras wore the same air, and so did Uncle Will, sorowfulness seeming especially odd somehow in a heavyset young man who at other times smoked a big cigar and was interested in the girls. I was standing close beside Mama. I didn't have to look at her to know how bad she was feeling, and I turned my eyes towards little Aunt Linnie. She was on my other side, sort of drawing her brood of small white-headed younguns around her while a tear crept down her soft crinkly pale-freckled cheek. Beyond her I caught sight of Aunt Myrtle. She was too young actually for me to call her anything but Myrtle, and usually on her visits to us she and Sallie didn't do much except get off in a corner and giggle around about their beaux. Here by the grave she was silent, and her companion was Troy, partly concealing himself behind her and drooping his head. Back of Troy, and still more hidden from the general view, was an old man with a ragged black beard. I stared for a minute, then with a start knew who it was—Uncle Berry Broadbent, tall, stooped, scarred and furrowed like the soil he tilled, and sad.

I couldn't take my eyes off him. Uncle Berry! I hadn't seen him since that fall morning, nearly a year ago, when Papa, Mama, Bruce and myself had driven away from his farm, all of us happy and smiling, leaving him and his wife Siller and all their little younguns clustered in their yard, backwoodsy and lonely-looking, watching us go, while Pussy and Little Berry waved me, as I felt it, a rather envious goodbye. Stealing a glance around Uncle Berry's neighborhood now, I noted thankfully that none of his family had come with him. For if I thought Granma's other children and grandchildren looked seedy and run-down in comparison with the Douds, how much more I'd be ashamed to own kinship with her brother Berry's family! It was bad enough to have just him there alone!

"Amen," he said, to something from the preacher, but so softly that I doubted it attracted attention to him from among the scattering of our neighbors round about.

Now I looked at them. How solemn and respectful their faces were! They'd be taking us all in, though, and it occurred to me that this was the stage for me to shed a few tears myself if I had them in me. One hand over my eyes, I waited a minute or two, but instead of blurry for grief I was becoming dryer and calmer than ever inside. Why was it that over two little cats I could weep so many hot hard tears, and have not even a moistening of the lids for Granma? Quickly I lowered my hand, relieved that apparently nobody had been observing my antics.

Preacher Maquiddy was praying now, his head bent low. Everyone was so quiet, and I'd got so used to the outdoors, that I could hear him distinctly say that God's love sometimes passed our understanding but we were aware of it in the love of husband, children and grandchildren gathered here. Tiny drops of sweat glistened among a few fluffy hairs on his round knobby bald spot. How did he know that we grandchildren loved Granma, since I, for one, wasn't sure that I did? My gaze fell to the yellow-flowered sheep's sorrel at his feet, and I thought how sour and fresh it would taste if I could eat some, only I'd be afraid of this particular sorrel, growing up as it was from all the dead bodies underneath, and Preacher Maquiddy continued his prayer, thanking the Lord that this woman, Rhodann Broadbent McNabb, had confessed her faith and been baptized, and also that He had made her fruitful during her lifetime. By fruitful the preacher

167

meant those thirteen children of hers. I knew better than he did about this subject, too, it was Granpa who'd made her fruitful, and he should have lain on his own side of the bed more, I'd heard Mama use those very words and others of the same color and from them it was clear to me that Granma would have lived longer if she'd been less fruitful. Preacher Maquiddy was so in the habit of thanking God for whole long lists of things, and of hardly ever making any suggestions for improvement unless maybe more rain for the crops, that I imagined he could be a little unthoughted about some of the items on his list. In fact, there'd been occasions in church when I got the idea that he was having to hunt around for extra points to fill out his prayer to the amount of time expected of it. He might be in a similar fix concerning Granma. She was a total stranger to him, and this alone might lead him to bring out the first handy reflection which came to him. Furthermore, I knew from myself that it was easier to bow your head humbly to misfortunes visited on other people, like Syrians and Armenians, say, than to those which befell yourself, and getting right down to it in the graveyard here today, it wasn't Preacher Maquiddy's life that was over.

These were plain thoughts, I couldn't deny it, and even as they flitted through my mind I was hearing the song in his voice drone on, peaceful and sad. Mingled with it was music of another kind. It came from the katydids in the grass, the wind in the cottonwoods, and the far-off beating of the oil wells, this part of the song being so slow and hot and dry it made me want to pant, and I squinted up at the sky with its fat flossy white clouds, hoping that one of them would trail its pale blue shadow across us, but they didn't move at all or not while they were being watched, and the hot yellow sunshine went on shaking over the rocky river bluffs in the distance and the scrub oaks which bordered the graveyard and the tall bent-over heavy-headed grasses and the gray and white stones all around. By reaching out my hand I could have touched the little lamb on Alma's stone. It was carved out on top, lying down meekly with its legs tucked under, and beneath were the words chosen by Papa such a long time ago:

> *Our darling one has gone before,*
> *To greet us on that other shore.*

In our room this morning Sallie had confided to me that she hoped Granma's burying would be different from Alma's, that day we'd stayed at the graveside until the last shovelful of earth had been thrown into the hole, she'd never be able to forget the thump of the clods against the little white casket, and she didn't want another such experience. This established that Sallie didn't have water in her veins, and I wished I could prove the same for myself. The truth was, I didn't remember Alma's burying very well, and I never thought about her except once a year, on Decoration Day. Always on this day Mama'd try to pick a few spring flowers and we'd bring them and put them in a Mason jar on the grave. It came back to me that only last May I had noticed Mama humming under her breath as she got water for the jar, and had asked her if she'd forgotten her little girl. "I'll never forget her, Delphie," was the reply, "but they's so much work an' pain for the livin', you can't grieve on forever for the dead."

Strolling among the other graves, we'd admired the flowers on them and remarked on the names, whether we knew the families or not, and who they were. It was the same stones around me today, but just as a few minutes ago I'd seemed to grasp for the first time that Uncle Berry wasn't a terrible old man at all but simply a poor one, rather ignorant and not too clean, so after that same manner now I was aware of the monuments around me in a new way, I was seeing them *more.* How gently that angel folded her dove-gray wings against an evergreen! How clear and straight that marble shaft went upward, as if to say, "Be still!" I read the words on a stone almost as small as Alma's, "Sleep, darling, sleep," and thought I might have murmured them myself to someone I loved, like Bruce. And gazing at a large flat block of marble, which covered the whole grave of a man named John Ray Riddle, 1862-1912, I gave a shiver of fear for him pinned down underneath. There were so many graves about me, and yet the people in them had been brought here one at a time, like Granma today. And their families had been as sorrowful as Granma's was this afternoon, but later they'd gone home and forgotten their grief in work and other pain, the same as Mama'd got over hers about Alma. For once they were left here, the dead people couldn't make anyone remember them, and they couldn't get away from the graveyard ever again. Through daylight and dark they stayed here, year in and year out, and sometimes there'd be flowers and greenness above them, as on Decoration Day last May, and sometimes a silky-golden coverlet of bowed-down grasses, like now. And while I'd never been here in fall or winter, I could picture them, too—the colored leaves in the scrub oaks about the sides, followed by silvery frost over all, and after that the wind whining through the tall bare cottonwoods, and snow sweeping among the evergreens and over the graves like a wavy white sea. But this was up above. From underneath nobody could see through to it any more, and the day was like the night, and the seasons were all the same, and one year no different from another, exactly as Preacher Maquiddy had been describing it, for this was eternity. It was awfully lonesome for the dead people down below if you let yourself think about it, all of them lying together down there in eternity and never stirring, the graves sinking in on them and no one here ever knowing how they felt.

"And we submit our lives to Thy guidance, knowing Thy mercy will not fail us," said Preacher Maquiddy. The sad words flowed up towards heaven through the wind and sunshine. "Amen," he said, and the burying was over. People stretched their stiff legs, and walked slowly away. I was watching the men who would lower Granma's box into its hole. Somehow I was afraid they wouldn't be careful enough, wouldn't bear in mind that they were doing something terribly important, that they had here a woman who'd been alive and now they were putting her into the cold dark earth and she couldn't do anything to hinder them. Maybe they wouldn't keep her coffin level, and her hands would come uncrossed for always, or maybe she'd slide from one side to the other, she was such a little person at the last, only skin and bones, and nowhere near filled the box. Then Uncle Berry strode past, blowing his nose on a grubby blue and white dotted handkerchief, and I had to move on. From the back seat of the surrey I craned to see what was happening to Granma, and this time was prevented by the line of cottonwoods as well as by a cloud of yellow dust which flew up as we pulled out into the road and which completely hid the graveyard from our view.

Mama settled down in the front seat beside Papa, remarking that she was glad none of the kinfolks were staying over, we sure were pinched for room last night, and that the first thing tomorrow she must get Granma's bedding out into the yard for a good airing and sunning. I couldn't put the graveyard from my thoughts so promptly, and I recalled once hearing Uncle Berry say, "I wonder how hit'll be when we're there, too, as we will be soon, each an ever' one of us." Such a wondering and prediction hadn't suited me at all, I did so love being alive and there was so much I was bent on doing. But Uncle Berry reckoned I didn't have any bigger plans for the future than a lot of other folks'd had when the Angel of Death pointed his finger at them, and he showed me by argument that everybody had his hour set for dying. I couldn't contradict him at the time, although in my heart I was sure that the hour hadn't been set very soon for anybody who mattered to me, and for myself I was unable to believe that it had been set at all. Deep inside, underneath the part of my mind which had to speak back to Uncle Berry, I was as convinced as ever that I was different from anything else in the world and that nothing could stop me from being myself. Yet today I believed more that it could, and the feeling was heavy in my heart and tight in my throat. I wanted to get out of the surrey and run back and tell Granma something, that I loved her and wouldn't forget her maybe, or something that would make it easier for her.

CHAPTER III

A Lonely Place

So I learned that I did love Granma after all and that, while I was mortified by my kin, still I couldn't deny sympathy for them. How could I ever put those two contrary feelings together and get a satisfactory answer? I didn't know. But I found that the farm was somewhat more lonesome with Granma gone and Granpa back in Gisper, setting himself to finish raising Myrtle and the boys who were still at home, by hand, as he put it. The boys in particular had lost the habit of being raised while Granma was sick, he declared, and it was like breaking in a houseful of young mules to wade in again. Uncle Bras wrote Sallie that it was almost butchering time, the smokehouse would soon be full of fresh pork joints, and she and I should come on down and get some good old-fashioned vittles whenever we liked. But Sallie said, "I'm not interested in his old-fashioned victuals, thank you," and I replied, "I never liked to go down to Gisper when Granma was alive, and I don't think I'd enjoy myself among a houseful of young mules now."

It was strange to recall that there'd been a time in my life when going to Granpa's had been my greatest delight. Fortunately, school had begun, and Sallie had a good excuse to say no to Uncle Bras's invitation. I was in the seventh grade this fall, and starting junior high. The new building and arrangements made me a little timid at first, but soon I was used to the change of rooms for different subjects under different teachers. The real problem was an old one, that the teachers asked us kids to buy a lot of books and paper, the one in domestic science also requiring us girls to bring a certain kind of apron, linen hand towels, heavy store dishcloths and so much else that I simply ignored it. Mama'd say, "I've used ol' flour sacks to dry my dishes on for many a year, an' a dishrag composed of a piece of your papa's ol' knit underwear, but a clean piece, that teacher can bet her sweet life, an' we ain't a-goin' to buy all that stuff. Do you think we're made o' money, child?" Rather than ask for anything more, it was better just to grin and worry along with the teachers as well as I could, without things, as usual.

The worrying wasn't long, this year, at Bridgewater. One evening at supper Papa announced that he and Mama had sold our house in town, and the crops being made, it wouldn't be many days till Ol' Man Abel could advertise for another tenant. Later in the evening, after I was in bed, Mama and Papa were talking further in theirs, and I heard him say, "What would you think of our goin' into the hotel business again, Brittie, providin' we can find a suitable location?"

She thought well of it. While they were hunting around for the location, they sent me and Sallie down to Granpa's.

"We may as well make the best of it," said Sallie, as we boarded the little local train nicknamed Oil Johnny, "as we can't get out of it." The distance was so short that we were scarcely well settled in our coach before the conductor passed through, calling, "Gi-i-isper!" He had a knack for making it sound like the dinky little jerkwater burg it was, with one street ankle-deep in sand and one piece of boardwalk in front of Scrugg's General Store, and we appreciated having someone as good-looking as Fred Frosting step out of the depot in time for the conductor and other passengers to witness his welcoming hello. Fred was the station agent and telegraph operator, and we were acquainted with him from earlier visits. His hair was dark and curly, and he had good teeth and a friendly smile. He also had a withered hand, but he seldom removed it from his coat pocket and was so pleasant that I hardly remembered it any more, and the reason for Sallie's ready acceptance of our stay at Granpa's seemed to speak for itself.

About halfway down the lane towards Granpa's we saw Myrtle galloping through their front gate. She was late because she'd had to get supper started for the boys, some of those good old-fashioned victuals, as I supposed. Leaving our grips in the front room, we followed her into the kitchen, where she could give one eye to the stove and one to Sallie. Quite a lot had happened to the girls since Granma's burying, and they had to catch up with it. Sallie's experiences were connected with her job at the telephone office, and I had a notion she'd have talked more about beaux if I hadn't been present and if Myrtle had had any, which she didn't right then, so far as I knew, unless you counted Roe LaTue. Myrtle's happenings, on the contrary, had all befallen her at home, and all of them were troubles, including the cooking and dishwashing and the boys' dirty stinking clothes to be got clean as sure as Monday rocked around every week.

"The work wouldn't be so bad if ever'thing hadn't got so run-down since Maw's gone," said Myrtle. "The stove's the worst."

She waved one chunky freckled paw at it. "Actually an' canally, I don't know sometimes whether it'll hang together for another cookin' or not. But my rub-board's worn out, too, an' one o' the washtubs has a hole in it might nigh beyond stopperin' up with a rag any longer. An' look at that ol' stump of a broom in the corner, will you?"

Neither did she have a stitch to wear. How could she go anywhere and have a good time without a decent garment to her back hardly?

Sallie was very interested and sympathetic, but I feared for the cooking. It was too early in the season to butcher, and far from being full of fresh pork joints, the smokehouse was

173

down to a slab of side meat cured last year. I knew how it would taste, salty and stale, and the rest of the victuals being more old-fashioned than good to begin with, for my appetite, and adding the condition of the stove onto Myrtle's, I wasn't surprised at final results.

The boys noticed nothing wrong. Every one of them had the digestion of a horse, and a day in the cotton patch had built up a matching hunger. To see them lace into those bowls full of greasy food discouraged me. Aware from the past, however, that I'd better lay in a supply the first time the bowls were handed 'round if I wanted anything from them at all, I ladled out a plateful of soupy stewed tomatoes.

"Delphie there needs sideboards for her plate," said Cousin Green.

This boy was Uncle Albert's son. I scarcely knew him, but he was about Sallie's age, and had come down to Granpa's to help the uncles with their crop.

"Now I consider that Delphie's got a real delicate birdlike appetite," said Bras, laughing at my efforts with the tomatoes, which were spilling over onto the oilcloth faster than I could spoon them up into my mouth. "I don't want to hear nobody referrin' disrespectful-like to Delphie's eatin' habits." And removing attention from me, he asked Green to shoot him the g.w. dogies.

The hard little biscuits which Myrtle had baked were the g.w. dogies, it appeared. Green tossed one of them across the table. He could act like that because Granpa was away from home, serving as night watchman at a mill, if I'd heard Myrtle rightly. He got home only on Sundays, and there was really nobody to keep order the rest of the week, although Will, the oldest, was supposed to. The biscuit landed in the gravy bowl.

"Some people haven't got the manners of a hog," said Sallie, scowling, and drawing back from the grease which flew out.

"That's my edgycated cousin speakin', fellers," said Green, grinning around the table.

"People that haven't got sense enough to pass the second grade don't need to claim kin with me," said Sallie.

"People that claim to be in the ninth grade orter have sense enough to know when they're about to get clunked," said Green.

"Set down, boy." Good-naturedly, Bras stretched across the table to shove Green back into his chair. "We got a rule in this family, we don't strike women." Turning to Sallie, he explained that it always riled Green to have it remarked that he couldn't pass the second grade. It was the third. " 'Course, he was a big ol' overgrown boy when he done that, but I allus thought if he could a took in a term or two more, he could a made it into the fourth."

Ras said no. There wasn't any call to beat around the bush, Sallie'd been right to start with and Green just didn't have any sense.

"Ain't none of us McNabbs got no sense, Sallie. Now you an' Delphie's got sense, I know yuns have or yuns wouldn't be 'way up in school like yuns are, but it comes from the Doud side o' the house, in my opinion. Green here favors the McNabbs."

After this fashion the twins brightened the mood of us all —of Myrtle in spite of her grievances, of Troy, who was such a hush-mouthed sort of boy and not very sociable in general, of Sallie and Green as well, though not towards each other, and even of Uncle Will, smoking a cigar as he leaned back, so big and brown and grown-up that I was pleasantly surprised to have him smile over the younger ones' pranking-around. Ras and Bras were telling tales about each other, Ras about Bras's old moth-et mule and how he was so ancient that he couldn't even hold up his ears any more, and Bras about Ras's purty little cow Moll and how Ras might nigh ruined her disposition the day he tied the tip of her purty little tail to the fence. I joined in the laughing, and presently, when some undue notice again fell on me, managed a slight contribution. " 'I should worry, I should care, I should marry a millionaire; he should worry, and he should die, and I should marry a regular guy!' " I quoted, to the general amusement. I didn't feel smart, I was just trying to fit in, and supper over, I helped Myrtle clear the dining room table.

Sallie had a date with Fred Frosting, and by meeting him up the lane a piece proposed to avoid Green McNabb's possible capers. Green was on the porch with the other boys when she clicked past in her high heels, and all he could bring out on the spur of the moment was something about his edgy-cated cousin was kind of struck on herself, hit looked to him.

Sallie strutted on, while I, in the kitchen, tried to raise Myrtle's spirits, cast down because Sallie, without half-trying, had carried off the best-looking man in town.

It seemed to me that Myrtle had no real call for jealousy. Hadn't she had plenty of time to catch Fred herself if she was going to do it? The fact was, Myrtle didn't have much to work from. Even if she'd had a store dress and new shoes, what could she have done with them and herself to compare with Sallie, stepping out in her ready-made blue serge suit and pink crepe de chine blouse, her black hair done up high and proud on the back of her head, and her black eyes snapping? It didn't seem fair, and remembering the sweet soft little kiss of greeting she'd given me in the lane, like Mama's in goodbye earlier in the day, I hated to admit it, but Myrtle did put me in mind of one of her own dumpy little red hens. Knowing of nothing to console her on that score, I changed the subject.

"Where did Uncle Will pull out for?" I said.

He'd gone to see his girl, Lena Frone. Lena had a hard name on account of having had a baby without being married, but this cut no ice with Will. Said Myrtle. And that package he had under his arm, well, my dear, that was a corset he was taking her. "I know in my own mind that's what it is. He buys her stuff like that, but he's as close as the next second so fur as I'm concerned."

If anything, her sulls had changed for the worse, and the dishdrying done, I gave up my efforts with her and went onto the front porch.

Ras had saddled his cayuse, as he referred to a spotted pony named Tippy Tight-Britches, and the boys were taking turns riding him around the yard while the others whooped it up from the steps. "Can I ride your cayuse, Ras?" I said. Here was something I might really enjoy at Granpa's, I was thinking, as Ras reined the pony in to the porch and I stuck one leg across the saddle. I didn't quite get seated. "Ride him, Delphie!" someone yelled, and a keen little hickory whistled down on Tippy's hindquarters. The pony sprang into the air, me with him, and the gate being open, down the lane we sped. "Whoa!" I cried, in vain. The reins slipped from my grasp and I grabbed the saddle horn and hung on for dear life, with a passing prayer that my insides wouldn't be bounced out of place for good, and a fleeting hope for my tee-hiney, which was taking a harder pounding than any ever applied to it before. Behind us the yells died away, and we might have wound up in the next county, the way that pony was splitting the wind, if all of a sudden, somehow, we hadn't arrived at another gate, this one shut. Tippy stopped as unexpectedly as he'd started. The wonder was that I didn't pitch over the gate head foremost.

"Are you all right, Delphie?"

Bras was gathering up the reins and helping me down. He must have been running after me from the first. Gingerly I slid to the ground, pulled up my stockings, and pushed the hair out of my eyes.

"You look kind o' like a battleship run into you."

He was trying to make me laugh, so he'd be more comfortable in his mind. I didn't answer. I could hardly keep from crying as it was. My hair ribbon was lodged on a dusty weed by the roadside, I rescued it and stalked stiffly ahead, back along the lane and across the yard, past the other boys on the steps and on into the front room, where I sat on the bed and listened to Myrtle use her sulls to give the boys the very dickens for their mistreatment of me. My pleasure in her remarks grew as my condition eased, and after a time, when Bras ducked into the room and sat down by me, slipping something which felt like a dime into my palm and saying, "Now you won't go tellin' yore maw on us, will you, Delphie?" I was able to reply, with almost as much friendliness as ever, "No, I won't, Uncle Bras."

That was the first evening among Granpa's young mules. The first night was ahead. Bras and the other boys went to their room, and Myrtle and I got into her bed in the front room. It was a huge old-fashioned wooden article, with a high foot and a higher head, set at an angle in one corner, next to the window which overlooked the side yard. Myrtle took the place next to the window, and I settled down in the middle, leaving the front for Sallie. For a while I mumbled replies to Myrtle's jabberings, and after another while was hazily aware that Sallie had climbed in and was scrunching her back parts against me. A long dark period of nothingness followed, splintered by a yell which would have waked the dead. I sat up, shaking my head to clear it of fuzz and so be in position to save myself from whatever there was to be saved from, and with another shriek you could have heard to Jericho, Myrtle lifted from beside me and surged over the foot of the bed. I didn't actually see her, but I felt her fan past, then came an awful crash as she struck something, probably the rocker, which I judged she'd broken into a dozen pieces, if she hadn't prit nigh killed herself.

"My foot," she was moaning. "Oh, my foot!"

Not a sound from Sallie. She'd merely soared after Myrtle, leaving me alone in the bed with God only knew what. Then somehow I was out, too, Sallie tripped on Myrtle, I tripped on Sallie, and the three of us rising up together landed in a body on the first bed we came to in the next room. Its slats groaned, and the bed sank to the floor. It took Will, springing from his bed and hastily lighting a lamp, to untangle us and haul us out, first us three girls, then Ras and Bras, trapped under the blanket and fighting for air.

"What the devil's goin' on here?"

"The winder!" Myrtle chattered. "Somebody at the winder by my bed!" She was nursing one foot in her hands. "I think I've broke my big toe," she told us, and gave a sob.

Will was already through the door, lamp in hand and nightshirt aflap. Ras and Bras trod on his heels, closely pursued by Troy and Green, groggy from sleep and batting their eyes. Sallie'd seized a quilt from the bed that fell down. With that around our shoulders, clutching each other and hampered by Myrtle on her one good foot, we girls peered from the doorway. Sure enough, on the far side of Myrtle's big wooden bed, the screen wire had been half ripped from the window.

"What's that?" said someone. Ras.

We froze where we stood. The noise came from the front porch. Will set the lamp on the sewing machine and yanked open a drawer. Whoever was on the porch scudded across it, thumped to the ground, and ran. Gun in hand, Will flung back the screen door.

"Don't shoot, Will!" Myrtle quavered.

The pistol clicked, and a terrible streak of red and yellow fire spat into the night.

"A stick!" Bras bellowed. "Git yoreselves a stick!"

Armed with pieces of the broken rocker, the four boys charged after Will. All were barefoot, and all in their nightshirts. Sallie, Myrtle and I clung together under the blanket, shaking like leaves. For more than an hour the boys roared around outside. They didn't find anybody, and it was only

178

the next morning that we made out the prints of a man's heavy boots in the damp earth below the window with the torn screen. Will was of the opinion that someone who knew that Granpa was away from home had thought to scare us.

"I don't think we'll be troubled again right soon," he said, shoving his pistol back into its drawer.

The window-screen scare had one good effect. It gave Sallie and Myrtle something to make up over. Myrtle hadn't broken her big toe, but she'd been the one to wake up first and save us, so she was the heroine, my dear, which led her to forget about Fred Frosting until Sallie had another date with him. Then she sulled again. I was betwixt and between the two girls, and, sympathetic in both directions, had to be careful not to go so far either way that it would turn me into a hypocrite. Where the boys were concerned, my new appreciation dwindled as a result of a further experience with them on the front porch. Ras alone was at fault, but I determined that except for Bras I'd keep strictly out of their territory unless Sallie and Myrtle were present. We were all together at mealtimes, of course, and very occasionally if we girls went to the field to pick cotton.

A week or so passed, and Sallie seemed perfectly content, but I *wished* that Mama would send for us. We did have a letter, written in pencil in her large crooked hand on tablet paper, saying Dear Daughters, her and Papa and Bruce were in Oklahoma City, no suitable location for a rooming house had shown up yet, and she hoped we were being good girls, as ever our mother, B.M. Doud. Nothing about how much longer Sallie and I might have to stay at Granpa's.

Then one day Bras came in and said that a whole bunch of us, Fred Frosting, Roe La Tue and Lena Frone included, was going to take in a country church social next Saturday evening. The uncles would fix seats in their spring wagon and hitch up the mule with Tippy Tight-Britches, and we'd have a bushel of fun all in one big party. At this particular social, Bras said, you'd pay a quarter and be allowed to eat all the ice cream you wanted. It sounded like a bargain to me, and I asked if he'd advance me twenty-five cents out of what I'd earned picking cotton, and began to plan ahead with Sallie and Myrtle. They were very tickled and pleased about the whole affair, until it dawned on Myrtle that it wouldn't mat-

179

ter how much all together we were in one wagon, Fred Frosting would still be dating Sallie while she'd be paired with Roe La Tue.

For several days she left us in doubt as to her intentions. But noting that she was in position to buy herself a new pair of shoes, to replace those which turned up at the toes like canoes, and finding her on Saturday morning pressing the blue lawn dress she kept for nice, I had reasonable hopes. My best dress was of pale pink tissue gingham, with silky-brown threads running through in a plaid pattern, and if it was some better than Myrtle's, it was so little that she'd not care. We were on the porch that evening, watching the boys hook up the team in the yard, and I thought she looked pretty good, all washed and powdered pink, except that not having a corset she was rather full and soft around the middle. Then Sallie came out of the house in her new red taffeta.

I burst into lively laughing talk—not that it did any good with Bras down in the yard pretending he was absolutely blinded, Ras tumbling over in a make-believe fainting fit, and Uncle Will, without any pretense at all, simply removing the cigar from his mouth to gape in admiration. At that moment also Roe and Fred chose to appear at the gate, and you didn't need to be told that it was the red dress which was lighting up their faces. As once before, I threw up my hands over Myrtle, and ran out to the wagon to make sure of my place beside Bras on the front seat.

"I thought anyhow you'd be willin' to stay home with me tonight."

It was Myrtle, wouldn't you know, plucking at my sleeve. I glanced around, and there was poor old Roe all by himself at the steps, where he'd thought to claim her.

The others climbed into the wagon. Sallie made room for Roe beside her and Fred, flinging Myrtle a glare as she did so, Bras clucked to the team, and the wagon lurched through the gate. At the bend in the road Bras and Fred looked back to wave, but Sallie only sat up straighter between her two men, her head in the air as proud as Lucifer and her dress shining redder than ever in the light of the going-down sun. After the wagon was lost to view, a rise of dust beyond the Osage orange trees of the hedge marked its passage towards Lena Frone's place, and in a few minutes we heard the boys singing.

> "If the train don't wreck and turn me upside down,
>   Sweet babe, I'm Alabama bound, I'm Alabama bound,
>   I'm Alabama bound. . . ."

It was as if the boom of their big honest voices, trying perhaps a little too hard to be carefree and gay, were stirring up
the dust. Gradually the sound died away in the distance, the
dust settled slowly on the goldenrod along the lane, and I
was alone with Myrtle in the deserted yard.

Slowly I turned my head to take it all in, from Myrtle's red
chickens already fluttering into the seedling peach trees, their
roost for the night, to the doors of the barn, wide to a dim
emptiness where the wagon had stood. What a lonely place it
is! I was thinking. Partly this was because night was advanc-
ing and I didn't belong here, and partly it had to do with my
being a little less than thirteen years old, not grown-up
enough to cope with others who were more so, yet not so
much of a child as to be willing to accept what was wrong for
me, which was a kind of not-belonging as well, and a lonely
place, an awfully lonely place, to be.

Myrtle was saying something about now she and I should go
uptown and have us a treat of our own. I didn't know what
she was talking about, but did it matter? I'll go on doing the
best I can, I thought, I'll hold on, and maybe, just maybe,
Mama will send for me in a couple of days. In my discour-
agement I scarcely noticed what Myrtle was doing until I discovered that it was my quarter which we'd spent at Scrugg's
General Store. She didn't even have hers along. That was
why she'd become so cheerful.

In the growing dusk we sauntered up to the boarding-
house, where Gisper's main street ended, and back down to
the store, where it began, gnawing on some hard peanut
squares and getting our shoes full of sand. "Now," said Myrtle, with an airy brush to her plump paws, "we'll pay a visit
to the La Tue girls." That she'd gone off and left their brother
standing on her steps an hour or so back troubled her not one
whit more than spending my quarter.

There were three of the La Tue sisters named, Lila, Lela
and Lulu, and they were all soft and chunky, like Myrtle.
Living in the country seemed to make girls like that. Li, Lee
and Lu, as they were called, lived with their parents at the

head of our lane, not far from the depot, in a boxcar which Roe and Ol' Man La Tue had made into a house. It resembled others I'd seen along a railroad track sometimes, for Mexicans to live in, with the difference that the La Tue car had a thin coat of white paint and a kind of picket-and-wire fence shutting off the yard from the ragged dusty tall surrounding weeds. There were also some morning glories straggling on twine strings towards the roof. Yet somehow those scrawny vines and odd pieces of twine knotted together, as well as the flimsy pickets and the yard itself, which couldn't boast a blade of grass but had recently been swept clean with a broom, leaving the dirt in neat little ridges except where the chickens had already tracked it up—somehow all these things made you feel sorry for the La Tues. And yet again, if put to it, what could I have suggested to improve the effect of their boxcar? It was as if they'd have to start all over again, and how was that possible?

They were all nice friendly people, though, and for two or three hours we sat in the lamplight around their table, laughing and joshing, while waiting for Roe to get in so we'd know our family was at home, too. Twelve o'clock came without him, and at last Ol' Man LaTue began to gap and stretch to such an extent that even Myrtle had to take the hint.

"We'll meet Roe an' Fred before we get home," she assured me, and arm-in-arm, as if we were chummier than I felt, we ventured into the lane and its shadows. "Ain't it them I hear now?" she said.

Straining my ears, I heard only the wind playing a soft little tune in the dry leaves of the Osage orange trees, while out in the fields somewhere a katydid sang off and on to itself. How welcome the sound of the boys' big country voices would have been at that moment! We reached our gate without it. Across the yard the house bulked up, gray in the night and silent as the grave, and it seemed to me that a dark cold breath ran out from it to meet us.

"Nobody'll be foolin' around here after what happened the other night," said Myrtle bravely. I let myself be drawn up onto the porch. "They's matches on the table right inside," she added. It occurred to me to wonder why she was whispering if she felt so safe, but that she meant for me to go ahead and light the lamp I realized only when she pulled back the screen door and gave me a little shove towards the dim inside of the front room.

In the dining room beyond, just above the table, was a black square hole into the place under the roof. I'd noticed it the first evening at Granpa's, and thought that if Granma's soul ever came back from the graveyard to see how things were going at home, that was where it would hide, to peer down with big black night eyes. Now, in the vague gray light, I could just make out the opening from where I wavered in the doorway to the porch. Maybe there wouldn't be any live person hanging around after Will's shooting off his pistol the other night, but what if Granma's soul should float down from that black hole and touch me with itself?

"We better go back," I whispered.

You could have heard a pin drop. Outside, the leaves of the cottonwoods went on rustling. Inside, a board squeaked. It was the sound a floor made when you tried to step on it without making a sound. I left the doorway. Myrtle left the porch. But where she'd rammed into the rocking chair the other night, on this one she missed a step and fell the rest of the way down. Served her right. Didn't hurt her anyhow, she was up in a flash, and from overtaking me, quickly regained the lead. For a short chunky person Myrtle was remarkably fleet. Churning along through the sand behind her, I recognized and gave her credit for that.

The LaTues were less put out than I'd feared at seeing us back so soon, and one of the *L's* got up and fixed us a pallet. It wasn't so hard that we didn't sleep through Roe's return, but it was sufficiently hard to wake us at the crack of dawn, and by that light we set off down the lane once more. To either side the last of the night was gathering under the trees and in the hollows, while in the sky above day was beginning, and the breeze coursing up the road from the river flowed around us with a cool morning murmur. In our best dresses, all crumpled from being slept in, with our hair mussed and eyelids half stuck together, Myrtle and I jogged silently along. The wagon would be in the barn, and Sallie and the boys in the house, though losing no sleep on our account, you could bet, and for the time being I had no concern either beyond my need to tumble into the good soft bed ahead and finish out my night's rest.

That was what it boiled down to for me, now, at Granpa's: the immediate practical need. Some hours later I woke to the next one, and after lying quietly for a few minutes between

183

Sallie and Myrtle, following their breathings and the louder ones rising and falling over in the boys' room, I crawled out. There would be plenty of milk in the storm cellar, cool and sweet in big gray crocks, but I wasn't keen about going down into that musty dark cave. As I hesitated on the back steps, I was surprised to see that one of the boys was up, after all, and sitting on a stump in the barn lot. It looked like Bras, and I went to tell him I was hungry.

"Well, come on in the barn an' I'll give you some o' Moll's milk right from the titty."

He'd seemed so likable and appealing, all spraddled out there, grinning and sleepy in the sunshine, and now he'd gone and spoiled it.

"I'll turn the titty up an' squirt the milk right in yore mouth, Delphie. I'm kind of an ex-pert at it. All you have to do is lean over close to the titty."

"I think I won't, Bras. I don't think I'd care for milk so direct."

"Aw, you don't know what nice clean little titties Moll's got. Hern ain't these little ol' dried-up repulsive things, Moll's are nice round soft pink titties."

I couldn't look him in the eye with that word standing between us. I remembered the other evening when Ras grabbed me up on the dark porch and tweaked at the bosom of my dress, saying he'd de-monstrate Fred sparking Sallie on their dates. It was Bras who'd come to my rescue, and I'd said to myself that he had a very different disposition from Ras and the other boys, and that I liked him ever so much more. Always, from my earliest recollections of Bras, I'd had this kind of feeling about him, and at bottom I hadn't changed in it either, but why did he have to go on repeating that word as if to rub it in? If only I had kinfolks who were always nice, people I could look up to and admire and love with all my heart! But I mustn't let Bras suspect my real thinking, it might hurt his feelings in case he meant no harm, or, on the other hand, it might only tickle him as it did Mama, who would talk like that, too, sometimes, in front of me and Sallie, and if she thought she'd embarrassed us, she'd get red in the face and laugh till she had to wipe her eyes, and even Papa would grin along with her, a little. No, the thing to do was not to hang your head at such times, but to pretend you appreciated the humor as much as anybody, be as sprightly as you could in your turn, and make your escape.

So I brought my eyes in from the distance, squinting into the sun to hide any giveaway expression in them, and stretched my mouth in a wide grin. "I don't want my milk warm from the pump, thank you!" I said, and soon found a chance to slip away to the house.

Meanwhile, Sallie and Myrtle had hauled themselves out of bed, and, busily repairing their friendship, had agreed that it was late and they were tired and it was enough to fix a big Sunday dinner, which had to be on time, too, since Granpa would be home for it. That Sallie was tired from having had a good time, whereas Myrtle was tired from not having had one, they must silently have united in overlooking. Myrtle brought us a glass of milk around, and the three of us fell to preparations for the noon meal, the girls agreeing now that the kitchen was hot as blue blazes and that the cookstove would try the patience of Job. However, they joined in the opinion that dinner was working up very well, and would be ready at the expected hour. By the time Granpa arrived, the two of them were so thick you couldn't have stirred them with a stick, and when he sat down to table, bowed his head and asked that this food be blessed to our use, the boys meekly bent their clean brown faces downward, too, and the entire meal was passed in general peace.

It lasted until Granpa vanished up the lane, and the boys behind the barn. Then Myrtle, handing dishes to me and Sallie for drying, remarked that others could go off to laze around in that old Arkansas River, but she had to stay in the kitchen and wash a stack of dishes a mile high. That was the usual difference between Sunday afternoon for the boys and Sunday afternoon for her, my dear. Sallie agreed that the way the boys treated her, putting so much work on her and not getting her a decent stove, or corset, or anything, was a sin and a crime.

"It sure is," said Myrtle, and dabbed at her eyes with one of her wet hands.

They were already swollen and soggy-looking from the hot dishwater and harsh homemade soap, and she was only well launched on her job. The kitchen was hot, too, from the thick sunlight pouring through the uncurtained window as well as from the fire dying in the stove. And the flies! We'd shooed them before dinner, cornering and waving them out with dishcloths and newspapers, but most of them had managed to dodge back in as one or another of the boys slammed through the screen door. Myrtle tossed her head to shake them off her nose, which seemed to attract them, and sweated till her dress between the shoulder blades was sopping wet.

"It's not fair," said Sallie. She was beginning to be very uncomfortable herself, and this made her a good deal madder than did Myrtle's state. "You know what I'd do, 'fise you? I— I'd *revolt!*"

Myrtle quit scratching away with her fingernails at a scrap of food glued to a skillet. In the stovepipe above her head were several rusty holes which allowed smoke to puff and bulge into the room, half-blinding and choking her whenever she cooked. Myrtle gave them a mean look. Then, stepping back from the stove, she pinched her mouth at a crack in the oven door which, to plague her the other way around, let so much air into the oven that it wouldn't bake evenly. Finally, a fist on either hip, she jerked her head at the stove legs, which looked all right to me, but she knew more about them than I did.

"They's times," she announced fierily, "when honest to God I got a good notion to pitch this stove out."

"If we did that," Sallie took her up promptly, "the boys'd *have* to get you a new one."

Myrtle stared at Sallie, Sallie at Myrtle, and me at both of them. Nobody said anything. Nobody had to. This was how it came to pass that we threw the stove into the backyard that Sunday afternoon at Gisper.

It was a considerable undertaking, and when we saw the stove lying upside down in the yellow dust, and what a huge empty space it had left in the kitchen, and how red in the face and sooty we all were, we broke into peals of laughter, pointing our fingers and flinging panfuls of wash water at each other as we skipped nimbly around the pump. Calmed down and cleaned up, we presently went back into the house and the girls rang up Fred to do some bragging. The telephone was on the wall of the dining room with a high stool below. Sallie'd sit and talk a while, then Myrtle, then Sallie again, and so on, and the one who was standing by couldn't wait and was always leaning forward to put her say into the mouthpiece. The tale they were telling grew funnier by the moment. Balanced on a nearby corner of the table, I giggled to hear. At the height of the tomfoolery, I glanced through the back door, and there was the whole drove of Granpa's fine brown mules coming from the direction of the river, looking wet and washed and fit for anything. Confessing to myself that I'd been more nervous than tickled from the outset, I got right down from my perch.

To my relief, Troy and Green turned into the barn and Uncle Will towards the front porch. I thought he might not even have noticed the change we'd wrought in the backyard. It was for the twins to march straight up to the ruins of the stove and give them the once-over.

"Couldn't you gals think o' nothin' better to do with yore Sunday afternoon?"

Ras flung the words in through the dining room window as he headed on around the house. He didn't sound so very dangerous to me. Bras came in.

"I don't know as I much blame yuns." Pausing in the doorway from the kitchen, one hand beneath an elbow, he fingered his chin with the other. I'd always liked Bras's big brown useful-looking hands, which had worked to pay for Granma's stay in the hospital at Tulsa. Knowing what it stood for in his life, I didn't even mind that his fingernails were ringed with the kind of black that wouldn't wash off. "It was a mighty pore excuse for a stove to start with," he said.

Myrtle was emboldened to declare that there wouldn't be arey other bite cooked around here till she got a new stove to cook it on.

"Then they won't be arey other bite cooked around here."

This was the law according to Will, in the front room. He'd taken in the situation in the back yard, all right.

Certainly something had to be cooked. Before dark the boys rigged up a grate out of the top of the old stove, built a fire under it and fixed their supper there. Sallie, Myrtle and I ate cold corn bread and milk in the house. The next morning, though, while the girls were still playing possum in bed, I took a chance on the boys around their breakfast fire. They were perfectly good-natured, and passed me some of their fried salt pork and potatoes in a tin pie plate, and a little of their strong black coffee in a mug. It was more than Myrtle and Sallie were able to scare up after the boys had gone to the field.

"They just laid theirselves out to eat ever'thing up from us," said Myrtle. "They ain't nothin' left but milk an' sugar."

"We'll have to get some stuff from the store," said Sallie.

To Myrtle's simple question, whose money did we use to

buy the stuff with, Sallie had an equally simple answer, and with their list in hand, my teeth chattering a trifle, I went off to Scrugg's General. By the time I got back with my sack of groceries, the dining room table had been decked out with Granma's big white cloth and the best of her dishes, and we sat down in style to oranges, gingersnaps, and Post Toasties with milk and sugar. The girls decided to leave the Post Toastie box in the middle of the table. Like the other left-overs, it was a rare sight there, and would speak for itself when the boys came in at noon.

On this occasion there was no business of one-boy-at-a-time, as yesterday. Like a small army, captained by Will, they tramped directly across the yard, up the steps, through the kitchen and into the dining room.

"Where'd that come from?" were Will's first words. The Post Toastie box had done its job.

Myrtle replied stoutly, where'd he think?

"Yuns didn't charge that stuff to us boys surely?" said Ras. Clearly he was having trouble laying such a dastardly deed at our door.

Nevertheless, as Myrtle was compelled to admit, that was where it had to be laid.

"I don't hardly think it's right for yuns to spend us boys' money before it's in our pockets to be spent," said Bras.

"They won't spend no more." Will was at the telephone and had rung through to central. In a moment Ol' Man Scrugg himself was on the line, and Will was telling him that the McNabb brothers didn't want any more grub charged to their account by anyone. "We'll pay what we're owin', Mister, but if you charge anything else, you can look elsewhere for yore money."

With that, he hauled a chair up to the table, the other boys followed suit, and before their powerful appetites the dainty food melted away like young snow under the sun. Sallie and Myrtle, with me hovering near, rocked to and fro on the front porch, carrying on a refined conversation, and only waiting for the boys to leave the dining room. Then they went in and called up Fred Frosting at the depot. This time they weren't tickled. They were mad. Maybe the boys were, too. In any case, they weren't picking any cotton that afternoon. How could you blame them, with no more in their stomachs than they had? Will, I observed, was striking off down the lane in the direction of Lena Frone's place, and I didn't know where

Troy had got to, but Ras, Bras and Green were in the side yard. Here in one spot two pieces of the telephone wire were loosely hooked together and drooped so low that the boys could reach up and by holding them apart break the connection. Sallie or Myrtle would be talking along, not knowing Fred had been cut off, then suddenly his voice would come on, asking what he'd missed. The effect was to make the girls, and Sallie in particular, talk louder and harder about the boys than ever. I didn't like it, and leaving them to carry on by themselves, pulled out for the henhouse.

"Are you goin' to let a couple of half-growed pullets boss the ranch?"

The voice was Green's, and through one of the dusty cobwebby windows of the henhouse, I saw that the three boys had left the side yard for the shade of a nearby cottonwood and were crouched, Indian style, in a semicircle, counseling together, I guessed, since Green was saying that what they ought to do now was to take the telephone down and carry it back to the office in Gisper. Ras didn't know. He was afraid Will wouldn't like it, he used the instrument almost every day to get in touch with Lena Frone. Bras thought it would be enough just to unscrew the phone from the wall and hide it for a day or two.

"Naw, let's go the whole hog while we're at hit," said Green, adding that what was saved on the phone bill would pay for the groceries charged to the boys at Scrugg's.

"They's some right on the girls' side," Bras replied. As he squatted, he was digging little holes in the dirt with his pocket-knife. "One o' the last things Maw remarked on was that we orter get Myrtle a new stove to cook for us on."

"Hit ain't Myrtle I'm thinkin' of," said Green. "Hit's that edgycated little slut Sallie. Come on, let's get hit done while they're off uptown reportin' to that telegraph-operator friend o'theirn."

I put down the eggs I'd gathered, and made for the back door. By the time Green opened it, I was on the high stool by the telephone, my arms clamped tight around it. "You can't have it," I gritted.

"I'll have to pull you an' the phone loose together then, you little leech," he told me, and was going to grab me under the arms in a way that would have hurt my dignity, but Bras spoke out, and Ras, for some reason, backed him up. "Come on, boy," he said, throwing an arm around Green's neck, "let's

189

go set in them easy chairs for a spell our own selves," and they all trailed onto the front porch, leaving me alone in the dining room.

I laid my head against the telephone and cried a little. Why didn't Mama send for me and Sallie? What was the matter? Didn't she know we didn't belong down here, neither myself, left to fight unaided against all the roughness and rudeness of the place, nor Sallie, ploughing up and down that sandy lane in her dainty high-heeled shoes, or bumping along in her red taffeta dress behind a spotted pony and a moth-eaten mule, and, in her absence, having a boy like Green call her by an ugly name, which she fiercely was not? Didn't Mama know what it could be like at Granpa's, or had she forgotten? Maybe it was both, she never came here herself for any length of stay any more, and if she'd known how it would be for her children with Granpa away, surely she'd not have let us come in the first place, and if she knew now, surely she'd send for us. When would that be? When?

My thoughts were so bent on themselves that I heard the quick light thump of feet across the yard, followed by Sallie's voice, not mad any longer but excited as she called out to the boys, and yet I didn't grasp for a moment that my waiting and worrying were at an end. Papa, Mama and Bruce were in a town named Enid, somewhere to the west of us but still in Oklahoma, and Sallie and I were to come on. The girls had been to the post office, and Sallie had Mama's letter open in her hand.

In the middle of the night Myrtle got up and lit the lamp, Sallie and I dressed and, with Bras carrying our grips, went up the black lane to the depot. A cold wind came from the river and went with us, tugging at the flame of our lantern and circling the little depot as though it felt at home in the silence and darkness there. "When do you reckon we'll see you in these parts again?" said Bras, lowering our grips to the platform. I had no answer, and left Sallie to say what she would for both of us.

Far away out in the country somewhere the train cried long and lonely at a crossing. I'd heard trains like that before, and sometimes seen one, a slender line of fire and blackness curving through the night, bound for unknown places with unknown people aboard. Now this one was coming to carry me to some strange new place as well, and who knew? who could tell?—mightn't I, with luck, find myself in the very spot most meant and best for me? My heart beat fast at the prospect, while beside us the rails hummed more strongly and Bras hopped down onto the track. To and fro he swung his lantern as the train broke around its final curve. The big white headlight flared over the platform, and over me and Sallie on the platform, Bras leaped from the track in the bare nick of time, or so it seemed to me, and with a terrible shudder, a burst of steam, a flurry of cinders and a grinding of brakes, the engine's mighty weight bore past. "A-a-all aboard!" At one of the coaches the conductor was wigwagging his lantern hurryingly. Sallie and I ran and jumped on, Bras handed us up our grips, the train jerked forward, and I nearly fell down the aisle. Searching the gloom from my window, I thought for a moment I made out Bras's little light, bobbing in the dark. I might have imagined it. All at once I remembered that early in our visit I'd wondered what *g.w. dogies* stood for, and also why Ras had named his pony Tippy Tight-Britches. I had forgotten to ask, and this, as I appreciated now, was just as well.

It was cold on the train, and I was all-over goose pimples until presently the sun came up and laid its rays across me through the grimy window. As their warmth increased, I relaxed against the dusty red plush seat and watched the fading fall countryside slip past, discovering that it was very pretty now that I was getting out of it. Even the brown patches speckled with white, meaning there was a lot of cotton yet to be picked by someone, wore a new complexion as they skimmed by. It was astonishing.

Equally so, for the opposite reason that we were getting into rather than out of it, was our house at Enid. First of all, it was large, painted white and located on a wide street lined with trees and other pretty houses. Then, besides a front door with a glass patterned in beautiful strange frosty flowers, it had windows which slid on little ropes and stayed up without being propped with a stick, also a cream-colored blind at every window, and electric lights that switched on and off from a pearly-topped button by the door. But the rent on this place was eighteen dollars a month, and with no more furniture than we had to sprinkle about its smooth glossy floors, the rooms looked bare and scarcely lived-in. As soon as our month was up, we moved.

The second house was small and gray, and more like always. We were still moving in when I went across the street to enroll in an elementary school a good deal dingier and more run-down than the one near the white house which I'd thought I was going to before. "Where do you live?" said the principal. I showed him from his window. With no word from him, I understood that he didn't think much of the place.

The woman who taught the seventh grade gave me a seat at the back of the room, and during the singing period I learned a song about "Hallowe'en is here again," while at recess I watched the kids play basketball on the schoolground. I didn't know who was on which side nor where to throw the ball unless somebody hollered at me, but I was so happy to be in any kind of school again, and happy to be allowed to play. In time I hoped to learn the game, and to join in at other times than just those when there wasn't anybody else.

I was hoping also to find the free public library. I'd heard there was one, and I set out to locate it, hunting up one street and down the next, but without success. The people who looked sort of ordinary and kind, as if it would be all right for someone like me to ask them a question, didn't seem to know anything about libraries. All I found was a lot of open sheds with piles of red apples smelling as sweet as could be in the cold fresh air.

I hadn't forgotten about Granpa's, and I wrote Myrtle and Bras a letter. In reply Myrtle said that Granpa had made the boys get her a new stove and that she'd wangled a corset out of them as well. At present she was keeping company with Roe LaTue, who was a very fine fellow, after all, my dear, and Fred Frosting had gone to Tulsa and married some girl or other, or anyhow got engaged. And she trusted this found us all well.

The letter was forwarded to me at Oilwell, Enid being as dead as a doornail so far as the hotel business was concerned, whereas Oilwell was booming. Papa leased a lot at one end of its main street, and put up a rooming house. At least, it was a kind of rooming house, with rows of cots to rent to men in a big dormitory across the back end. We lived in a couple of rooms partitioned off at one of the front corners, and rented the other corner to an old man who sold candy, gum, cigars and odds and ends of groceries. Papa didn't bother to paint the place, or give it a name. He hung out a sign, *Cots, 25 cents*, and every night he could hang out another, *Cots All*

192

Taken, and go to bed as early as he pleased, in the dormitory section with the men where he could look after things. On the lot next to ours some people set up a big brown canvas tent, like one for a revival or carnival, and they made so much money with their twenty-five cent cots that the woman went to a picture show almost every week. Once she spent a whole quarter to see *The Birth of a Nation.* She told me so herself. But then she and her husband didn't have any younguns, nor did Mama suppose they'd invested every last red cent they possessed in their tent and cots, and so laid themselves under the necessity of getting their stake back out of the business as fast as possible.

We made the move from Enid to Oilwell shortly before Thanksgiving, and I missed only a few days of school. Sallie decided to drop out of school entirely, and soon she was taken on at the telephone office. She got to be a long-distance operator, too, with more pay, and she'd be saying, "Hetto, Kickapoo, hetto, Wichita, hetto, Tulsa, hetto, hetto," all night long in her sleep. She had a new black and white checked sport coat with green piping, and high-heeled white kid shoes that laced halfway up those slim legs of hers. She had a figure like a little goddess. She looked like a little queen. George Croney was always telling her so.

He was the only one of her beaux she'd let come to the house. Having met her while he was renting one of our twenty-five cent cots, he knew all about us already, and Sallie knew about him. He worked at a smelter, sometimes on the day shift and sometimes on the night, getting his face blistery-red from the heat but making good money and wanting to take her places his every free moment. Sallie didn't often consent. She could afford to be picky and choosy about men, she met so many putting through their long-distance calls at the telephone office, and so many of them liked her.

The fellow she was craziest about was Doug Cunningham. He went around for oil companies, finding likely places for wells and getting leases on them, and did such wonderful things as make trips to South America. We never saw him, but he wrote to Sallie on fine gray paper, and sent her presents—silk stockings, and boxes of chocolates which she kept hid in her drawer of the bureau. So what difference did Fred Frosting with the withered hand make to her now? She just said, "Poor old Myrt. So all she's got is Roe LaTue."

I felt sorry for Myrtle, though, down there in all that sand with only a corset and a new stove to make her feel as if she amounted to something, and I'd have written her another letter if I'd had an envelope and a two-cent stamp. It was easier to get blood out of a turnip than money out of Papa these days, which was normal in his case but worse than usual in mine, with matters shaping as they were for me in the seventh grade here at Oilwell, Oklahoma.

CHAPTER IV

Two Times, So Different

"What are you doing, Delpha?" said Mrs. Zickey, frowning at me down both sides of her long red nose.

I'd taken off a string of little gold-colored beads which Jennie'd sent me for Christmas, and was fiddling with them on my desk. The idea was that Hilya Hite, the girl who sat in front of me, should understand on this first day of school after vacation that I'd got a pretty gift the same as other kids.

"You may sit on the front seat until the bell rings," said Mrs. Zickey.

It wasn't the first time she'd ordered me up there during my few weeks with her. There nearly always was someone in a room the teacher picked on, usually someone who was ugly or a dunce or mean, and it hadn't entered my head that it could ever possibly be myself. It might have been that I was especially ugly right then from having sties, combined with the fact that I was the new one in her class. I tried to give the impression that she didn't bother me, but it was hard, exposed to full view there in front of the room, with no desk to the seat to shelter me in some dress that Mama'd managed to cobble up with a bulge right over the stomach and the sleeves a little too short, so that my hands stuck out larger and redder-looking than ever. Worst of all was those sties.

All through the winter they'd been plaguing me. I'd have two or three at a time, on the upper lids usually, the size of boils and so red and festery that I could scarcely endure a glimpse of myself in the looking glass. Mama said I was reading too much in those old love-story and western magazines which the men who rented our cots would go off and leave behind. Between school-out in the afternoon and bedtime after supper I could read an issue through, and on Saturday and Sunday I'd finish several.

Reading matter of any other sort seldom came into our house. I did have a Sunday school magazine, small and quickly read, but an important reason for my going to Sunday school at all, in Oilwell. I certainly wouldn't have gone for the pleasure of seeing Clara Shane sit up, bright and stiff, her yellow hair in two flat braids around her head, and show herself as smart as she looked, which was about two percent smarter than I was. She wasn't any smarter by nature so far as I could tell, but she was eternally applying herself to lessons, and just sometimes I let myself off, either my eyes hurt or I'd suddenly be overcome by a strong distaste for resembling too closely a girl like Clara Shane.

The other children in my grade might like me well enough in time, I thought, if only Mrs. Zickey would stop picking on me. Clara Shane would never like me. Possibly she was against me because without trying I was almost as smart as she was with. Or possibly if other people were going to be smart, she felt they should be as starched and shining as herself. In any event, unable to avoid the sight of her on five school days of the week, I'd not without good reason have made myself put up with it on Sunday, too.

It was also doubtful that without that little Sunday school paper I'd have kept on so regularly attending a class which had voted we should bring two cents apiece for the collection every Sunday. Since I was the only one who brought nothing, or next to nothing, the vote had to be on account of me, and if I wasn't mistaken, Clara Shane had put the others up to it. Did she know I couldn't get the two cents, and was she trying to force me out of the class? Let her try. I didn't aim to quit Sunday school on account of her and her two old pennies. I just went on pretending that I was stubborn about being compelled to bring a certain sum and so wouldn't bring anything at all. And it was because I didn't quit going that a marvellous book fell into my hands.

It was lying open on the sidewalk with its leaves fluttering in the breeze one morning as I was returning from Sunday school. I picked it up, charmed by its fresh white pages and clean black print, and leafing through, saw that they contained poems and other pieces divided into sections with such headings as *Gay, Humorous, Pathetic, Solemn, Oratorical, Abrupt and Startling Selections,* and *Selections of Beauty, Serenity and Love.* The cover was blue, a beautiful medium blue. Printed on it was the title: *The Cumnock Reader.* Like Moses in the Sunday school lesson before he slew the Egyptian, I looked this way and I looked that way. Still no one appeared to claim the book, and after a few minutes I tucked it under my arm and took it home with me. It was the best thing that had happened to me in Oilwell. With all those different selections from various authors, it was like owning a private library. For it I had what to myself I christened Delphie Doud's private reading room.

This was a big wooden dry goods box with the top off, in the yard out behind our house. From a sitting position inside I could neither see out nor be seen, and on days that weren't too cold I'd climb in and be alone there with my blue-backed reader. In the middle of the day the sun struck down into the box, the golden warmth gathered around me, and if a little wind puffed in now and again, its main effect was to stir up the new clean smell of splintery wood. I'd have on my heavy black and green plaid coat. At the time Mama bought it for me, I'd simply despised that coat, but I'd grown used to it, having worn off the stiff new-ugliness and toned down the old-ugliness to a better fit. Snug in the coat and the sunshine, I'd prop the book on my knees and read.

More often than not during those February days at Oilwell I was disposed to feel sad, and I frequently reread the death scenes, sometimes the one about Connor, an Irishman who got his death because after he'd worked and saved to bring them over to America, his Nora and Jamesy died on shipboard; and sometimes another favorite about a rich little boy, Paul Dombey, whose lovely sister Floy held him in her arms before he went away on the dark and unknown sea. These pieces in prose were especially piteous, it was as if nothing stood between you and their sadness as it did in such a poem as the one called *Enoch Arden,* where somehow there was comfort in the beautiful swaying of the lines themselves.

Among the sad poems, however, the one that meant most to me was *Pictures of Memory.* It told of a girl who walked in a tall old forest with her little brother before he died, and of how once when he was tired, she made him a bed of the yellow leaves. I remembered Bruce the time we had nearly lost him, and the girl became me. But the poems didn't have to have someone who was that much like myself in order for me to love them. If they were sad at all, my own sadness went to meet theirs, all of it melted together in my heart, and I'd feel pale and perfect within regardless of my appearance without.

Poetry at school wasn't like that. Take a poem we were reading now, about Sandalphon, the Angel of Glory, Sandalphon, the Angel of Prayer. In this poem there was something long and rolling which might have appealed to me, in spite of my ignorance of the Talmud and rabbis and legends it mentioned, but for the way it was taught by Mrs. Zickey-Dickey-Hickey-Lickey-Pickey. I called her that now, in secret. Her way with poetry was to have the children read it aloud in turns, a verse at a time, or, as she said, stanza. We read the same poem so many times that you knew it by heart whether you wanted to or not, and afterwards it was wearisome to have the lines go on endlessly repeating themselves in your brain. Mrs. Zickey-Lickey-Pickey said not to memorize the poems, that caused you to read them singsong. You were supposed to read as if the line didn't break where a break was printed on the page. You'd draw a big breath and go fast at the end of a line so as to be well into the next before she could hear a pause. Running out of breath at the end of a line was the same to her as a pause on purpose.

Mrs. Zickey-Pickey's pronouncements didn't convince me. Nevertheless, during my hours in class I did my best to please her. And to my own ears it seemed as if I read exactly like Clara Shane, only more gently, from loving poetry so much as well as from not wishing to call attention to myself, but Clara, standing up so straight in her blue serge dress with its starched white collar and cuffs, and speaking out so bright and clear—Clara was always perfect the first try, and after several efforts I never was, according to Mrs. Pickey.

There was a discussion of how to speak in public in my *Cumnock Reader*, but what was the use of studying it so long as I was in that woman's room? Alone in the back yard and hidden in my box, I opened the blue-backed book to poems that pleased me and read them to please myself, sometimes in a whisper and sometimes aloud, and if I yearned to hear and pleasure in the rhymes, I'd hold very still and listen, as you might say backwards, at the end of lines, and if the poem had the sound of singing strong in it, I'd let it sing to some little tune I made up for it. I read about the sea breaking on its cold gray stones and about wild bells ringing to a wild sky, about stately ships that passed to their haven under the hill, and about the bleak December when each separate dying ember wrought its ghost upon the floor. At this point, with the raven's croak echoing in my ears, hastily I'd rise to my knees to peek over the top of my box.

Nothing would have changed in the muddy littered yard around me. Here was the back wall of our building, its bare planks streaked from rain, there to one side the brown canvas of our neighbor's tent, mildly sucking and swelling in the wind, there to the opposite side the solid red brick wall of the laundry and beside it, at the very end of the lot and next to the alley, the toilet, with a line of boards thrown down as a walk between it and our own back door and now half sunk in mud. Resettling myself in Delphie Doud's private reading room, well-bedded, too, in its safe though disagreeable muck, I'd go back to the poems.

Some I learned by heart, including the one about the Admiral who peered through the darkness over the mad sea. "'Sail on! sail on! sail on! and on!'" I'd cry out the words that leapt like a leaping sword, flinging my sword arm into the air with their greatness, then taking it down quickly lest somebody passing through the alley should see and wonder what on earth was going on in that box. Poems which roused me after this fashion were easy to recall, the words stayed in me together with the feeling, both were so one and so true. "Build me straight, O worthy Master!" was a similar instance. But that phrase I remembered like a prayer, and along with others from the most beautiful of the poems it would come back whenever I was alone.

Aside from what my dry goods box afforded, there wasn't much chance to be alone at our house, but it could occur on certain mornings at the moment of waking. Warm and cozy, I'd swim up from the night's rest, and bits of the poems would be hovering in the silence that was always there, back of my sleep and the sun growing red beyond the frosty window-panes . . . "The splendor falls on castle walls and snowy summits old in story . . ." I saw it, I felt it, that tingling glory, then dreamingly my thoughts would lift and linger on another lovely line . . . "Shine out, little head, sunning over with curls, to the flowers and be their sun . . ."

They were just wisps, little broken snatches of poems, so cloudy and frail that no more than a "Hetto, Tulsa, hetto, hetto," from Sallie in her sleep would scatter them. But so long as she lay quietly beside me in our bed in the kitchen, so long as Mama and Bruce hadn't stirred in their bed in the front room, and before Papa'd come in from the men's part of the house, during that short blurry brush of time the flowers and music and sweetness were all around, glimmering between me and the day ahead in Oilwell.

I never woke without dreading that day ahead. Oilwell was such a cold new ugly place, its streets were so black and muddy, there were drippings of crude oil everywhere to foul the air and mess your shoes, always you heard the beat of the pumps as they sucked the thick black liquid up out of the ground, and if you walked to the edge of the town you saw that it wasn't country there any longer but groups of steel tanks, hot flaring smelters and wooden derricks reaching so high that even the sky wasn't free to be itself, pure and blue. Our house and everything about our living in it matched Oilwell, to the very air we breathed, which was chilly, and damp from Mama's washing. For when it rained—and it was forever raining all that long month of March at Oilwell— Mama had to hang her wash indoors, and every nail, door knob and chair back would be three or four deep in dresses, shirts and underwear, which were scarcely dry before the next week's accumulation was due. As for the seventh grade at school, it continued to be of a piece with the town and our home. My single refuge was that blue-backed reader, and as the days dragged by, cold and drizzly, fighting and holding back the brightness and warmth that surely ought to be arriving by now, the more it was the sad poems I turned to and the more they made me want to cry.

Crying, in truth, could hardly be termed a comfort, with sties. The salt tears stung my sore eyelids so badly that I resisted crying altogether, as much as possible. Then at last I got rid of the sties. I was reading on our front step above the sidewalk on one of the few mild evenings we'd had this spring, and a man striding by glanced at me, hesitated, and said, "Would you like me to tell you how to cure those sties your girl's got, Missus?" Mama was in the doorway, behind me. "Why, sure," she replied, as surprised as myself. In line with his instructions, she bought me a nickel's worth of nutmegs. They proved to be small brown nuts with white dust in their cracks and wrinkles. I gnawed at one of them off and on for several days, and by the time I'd eaten about half of that one nut I didn't have a sty left. So why shouldn't I compare this stranger who'd helped me with Mrs. Pickey? Oh, she'd noticed my sties, all right. She'd noticed them by coming back to my seat one day and bending cautiously to squint at my eyelids as if what I had might be leprosy or lice, or both, and both catching.

It was so good to have a pair of strong healthy eyes once more, and to be able to cry again, if I had to. And have to I did, it was certain that in Oilwell one thing couldn't be right without another's going wrong, and no sooner was I shut of sties than on came the toothache. The tooth hurt all night, and I cried and nursed my jaw in one hand and paced the floor in front of the oven fire which Mama got up and lit for me in our gas-burning range, and the next morning Papa went with me to find a dentist. We located one just unlocking his office door. Good morning, said Papa politely, and how much would he charge for pulling a tooth.

"Let's see the tooth," said the dentist, and obediently I opened my mouth. "Fifty cents," he said, peering in, "on account of this particular molar belongs to Helen here."

He was chuckling as though he found the whole business mightily entertaining. I was so distracted by this, as well as enchanted with being called by that pretty name Helen, that without my noticing quite how he'd done it, there I was firmly installed in his dentist's chair, the first of the sort I'd ever occupied, and he was reaching into my mouth with something hard and cold. "Hold your breath now, Louise," he told me, chuckling away. "It won't hurt a bit if you hold your breath." With all my power I held it, but a little air must have got in after all. I felt an awful tug and wrench, Papa tightened his grip on my shoulders, I tried to holler and couldn't, my mouth being stretched so wide, but I heard a long *a-aah-ah* coming out of my throat, and then the dentist was saying, "There now, Gracie, that wasn't so bad, was it, and see what I've got." I unsqueezed my eyes, and there in his pinchers he had a tooth, bigger than any I'd ever suspected was harbored in my own head. Besides the part which I knew about, it had long stout prongs dripping with what I judged to be my blood, and trailing some spongy-looking stuff likewise bloody and definitely unpleasant, but which must have been me, too, before it was ripped from my jaw along with the roots. I shuddered, but couldn't tear my gaze from the sight. What impressed me most was that the roots were really the main part, while the hole, which had felt absolutely enormous to my tongue in the middle of the night, seemed far too small to be responsible for so much misery. But I was in position to testify that it had been, and I couldn't help eyeing it with immense respect.

Papa watched me spitting blood and not saying much as we went back down the street. "You behaved well, Delphie," he said, adding that I'd better not try to go to school today. After a moment he added also that he thought Mama would consent to my going over to Ponca City to visit Jennie. Cecil was away and she'd sent money for my fare, which wasn't much as it was only a twenty-eight mile trip and I was still allowed to travel for half. It was Friday, and I could stay till Sunday.

By evening I'd perked up sufficiently to enjoy the train ride, and to toy further with the idea, how would it be if I really were Helen-something-or-other, or Louise, or even Gracie? In my opinion there was more in a name than you'd think, unless you did think, although someone—could it have been Shakespeare in my *Cumnock Reader?*—had remarked to the contrary. Before I was through with this interesting reflection, we arrived in Ponca City.

Darkness hindered a full view of the town until the following morning. The play of sunshine on my eyelids brought me awake, and sitting up, I saw that it was striking across Jennie's front porch and weaving through the dark and light pattern of the lace curtains at her windows. Unusual as the yellow light on my face was the dry soft air I was breathing. "So this is Ponca City," I said to myself, and after breakfast I stepped onto the porch to find out more.

The porch ran the whole length of the building where Jennie's light housekeeping rooms were located, and from its height a few feet above the sidewalk I surveyed the business district, where all the streets seemed to be paved and entirely free from mud and oil. Presently I sorted out another difference between Oilwell and Ponca City. There was no sound here of beating pumps nor any smell of crude oil. On the other hand, I noted the presence of Indians, in bright striped blankets, straggling along Main Street or sitting, either on the curb or flat on the sidewalk with their backs to the wall of a store. They had come in from a nearby reservation to do their Saturday trading, I supposed, and strolling towards them for a closer look, was somewhat put off by their grim weathered faces.

Better Indians than oil wells at that, was my second thought, and invited by the quiet and openness, as well as by the sunlight which seemed especially thick and warm in the side street at the next intersection, I turned and wandered along it. A block away I blundered upon the Elite Hotel.

A big old rambling white frame house, it was built close against the sidewalk on the cross street and fronting to the next, parallel to Main. There a neat little board with the name, painted black on white, swayed lightly above the steps to a porch, which was wide and deep, with a low white rail, a swing and chairs. It was quite chilly-looking now, but what a nice spot it would be in hot weather, with that sweep of yard to the far side, where several trees were fulling pink and tufty towards the tips of their boughs, and the grass, though wintry-green in color still, was swelling and pushing in rough uneven humps! A little path wound on around the house. I knew where it went—to a garden, a pale green garden, shut in by frosty purple-pink raspberry canes and gooseberry bushes sprouting tiny green leaves, and set in its very midst with some kind of early fruit tree flowering out as if with young snow all over its slim bare black boughs. I'd glimpsed the garden from the side street as I approached, and on my way back to Jennie's I lingered alongside, enticed by that beautiful white-flowering tree and pondering what it might be like to live in that friendly white hotel and have that sunny garden for my very own, though of course I never should.

"E-light, you pronounce it E-light, the E-light Hotel," Jennie answered my question. "It use to be a hotel. Now it's a roomin' house."

She was fixing to make me a tam o' shanter out of some brown velvet scraps, to replace the old wool cap I'd worn over from Oilwell. Francis played on the floor and I sat on the edge of the bed and watched her lay two or three sheets of newspaper flat on the arm of her sewing machine and, cutting them to the right size, stitch them inside the lining to hold the tam's saucy shape. As she sewed, she was telling me something. At first I didn't listen closely, not grasping what she was talking about, and when it began to sink in, I wished I didn't have to listen at all. She said she was warning me beforehand, I wouldn't be a child much longer, the difference could happen any day now and I might be scared. Nobody'd told her, and it'd happened on a train trip, she'd soiled her coat even, and there were men around to see. She was sure she'd caught some terrible disease, and when she was alone she nearly cried her eyes out, from humiliation and fright.

"I guess Mama was embarrassed to speak of it to me," said Jennie, and gave a sigh. "But she orter done it."

Thank goodness, my information was coming from Jennie! From Mama I just couldn't have borne it. If only men didn't know anything about such an offensive state of affairs! But Jennie was sure they did know, at least the husbands did. They'd have found out from their wives.

"My husband won't find out from his," I declared, maintaining myself in her presence with huffiness. "He can 'tend to his business, an' I'll 'tend to mine."

That brought Jennie to another subject she wanted to talk to me about, and I hoped I liked it better. Boys. After I started going with them, it was perfectly O.K. for me to have a good time and enjoy myself, but I mustn't ever do anything that would get me in a family way.

I'd heard Papa and Mama apply that term, *in a family way*, to certain poor-quality women in backwoods Arkansas, and it was disagreeable to me, like the word *titty* in Bras's mouth. Wasn't there some other way of expressing Jennie's fact, I didn't mean nicey-nice, but some natural way that would keep it from sounding like a shameful and contemptible secret? If so, Jennie didn't know it, and even from her kindly meant use of the unpleasant phrase, I felt a little furtive and dirtied. To escape the feeling rather than from so much ignorance, I said laughingly, "Could you go as far as a kiss, Jennie?" and succeeded in breaking her seriousness into a smile.

"You needn't shy off from kissin' a boy like I done. Just so you know where to draw the line."

"Oh, I can draw the line, all right," I joked to her, and to myself, I'll draw it on the other side of quite a few kisses. First on my hand, then on my cheek. By moonlight, if possible. By moonlight I imagined that I could look very pretty, and if I looked pretty, I could act pretty, and everything would be most enjoyable.

Nonetheless, underneath all my attempts at lightheartedness, the burden that Jennie'd laid on me hung like one more cloud around my horizon at Oilwell, where, if spring had touched down during my absence, it had left behind no such traces as had welcomed me at Ponca City. Oilwell on Monday was the same as Oilwell on Friday—muddy, drizzly, and cold. Donning my new brown velvet tam, I set off for school.

"Where'd you get your umbrella, Red?"

Oilwell's greeting was tossed at me by the first big boy I met on the schoolground. Straight to the girls' toilet room in the basement I went and wadded the tam in my hands. "Now will you behave?" I muttered, to its reflection in the looking glass. It dealt me a pang, though, to see what had been so jaunty now droop so meekly over one ear, and I was glad that Jennie would never know how I'd abused those stiff newspaper linings which she'd been at such pains to sew well.

Outside the building the kids in the seventh grade were clustered together, planning a handkerchief shower for Mrs. Zickey-Pickey. Clara Shane had thought it up. Naturally.

"We'll bring our handkerchiefs at noon," she was saying, bright and bossy as usual, "and put them on Mrs. Zickey's desk when she leaves the room at recess."

"I may not bring one," I said, with the air of stubbornness I used against her at Sunday school.

"You have to."

"No, I don't."

"Please bring one, Delpha."

John Charles Thomas had turned to me. He was such a winning boy, always so fresh and warm-looking, with a quick smile in among freckles, and one of the few children in my room who'd been friendly from the first. I wished so much I could please him! For his sake I bothered to ask Papa for a nickel at noon, and was told that he wasn't earning sufficient to buy that teacher arey handkerchief to blow her nose on, while Mama chimed in, "You don't have to be a-spendin' money for ever'thing them little ol' kids think up. If they say anything to you, you can tell 'em I said so. That'll be answer enough for 'em."

I hadn't expected them to understand. As I returned to school, I stepped into a store which had handkerchiefs spread out on a counter. I looked at them for quite a while, and presently found a chance to slip one into my pocket.

Mrs. Pickey's scowl had dug itself in so deep between her eyebrows, it was a wonder to me that it could ever unclinch, yet I'd seen it do so on a few happy occasions. The handkerchief shower loosened it again, as she caught sight of all the pretty squares of linen and cotton heaped on her desk her face broke up into a whole different set of lines and wrinkles. "Thank you, thank you all very much indeed," were her special words of pleasure, and after admiring several of the handkerchiefs on top, she told us that she needed this last period of the afternoon to practice with the girls who were singing at the high school tonight, and the rest of us had permission to draw or watercolor or read, whichever we wished.

Everybody clapped, because we'd been so nice and now she was being nice back to us, and Clara Shane and seven other girls grouped themselves around her desk.

"Oklahoma, Oklahoma, fairest daughter of the West,"

they sang, and the rest of it. I didn't care. I knew I couldn't sing. And since I didn't have any watercolors or drawing pad, and was tired of my reader, I got out my geography and a piece of thin white paper which I laid on top of a map we were supposed to draw. Hilya Hite twisted around in her seat immediately in front and watched me trace the lines which showed through. Hilya was a tall skinny unfriendly girl, with a very sharp backbone under a dark red wool dress. I didn't trouble to glance up.

I wasn't very proud of myself. I had stolen once before, really stolen, when I knew it was stealing. It was in the fifth grade at Bridgewater, for Valentine's Day. There was a boy in our room named Frank, who was much too big to be in with all us little kids, and for this reaon reminded me of Jennie when she was in the same fix at school. Also, this boy had a brown complexion and a sort of timid air, like my half brother of the same name. I didn't think that anybody would remember him, and I took a valentine from a drug store and wrote his name on it without signing my own, and dropped it in the valentine box in our room at school. But the reasons for giving it to Frank came later. I didn't have them when I took it. That slipped up on me. It was the ugliness in me coming out. I hadn't intended to take the valentine, at least there

205

wasn't a plan in the back of my head when I entered the store, as there'd been about the handkerchief today. I was just looking at the valentines, and after a bit I put one of them into my pocket and walked out. But I knew it was stealing well enough. And it wasn't even the right valentine for Frank. It was a cutout pipe with smoke rising up from it, which said, "Let us smoke the pipe of peace." There was no sense in my saying this to Frank, we hadn't been mad at each other, and as a matter of fact weren't very well acquainted, but it did please him to receive the valentine, and as I peeped around, he guessed who'd sent it, and laughed and shook one long brown finger at me. Recalling it now, it seemed to me that the thought of my half brother should have been a stern warning against the very act I'd committed, instead of which it seemed to have had exactly the contrary effect, helping to bring the act on by suggesting it. And I couldn't say I'd felt really bad over the matter until today, remembering, and after I'd done the same thing again, but this time in a worse way, more on purpose.

It was a pretty come-off for a person who hoped to amount to something some day. No wonder the kids hadn't taken to me. At Sunday school they said it showed on your face what you were. It was on my face probably, clear as day, what I was. How could it help being, when I knew it so well myself? I was ugly, inside and out. I didn't aim to be, I didn't want to be, but I was.

Even so, why should Hilya Hite feel privileged to squirm around and stare her head off without a word? I wasn't doing her any harm. And you could be civil even to low-down people. At last she turned her spiny old red wool back again, and I made a face at it. But not a very big face, because my heart wasn't in it, and it cheered me up hardly at all.

I was never very cheerful in Mrs. Zickey-Pickey's class at best, however, and by the next afternoon the new bad feeling over the handkerchief had already sunk down and was lost among the other mixed-together bad feelings so familiar to me. So after recess, when Mrs. Pickey failed to tell us to open our readers to the lesson but sat down at her desk, clasping her hands on top of it and frowning down at them, there was nothing much in the fore of my mind beyond an idle wondering as to whether she was truly as much redness and glower as she seemed to me, or whether she looked otherwise to children she liked.

"Someone in this room has been dishonest in school work. I'm not going to say how I found out, and I'm not going to say who is dishonest, because that person will know. I feel very bad about it. I trusted you. I didn't think that any of my boys and girls would do such a thing to me."

She opened out her hands as if to see what they were like on the inside, then lifted her gaze and let it run over the room. "I shall say nothing more, but I hope that the person who is guilty will do what ought to be done."

Hilya Hite turned and looked back. So did everyone else. So did I. There was only one person behind me. He was looking at me.

"Now I want the rest of you to forget this," came Mrs. Zickey's voice. "Let's see how we're getting along with our reading."

Different ones rose and read,

> *"Half a league, half a league,*
> *Half a league onward,*
> *All in the valley of Death*
> *Rode the six hundred . . ."*

After a while Mrs. Zickey had to write something on the blackboard, and I leaned forward and whispered to Hilya Hite. I never would have done it if my head hadn't been so light and full of fuzz.

"You certainly have done something," said Hilya, in a satisfied hiss over her shoulder. I hadn't realized she hated me that much. "I should think you'd know after showin' off doin' it yesterday. You're a disgrace to the class. Mrs. Zickey said so."

"I am not!"

I tried to say it, and I felt my mouth open and move, but nothing came out. So God had noticed the handkerchief and was punishing me. "Dear Jesus," I prayed in my mind, but I didn't feel as if I had any real right to ask Him to look after me. Still, I did it, in a wordless sort of way. All the time I was staring at my book without seeing the page. There seemed to be a mist before my eyes. But I heard the words of the poem as they were read out over and over:

> *"Storm'd at with shot and shell,*
> *Boldly they rode and well,*
> *Into the jaws of Death,*
> *Into the mouth of Hell . . ."*

I went off the schoolground with the other children, but slowly, and after they had gone on, I started back. Mrs. Zickey was just coming through the front door of the schoolhouse. Another teacher was with her. It would have been easier if she'd been by herself, but it couldn't be helped, I had it to do in any case. When she was almost even with me on the walk, I said, "Were you talking about me this afternoon, Mrs. Zickey?"

"You should know that better than anyone else," she said, keeping on with the other teacher. There wasn't any room beside them. I walked behind.

"I didn't think you meant me," I said.

"I didn't say I meant you." She moved her head a little in my direction. "You know whether or not you've been dishonest."

"I didn't think I'd been. I don't know what it could be—"

"You certainly do know if you've done something."

"—unless it was tracing my map. But we always traced our maps where I went to school before."

"We don't trace maps here. You should know that by now. It's dishonest."

If it was, it was, that was all.

"Then what'd I better do?"

"Don't you have any idea what you'd better do?"

"I expect I could draw another map."

"I expect you could."

"Would that make it all right then?"

She didn't say. I waited until we were across the street from the post office. Then I stopped and watched her and the other woman walk on and round the corner onto Main Street. They never noticed.

There was a letter in the post office for me, from Edna Deed. Taking up a question I'd asked, Edna wrote that if she was me she'd save her money and come back to visit her and my other friends at Bridgewater rather than buy a pair of roller skates. It had been a purely fanciful question, my savings at this point amounting to exactly one cent. At home I removed it from hiding and went into old Mr. Harpwell's store in the corner of our building and spent it for a green candy fish on a stick.

A big man in an overcoat was buying a cigar at the same time, and taking up most of the room in front of the counter. As I reached for the candy, he began to ask me questions—who I was, where I lived, how old I was, and so on—which led me to notice that he was another of those red-faced people like Mrs. Zickey, and furthermore was possessed of a pair of right down slinky eyes. *The Cumnock Reader* was under my arm and I was ready to leave, but behind the other man's back old Mr. Harpwell, with a very cross expression, was shaking his head and making motions at me. It didn't seem polite to go without learning what he wanted, so I waited, replying to questions in the meantime, then, not being able to figure it out after all, I did leave, and went on around the house to my dry goods box and climbed in. The green candy fish was in my mouth and the reader open on my knees when, happening to glance up, I looked straight into the slinky little eyes of the red-faced man in the overcoat. I nearly jumped out of my skin.

"What are you doing here?" I snapped.

He said nothing, and after a minute, in which his hard little eyes roamed over the yard and he shifted his cigar from one ugly wet corner of his mouth to the other, he took himself off. I settled back. I hadn't known I could be so effective, and it lifted my spirits, a trifle.

> *Come into the garden, Maud,*
> *For the black bat, night, has flown . . .*

Reading the whole beautiful poem aloud, I paused now and again to lick the candy fish and to picture the garden as the delicate pale green one I'd seen at Ponca City, and myself as Maud, invited to come in. Gradually the memory of the afternoon at school was getting pushed towards the fringes of my brain, where it stabbed less sharply. As for the man in the overcoat, I might not have given him another thought but for old Mr. Harpwell's reminder later in the evening.

"I tried to get you to go on out." He was so worked up to this moment that he kept tugging away at the ends of his

209

floppy old gray moustache. "Don't you know a feller o' that stamp don't have no good purpose in makin' up to a young girl? But you wouldn't take the hint."

I laid my dime on the counter and picked up the box of Arm & Hammer soda I'd been sent for. "How'd I know what all your nods and winks meant?" I said stiffly. "Anyhow, I'm not a young girl. I'm a child."

I was, too, I didn't care what he said, or Jennie either, for the matter of that, and I yearned only that spring should come. And without warning it was there, just overnight. One evening I went to bed in the chilly dampness, and the next morning woke to sparkling sunlight. Oilwell might not be the best place in the world for it to sparkle, but my heart danced anyway. On the schoolground the little kids were as happy as myself, and showing it, laughing and hollering and scampering about like mad, and when I came back from home at noon I found a bunch of the seventh graders merrily forming a circle to play *The Farmer Chose A Wife*. I knew I wouldn't be singled out until the cat chose the rat or the rat chose the cheese, and maybe not then, but I wanted to skip and sing in the sun with the others. I ran up to Isabel Gilbert in the line.

Isabel was a girl with red cheeks who'd never looked quite warm to me, but must have been, as she had fur on her coat and two pairs of red mittens, and I knew her feelings weren't cold because one day last winter we were playing in the snow and she'd insisted that I put on the extra mittens.

"Let me in," I said to her, in the circle.

She skipped on as if she hadn't heard me. I must have been mistaken in thinking that she liked me because she'd lent me her mittens that day.

Clara Shane was next in line. "You can't have in," she said. "Yes, I can."

Usually I wouldn't have asked a boy to let me in beside him. Boys wanted to be next to the pretty girls or at least to someone smart and shiny with proud parents at her back, like Clara, if they were by girls at all. But I wasn't so afraid of John Charles Thomas, and as I held out my hand he dropped Clara's for mine.

"Don't, John Charles!" Before I could take it, Clara'd seized his hand again. "You know what we said!"

I went around the schoolhouse to a cold cemented corner

where the sun didn't shine. Only a few little kids were near to see. Until Alice Pinney followed me. Alice had red hair like me, and I'd sometimes gazed at her and thought how pleasant it would be if only I'd got cut out as small and fine and pretty as she was, and after our class had its picture taken, and I saw how I looked, with my chin down and one shoulder raised and a kind of silly grin on my face as though I was trying to make the best of a bad job, I hated myself so much that I took a pin and scratched myself off the copy which Mama'd given me ten cents to buy, and in future I pretended that Alice Pinney in the picture was me to anybody I thought wouldn't know better. Alice herself sat clear across the room from me, and up to now we'd done little more than say hello to one another. Seeing her approach, I turned my back.

"What did they do?" She came close and put her arm around me.

All the hardness holding up my heart melted into tears and I had to face even more to the wall.

"They wouldn't let me play," I whispered.

"They're mean!" she cried, stamping her foot. "They will, too, let you play! I'll make them!"

But she didn't make them. After a while I got over wanting so much to play. I got used to things, and managed. I didn't go to school until nearly belltime, and at recess, if I fooled around long enough and a teacher didn't come in and send me out to get some fresh air, I could spend most of the time in the girls' toilet room.

My sole wish now was that it would hurry up and come summer, so that school would let out and I could be through with the seventh grade and Mrs. Zickey. But you couldn't hurry a month. You couldn't hurry a day, or a minute. You had to live through it, there was no getting away from it, and the worse it was, and the faster you wanted it to go, the slower it went as if on purpose. And although I honestly had lost the desire to play with these children any more, I got tired of putting up a show of being satisfied just as I was, of liking to stand around by myself, and of not even being interested in running and jumping with the rest.

Earlier experience had taught me how to pretend after that fashion, of course. But on valentine days at Bridgewater, my fear that I might not receive any valentine at all stemmed

211

from my not having sent any, and at Enid I'd been left out of the basketball playing because I didn't know the game. There wasn't anything wrong with me.

Now there was. I was left out because there was something wrong with me, something terribly wrong. The mean big boys yelled, "Hi, Red!" more than ever. The girls stared at me and said things in whispers. If I came near, they didn't say anything at all, and after a moment moved off and left me.

I hadn't done anything bad since tracing my map, that I knew of. I went along every day, acting as well as I knew how, and matters didn't get right. I was smarter in my books, too, now that I had so much time for them, and would get one hundred in arithmetic as regularly as Clara Shane. But nobody even asked to copy my problems.

I had thought that in time most of these children would like me well enough, if only Mrs. Zickey would stop picking on me. I saw now how mistaken I'd been. Maybe Clara Shane was to blame. Maybe it was Oilwell. Maybe it was mostly myself, after all, without my understanding why.

I remembered Keta Cleck, a big old girl at Bridgewater with a square end to her nose and freckles and oily hair, who was so ignorant she couldn't tell when the kids were making fun of her. But I could tell. And I wouldn't stand for it. Not from these Oilwell kids or from anybody else. Even if I had been born in the sticks. Even if I was as ugly as a mud fence, which was uglier than I was. My whole mind clenched itself and said they couldn't do it. I'd fight.

Only I couldn't fight. These kids weren't making fun of me, anyhow. They were saying things about me in whispers, and I couldn't find out what.

I kept trying to, from a girl named Daisy Post. Nobody else would talk to me. She wouldn't have done so either probably, if she hadn't been new to the school. Then, too, she was older than the other boys and girls, and you'd expect her to be kinder. In the past I'd never have sought out a girl like Daisy, who wore thick round glasses and never did anything at recess except stroll around looking earnest, but I turned to her now, thankfully.

"You ought to tell me," I said to her one afternoon when she was allowing me to walk off the school ground with her.

"Don't you think you ought to tell me so I can see about fixing things up?"

"I'm not saying you oughtn't to know," she replied, "but I wouldn't want to be the one to tell you."

"Why not, Daisy? Why wouldn't you?"

"I just wouldn't, that's all."

"Then give me a hint. If I ought to know, you ought to tell me enough so I can guess the rest. Is it something I could guess if you told me a part?"

"I should think so. You know it better than anyone else."

Those were the very words used by Mrs. Zickey and Hilya Hite the day they were talking about my map-tracing. It looked as if people could at least tell you what you were supposed to have done if they were going to accuse you of it, and not leave you to wonder and worry and imagine until you were half sick. And at the same time that I was grateful to Daisy along one line, along another I hated her for being so calm and far-off and sure of herself behind her heavy spectacles and for making me work so hard to worm the thing out of her, even having to act as though I might really be guilty of something and have to improve my conduct. I knew better than to give her an inkling of my true feelings, and I'd thought of another way of coming at her.

"Then don't you think it's your Christian duty to give me a hint, Daisy?"

This idea seemed to impress her, and I said more to the same effect, putting a lot of her kind of earnestness into it, and trying to pin her eyes to a straight steady look. This in itself was difficult, as her eyes were so large and unnatural behind those thick lenses that I couldn't get hold of their exact center.

"I'll tell you this much," she said at length. "It's something to do with a man."

"A man?"

"Some man over at your place. You must've been doing something you shouldn't. In a box out behind, maybe."

I took it in. Then: "I haven't! I haven't!" I cried. "I don't know what you're talking about!"

She wouldn't tell me another word. She thought I had done it, whatever it was, whatever somebody had made up about me, oh, I couldn't think exactly what, but the ugliest kind of thing, like letting a man put his hands on you maybe, which I'd never, never let happen to me! But I couldn't make Daisy believe me. There wasn't a spark of liking under her words which could see how it was with me. She was only doing her Christian duty in talking to me at all, the same as Isabel Gilbert was only being kind the day she'd lent me her mittens.

"A person thinks that where there's so much smoke, there must be a little fire," said Daisy.

There was a corner in our backyard between the toilet and the laundry wall, not an agreeable place, but Mama couldn't see it from the house, and I ran and stood there and cried. It had rained again, and my dry goods box was wet. Besides, I didn't want in it. Somebody had seen the red-faced man in the overcoat there, bending over me with the cigar in his mouth and his mean little eyes roving the yard, and had made something bad out of it, though it wasn't, it wasn't! If growing up was going to be like this, I wished—more than I had at Jennie's, more than I had the other evening in talking to old Mr. Harpwell—I wished I could never stop being a child.

Never stop being a child! What a silly childish thought *that* was to have! As if there hadn't been times when desperately I'd felt the need to be grown-up! And, in any case, as if you could hold time back any more than you could push it forward! I remembered the fateful day at Bridgewater when I learned the full story of the disgrace that Frank had brought on our family, and of the terrible ordeal that Papa'd suffered at the same time, both of which events had helped to lay our family so low. I remembered thinking that in the learning I'd grown much older, and crossed to the other side of something. What would it be like on this new side? I'd wondered then, filled with vague hopes and nervous fears. Now I knew. It was exactly the difference between being altogether a child and starting to be grown-up.

I remembered also that on the dark night when Sallie and I ended our visit to Granpa's, and stood shivering on the drafty platform of the little depot at Gisper, waiting for the train which would bear us away from that spot where neither of us belonged—I remembered what deep excitement I'd felt because *out there* somewhere that I was going I might find the very place most meant and happiest for me. Most meant and happiest! How I'd have laughed over that childish non-

214

sense in the place it had been mine to find at Oilwell, if I'd had it in me to laugh at all at this stage.

But being the failure that I was in Oilwell, wasn't it queer that I didn't welcome the chance, when it came a little later, to escape to another town, to any town, but especially to Ponca City? It was a pleasant place, on my visit to Jennie I'd seen its wide sunny paved streets, the beautiful home of an oil millionaire set on sweeping green lawns, and a municipal auditorium where tall evergreens rose against white walls. My fear concerned only myself, in it. What would I be able to do there? Here at Oilwell I knew what I had to contend with, and was used to putting up with it. What reason was there to suppose conditions would be better in Ponca City, for me at any rate? Furthermore, in a very short while school would be over for the summer. I said this to Papa one evening at bedtime after he had announced that we were making the move.

"Couldn't we stay here till then?"

"No, we couldn't, Delphie."

Had he even heard my question? "Why couldn't we?" I persisted.

"Because we couldn't." Now he did pause, however, actually to consider me. "We have to go when we can to wherever me an' your maw can make the best livin' for us all."

"I can't see as you do any better one place'n another, we never do have anything like other people." It wasn't my wish to be bitter and reproachful, but it helped me not to cry.

"You've got an awful sassy tongue in your head," said Mama.

"They ain't no use tryin' to reason with a child," said Papa.

"I can't see as your reasoning is any better'n mine," I said. "Don't you want me to get promoted and grow up and amount to something?"

"Ain't it possible for you to get your promotin' done anywhere else than at Oilwell?" said Papa. "So fur as amountin' to somethin' is concerned, sure I want you to, if you can."

"What you in such a killin' big rush for?" said Mama. "You're just a kid of a youngun yet. You've got all the time in the world to amount to somethin' in."

"No, I haven't. I've got to get through the seventh grade and after that the eighth before I can even go to high school."

215

"Well, what makes you think you're goin' to amount to so everlastin' much, anyway? You're a smart-enough youngun, I don't aim to say you ain't, but Jennie nor Sallie neither one went to high school, an' me an' your papa don't have no assurance we'll be able to put you through."

" 'Course, we're willin' to send you to school as long as we're situated so we can," said Papa, "providin' you act like you appreciate it."

"Well, I do appreciate it."

"I incline to think you do. It's like this, Delphie. We're willin' to give, within reason, while we've got it to give. But we can't make you no promises about high school at this time. It all depends."

He folded his arms and looked at me gravely. There wasn't anything there for me or against me. It did just depend.

"The chances are prit nigh even you won't get to go, though," said Mama. "They ain't no call to look so fur ahead nohow, settin' your heart on what more'n likely you won't get. We're just poor folks, child. We can't provide all them things rich people give their childern. We'd like to, all right, but we ain't got the means. We have to be content with what we've got."

"What've we got?"

"Enough to be thankful for," said Papa. "Things you take so much for granted ain't so easy come by, as you're goin' to find out before many years when you're earnin' them for yourself."

"We've got plenty to eat an' wear, an' a place to sleep," said Mama. "I figger that's about as much as common ol' folks like us can hope for. An' that applies to you, Miss Delphie."

It didn't either apply to me. I wasn't common old folks and I didn't figure like that. I wouldn't be content with what I had. It wasn't enough. I wasn't going to let her and Papa turn my heart into lead. There was all the world before me, things I knew and others strange to me. I *would* do some good hard work, and then amount to something. Hadn't Mama herself set me an example, growing away from her brothers and sisters, and making something better out of her life than they had out of their lives? Hadn't her mother before her left *her* family, and improved upon its situation as I'd seen that represented at Uncle Berry Broadbent's? All right then. So could I, in my turn. "I'll show 'em!" I vowed into my pillow, all my muscles tightened as if for the fight ahead. "They aren't going to make me fail the seventh grade! They'll see! I'll go to high school, too, I will, I will, I *will!* I'll go away, and I'll *never* come back!"

But I didn't see how I was going to do it. If Mama hadn't meant all she'd said, she'd meant enough. And Papa meant exactly what he'd said. I knew them both. For it had always been like this, ever since I started to school at Urbanette, Arkansas. I couldn't remember where I'd learned to read and write, but it wasn't at Urbanette, and maybe I hadn't been taught how to at all but had merely picked up the ability by myself and it was only somehow, among all those places we'd lived, that I got shuffled out of one grade and into the next, depending, at Bonnot's Grove, on Jennie's and Sallie's persuasion of the teacher, losing that advantage and being put back at Claremore, and finally getting a chance more or less like other children when we settled for a few years at Bridgewater. There, during those few years, the only move was from town to the farm and the only break a few weeks of cotton-picking at Uncle Berry Broadbent's, I went along in a normal manner through three straight grades and had friends and quite a bit of fun besides in spite of everything. Yet it was all slipshod and by accident in the whole general way that Mama and Papa lived, which was out of one place that didn't suit them into another that suited no better, and except for those Bridgewater years my life had been nothing but a constant go-go-go, from one set of books I didn't possess to another I didn't possess either, and from one bunch of kids who had small use for me to another who had no use at all. It was a God's wonder I'd got along as well as I had, and there wasn't much to thank Papa and Mama for in this as in anything else.

They didn't care. They just didn't care, that was all. They wanted the teacher and kids not to pick on me, and I guessed they wanted me not to fail my grade, but they'd do very little to prevent either. Papa didn't want me to tell him a lie, though he told lies to other people, not very often, but sometimes, yes, he did, I'd seen him do it without cracking a muscle, and he didn't want me to say swear words or take things that didn't belong to me or let men monkey around with me, but after that he didn't care what happened. Mama wanted me to have enough clothes to be warm, and to have them clean, but it hardly mattered to her how she cobbled them up in the sewing or what people thought of them. Together with

217

Papa she wanted me to have enough to eat, and I did, such as it was, but I never had a banana or an apple for a fruit shower on the teacher, and I had to steal a handkerchief. Mama was always priding herself on raising her children better than the folks down in Arkansas did theirs, but if she thought she'd done much more than jerk me up by the hair of the head at that, let her take a look at the people we were living among now, in Oklahoma.

People around us here weren't like that. I didn't see anybody at school like that. The other kids had families who thought the world and all of them, who gave them good clothes and parties and music lessons, and bicycles and roller skates, and bought them every last unnecessary the teacher asked for, and were proud of every solitary little thing they did. Mama and Papa loved me, too, I supposed, after their fashion. They'd even be rather proud if I got the highest grade in class, and might even brag a bit to some neighbor person, I'd heard them do that. But their love for me was a whole lot like Granpa's for Granma, which Mama herself criticized because it hadn't been very much concerned with Granma's real welfare. As for the grades, they were the part I could take care of by myself, without any help from home.

All I wanted from home was a chance. I didn't want Papa and Mama to do anything directly. They wouldn't know how. And I could get along with awfully little. I didn't have to have so many clothes, just enough and good enough for me to feel all right walking across the front of the room at school. I knew I couldn't have a bicycle or take violin lessons, and I did very well without roller skates, but I would like to have a toothbrush and a pair of mittens.

Papa and Mama didn't look at matters in that light. They didn't want me to turn out bad, they'd be the first to condemn me if I did, but they really didn't care whether I amounted to something or not. They wouldn't stand in my way on purpose, and if I succeeded in spite of them, they'd say, that's fine. I expected they'd be willing to help me enjoy it. But if I failed, they'd feel it wasn't their responsibility, and I could just grin and bear it. As soon as I was a little older, they'd stop sending me to school and make me go to work at anything that came along whether it suited what I was best able to do or not. Wasn't that what they'd said? They'd said I'd find out before many years. It was the way things had gone in their own lives, I supposed, and they were passing it on to me. And how I could go to school and make something of myself unless they'd pull with me instead of against me, I didn't see.

Maybe they were right. Maybe the good things couldn't happen to people like us. We were just clodhoppers. We looked as if we came from the backwoods. We acted like it. Mama chewed tobacco and said ugly words, even if she did have an ancestor she claimed had almost been president of the United States. Papa's old striped pants had patches at the knees and his old red sweater was out at the elbows, I didn't care if he had taught school once upon a time. Bruce kept his blouse dirtied up half the time and was always begging to move back onto the farm where there might not be any chance at all to go to school. As if school weren't something that belonged to everyone who wanted it and could make good use of it, as if it weren't a thing that nobody, *nobody*, had a right to take away from me! As for Jennie, I knew she was good and I loved her, but she did look like a hayseed when you got right down to it, with her big hands and feet and pile of red hair that she couldn't get a hat large enough to come down over, which left it sitting on top of her head, held on by a hat pin. And George Croney wouldn't think Sallie was such a little queen if he could see her blowing her nose when company wasn't around.

I wasn't any better. I had red hands and an ugly nose that squared off at the end and kept getting pimples along the sides of late. I took what wasn't mine. I might as well call it by its right name. I stole. I was a thief, and the difference between me and Frank, that half brother I was so ashamed of, was only a matter of how much, and if he had bad blood in him, then there was a chance I had it in me, too.

That was the kind of family we were. There wasn't any need to pretend it wasn't so.

But I could cry because it was so. I could cry till I was shaking all over and my head ached. Because Bruce couldn't ever be president, or me make a trip to South America, like Doug Cunningham, or have a parlor with a rug. Just because Mama would give in to such outcomes instead of putting up some kind of fight about it. Because we came from Arkansas where everybody was poor as a church mouse and because people made fun of you if they found out you were born there, and Mama and Papa were always letting the cat out of the bag. Because we had such a peculiar last name, a little old stub of a name, that simply asked the kids to laugh at it and call me Delphie Doudy. Because they were able to insult me, seeing how everything was with me, and there were lots of them while I was only one, and I didn't have anybody to scorn them to. Because I hated Mama and Papa for being what they were, and couldn't do anything about it. We were wrong, and Oilwell was wrong, and my whole life would be wrong. I could see the days coming, all put together the way Papa and Mama lived, and I could feel their way hardening around me like a crust that I'd never, never, be able to break through, to get away to a place where I wouldn't have to lie about what I had and certainly not to steal because I'd have earned enough, and more than enough, to buy what I needed, and where I wouldn't have to hide anything important in my life because I'd be so straight and right within myself that even with unavoidable mistakes I could still stand on that. It was all a dream, and there wasn't any need to yearn for it any longer. I was caught, my people and all that was past—they had me, I wouldn't ever get away. So I didn't try to stop my heart if it wanted to break. I let it cry into my pillow until at last it lay down inside of me with a sigh and went to sleep, being too tired to fight and hate and resolve and despair any more that night.

My face was still red and swollen the next morning. Mama took a look at it and said, "Here's three dollars, Puss. Go up-town an' buy yourself a pair o' them Mary Jane shoes."

They were black patent leather with heavy white soles and white piping around the straps. I wore them the morning we moved over to Ponca City. Beside Papa on a mattress on top of our truckload of furniture, I stretched my feet out in front of me, and I couldn't help admiring them in those new slippers, which helped the soreness in my heart. And after a while I was looking at the other trucks on the road, most of them loaded down with huge iron pipes and machinery for the new oil districts, and at the fields to either side where the great wooden arms of active wells went around and around, and sometimes over my shoulder at the black lane ahead, thinking of the quiet town at the end of it.

Papa had bought us a rooming house there, but nobody had told me as yet that it was the very same old white Elite Hotel, pronounced E-light, in a grassy yard beside a pale green garden, which I'd chanced on in the early spring and thought too warm and good ever to be mine. Nor did I know as yet that up the street from the hotel was a free Carnegie library, with an absolute treasury of books which had everything in the world to tell me and which, so it seemed to me, had been waiting for me all my life long just as I had for them. Beyond the library was a friendly stone schoolhouse, where the junior high children changed every hour from one room to another for a fresh subject and another teacher, just as they had at Bridgewater. This I didn't know either, as yet. Or that one of the teachers, a dark plain likeable woman named Mrs. Busch, would say to me quite soon, "Your composition was excellent, and I want you to read it to the other section in civics. Then I'm going to have it printed in the *Ponca City Courier.*" Mrs. Busch's husband ran the *Courier,* and one day he met Papa on the street and congratulated him on his daughter's article, *Ponca City—Then and Now.* Papa was surprised but also tickled, and had to brush at his moustache to hide the pleasedness in his grin as he related the occurrence to Mama.

What astonished me was having the boys and girls start clapping after I read my composition to them. But my classmates at Ponca City were an altogether new sort for me, they were smarter and more brimming with ideas and plans for carrying them out than any I'd known before. An idea which eight of us girls carried out was to take part in a patriotic program in the city auditorium. Dressed alike in dark pleated skirts and white middy blouses, we marched onto the platform and sang a song about

> *He was just a long lean country gink*
> *From away out West where the hoptoads wink,*

and no one seemed to think I didn't sing about as well as anybody else. Later I was called upon to write a poem for a thrift-stamp campaign at school, and did so, though without any particular success so far as poetry went, the rhymes being about what you'd expect, like wheat, meat and eat, and slacker and Sammy-backer. I had a number of friends, and one special chum, Rachel Faris, whose father was a lawyer. Both Rachel and I were in the group of eighth graders who were permitted to begin ninth-grade algebra in the middle of

221

the year, and when I brought her home with me and Mama saw how much better Rachel's clothes were than mine, she was put out, and after that my own improved.

All that would be change in plenty from Oilwell. There was more. Close by the Carnegie library a small white church lifted its slim white spire towards the sky. Here I went to Sunday school, often staying on for the main service in order to hear my teacher play her great golden harp. What a wonderful woman she was! large and kind and fair-complected, whose full name was Mrs. Martha Baker Barr. Sometimes she drove past the Elite in her car and took me with her out into the country to see how the crops were coming along on the famous 202 Ranch, which she and her brothers owned. The girls in her Sunday school class were invited to her house every month for a party with refreshments served by a real Japanese butler, and once she offered a prize to the girl or boy in our church who wrote the best story based on an incident in the Bible, the prize being five dollars and the winner me, and she said, "Always remember, Delpha, that any bright American girl may go to college if she will make the effort."

It was a magical word, *college!* No one had ever spoken it to me, about me, before. I would remember, and I would make the effort. Of course. This was the way forward, for me. I'd been right in my thinking about myself all along, about where I didn't belong and where I did.

I wouldn't forget the winter at Oilwell which had made the world seem such a bad place, nor the black night when I found myself hating Papa and Mama and our whole family and kin and most of all myself. That winter and that night would teach me through what followed that I must never sink down to the bottom of despair through feeling that one part of my life was the whole of it, and never forget what was good in my family, or even in myself, through thinking only about what was bad. When I was altogether grown-up, I'd reflect more on this, and on all the other important things which I remembered from earlier in my life, from that long-ago beginning when I rushed bellowing to Mama if something went wrong, here to the very end of childhood when I kept my crying to myself if I could. I'd think about them until I understood them better, until I got them outside myself, so to speak, like that aching tooth with the hole in it, and could see what their meaning looked like.

When I was altogether grown-up. That time and all its

thoughts and acts were far, far ahead, of course. At the moment I was able, as always, to do little more than to store up and lay away, for later, while it was the year in the eighth grade at Ponca City which was at hand, which was almost upon me. It was hard to imagine there could be two times, so close together, so paper-thin between, and yet so different as those at Oilwell and at Ponca City were for me. I never would have dreamed it on that May morning as I sat on the truck beside Papa, with Mama, Sallie and Bruce tucked into the cab by the driver down below, and watched the black oily road unwind and narrow into the distance as it returned to Oilwell. From Oilwell there were other roads, I could see them in my mind's eye, leading back to Enid, and Gisper, and Bridgewater, and Claremore, and Bonnot's Grove, and Arkansas. On those roads a lot had happened to me, all I'd had of life so far, thirteen years. And with no idea of what was ahead, I knew all too well what was behind, and knew also that it was over and done with. Raising my eyes to the blue sky, I breathed in deep of the air which was growing fresher and softer with our passage out of the oil district, and felt the sunlight which lay on my shoulder like a warm hand, coaxing me to turn and face the forward road. The sun was shining at the same moment, I supposed, on the old red brick school-house where Mrs. Pickey was doubtless casting about for some handy person to pick on, but that person would never be me any more, and it heartened me almost as much as my bran-new shoes to find that I was able to think of her as Mrs. Pickey again.

THE MOST
UP-TO-DATE OF ALL
PAPERBACK
DICTIONARIES

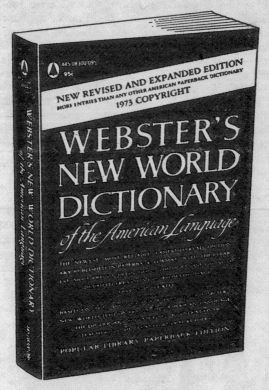

ALL NEW!
Completely Revised
Now On Sale Wherever
Paperbacks Are Sold